Praise for *Bring Me Back*

One of *Good Morning America*'s "Best Books to Bring to the Beach This Summer" on GoodMorningAmerica.com

A *Bustle* Best Books of the Week Pick

A *Lit Hub CrimeReads* "Summer's Most Anticipated" Pick

"We're in a new golden age of suspense writing now, because of amazing books like *Bring Me Back*, and I, for one, am loving it." —Lee Child

"[Paris] builds a nice plot and brings some originality to the old 'good sister, bad sister' character dynamic."

—*The New York Times Book Review*

"A twisty and seductive new psychological thriller you won't want to miss." —*Bustle*

"B. A. Paris is back with another twisted psychological thriller."

—*The Daily Beast*

"B. A. Paris . . . is a consistent whiz at stitching any number of random events and devious characters into a winner of a plot." —*Toronto Star*

"Paris once again proves her suspense chops with this can't-put-down psychological thriller." —*Library Journal* (starred review)

"Paris adroitly ramps up tension. . . . Compelling." —*Booklist*

"[An] outstanding Hitchcockian thriller . . . Paris plays fair with the reader as she builds to a satisfying resolution. Fans of intelligent psychological suspense will be richly rewarded."

—*Publishers Weekly* (starred and boxed review)

"A daring, stay-up-all-night love story. This should be next on your reading list if you love to read thrilling love stories."

—*The Washington BookReview*

Praise for *The Breakdown*

A Barnes & Noble Best Book of 2017: Mysteries and Thrillers

"A story with a ratcheting sense of unease—a tale of friendship and love, sanity and the terrible unravelling of it." —*USA Today*

"This novel will keep you on the edge of your seat from page one." —*BookTrib* (Top 10 July Reads)

"B. A. Paris has done it again! *The Breakdown* is a page-turning thriller that will leave you questioning the family you love, the friends you trust, and even your own mind."
—Wendy Walker, author of the *USA Today* bestselling novel *All Is Not Forgotten*

"In the same vein as the author's acclaimed debut, *Behind Closed Doors,* this riveting psychological thriller pulls readers into an engrossing narrative in which every character is suspect. With its well-formed protagonists, snappy, authentic dialog, and clever and twisty plot, this is one not to miss." —*Library Journal* (starred review)

"This psychological thriller is even harder to put down than Paris's 2016 bestseller debut *Behind Closed Doors*; schedule reading time accordingly. . . . A skillfully plotted thriller. With two in a row, Paris moves directly to the thriller A-list." —*Booklist* (starred review)

"British author Paris follows her bestselling debut, 2016's *Behind Closed Doors,* with another first-rate psychological thriller. . . . Tension quickly builds to a crescendo as Cass's fears . . . become palpable."
—*Publishers Weekly* (starred review)

Praise for *Behind Closed Doors*

August Amazon Best Books of the Month: Mystery, Thriller & Suspense

August 2016 Indie Next Pick

Selected for the August 2016 LibraryReads List

Real Simple Best Book of the Month for August

iBooks Best Books of August

23 Weeks on the *Publishers Weekly* Bestseller List in 2017

"In B. A. Paris's hair-raising debut, a woman falls in love with a psychopath, only realizing his true nature when she's hidden from the world and suffering unthinkable horrors at the hands of a seemingly perfect man. *Behind Closed Doors* is both unsettling and addictive, as I raced through the pages to find out Grace's fate. A chilling thriller that will keep you reading long into the night." —Mary Kubica, *New York Times* and *USA Today* bestselling author of *The Good Girl*

"Newlyweds Grace and Jack Angel seem to lead a perfect life in British author Paris's gripping debut, but appearances can be deceiving. . . . Grace's terror is contagious, and [her sister] Millie's impending peril creates a ticking clock that propels this claustrophobic cat-and-mouse tale toward its grisly, gratifying conclusion." —*Publishers Weekly*

"Making her smash debut, Paris [keeps] the suspense level high. In the same vein as *Gone Girl* or *The Girl on the Train,* this is a can't-put-down psychological thriller." —*Library Journal* (starred review)

"A clever heroine." —*Kirkus Reviews*

"Debut novelist Paris adroitly toggles between the recent past and the present in building the suspense of Grace's increasingly unbearable situation, as time becomes critical and her possible solutions narrow. This is one readers won't be able to put down."

—*Booklist* (starred review)

"A frighteningly cool portrait of a serious sadist, *Behind Closed Doors* is a gripping, claustrophobia-inducing thriller . . . Read at the risk of running from every handsome British lawyer who crosses your path."

—*RT Book Reviews*

"B. A. Paris's debut, *Behind Closed Doors,* is a chilling confirmation of the adage that no one ever really knows what transpires in other people's private lives. . . . Paris has created one of the most heinous villains in recent memory, upon whom even the most pacifist of readers might wish torturous revenge. They'll likely remain behind their own closed doors as they race through this thriller to see how, or if, the nightmare ends."

—*Shelf Awareness*

"A gripping domestic thriller . . . the sense of believably and terror that engulfs *Behind Closed Doors* doesn't waver." —Associated Press

"If you're hunting for a thriller to give you chills in August, look no further than this book, which is already a big hit in the United Kingdom."

—*Real Simple*

"*Behind Closed Doors* takes a classic tale to a whole new level. . . . This was one of the best and [most] terrifying psychological thrillers I have ever read. . . . Each chapter brings you further in, to the point where you feel how Grace must feel. The desperation, the feeling that no one will believe you and yet still wanting to fight because someone you care deeply about will get hurt." —*San Francisco Book Review*

"Paris grabs the reader from the beginning with a powerful and electrifying tale. *Behind Closed Doors,* a novel sure to make one's skin crawl, also reveals no one truly knows what does go on behind closed doors."

—*New York Journal of Books*

"B. A. Paris takes the cliché about not knowing what goes on beyond closed doors to nightmarish place. . . . Each chapter escalates the tensions and stakes faced by Grace in the nightmare that is her new 'perfect' marriage to Jack." —*HuffPost*

"This debut is guaranteed to haunt you—especially if you're about to tie the knot. Paris's thriller asks the question: 'The perfect marriage or the perfect lie?' Jack and Grace, the couple at the center of this totally enthralling novel, are so clearly not what they seem you'll have no choice but to read and read and read until their darkest secrets are revealed. Warning: brace yourself."

—*Bustle* (10 New Thrillers to Read This Summer)

"This dark and twisted thriller will keep you on your toes and have you wondering exactly what goes on behind your neighbor's door."

—*BuzzFeed* (6 Thriller/Mystery Reads That Will Have You Sleeping with the Lights On)

"Really freaking creepy. And really good. Until the end, which was an honest gasp and imaginary pearl-clutching moment. Yes, that good. Reader, if you want to read the thriller that enthralled even this jaded soul, pick up *Behind Closed Doors* by B. A. Paris. . . . Then draw the blinds and turn off your phone because you will not want any interruptions."

—*Literary Hub* (18 Books You Should Read This August)

"This book proves that looks are most definitely deceiving. . . . Disturbing, to say the least, readers will definitely be shaken as the story commences and they become immediately absorbed. The writing was incredible, and the pace is quick, offering up too many chills to count. . . . *Behind Closed Doors* screams: 'Stay single!'"

—*Suspense Magazine*

"The book dishes out endless tension [and] much creepiness."

—*Toronto Star*

"Oh wow. What a story. What pacing. Already a runaway bestseller in the United Kingdom with movie rights sold, B. A. Paris's debut psychological thriller is sure to top many 'must-read summer lists.' And it should. *Behind Closed Doors* is completely unsettling and addictive, a true page-turner."

—Leslie Lindsay, leslielindsay.com

Also by B. A. Paris

Behind Closed Doors
The Breakdown

BRING ME BACK

B. A. PARIS

ST. MARTIN'S GRIFFIN NEW YORK

For Christine, my sister and best friend

This is a work of fiction. All of the characters, organizations, and events portrayed in this novel are either products of the author's imagination or are used fictitiously.

Printed in the United States of America. For information, address St. Martin's Press, 175 Fifth Avenue, New York, N.Y. 10010.

www.stmartins.com

The Library of Congress has cataloged the hardcover edition as follows:

Names: Paris, B. A., author.
Title: Bring me back : a novel / B. A. Paris.
Description: First U.S. Edition. | New York : St. Martin's Press, 2018.
Identifiers: LCCN 2017060169 | ISBN 9781250151339 (hardcover) | ISBN 9781250193506 (international, sold outside the U.S., subject to rights availability) | ISBN 9781250151353 (ebook)
Classification: LCC PR9105.9.P34 B75 2018 | DDC 813'.6—dc23
LC record available at https://lccn.loc.gov/2017060169

ISBN 978-1-250-15134-6 (trade paperback)

First published in the United Kingdom by MIRA/Harlequin, HarperCollins UK

First St. Martin's Griffin Edition: May 2019

10 9 8 7 6 5 4 3 2 1

TWELVE YEARS BEFORE

Interview: Finn McQuaid
Date: 15/03/2006
Time: 03.45
Location: Fonches

We were on our way back from skiing in Megève. I decided to stop in Paris on the way up as a surprise for Layla, because she had never been there before. We had dinner in a restaurant by the Notre-Dame Cathedral and then went for a walk along the Seine. We could have stayed the night there—now, I wish we had—but we were both eager to get home to our cottage in St. Mary's, in Devon.

It must have been around midnight by the time we left Paris. About an hour and a half into our journey I wanted to go to the toilet so I pulled off the motorway, into the picnic area at Fonches. It's not a service station, you can't get petrol there or anything, but I knew it had toilets because I'd stopped there before, on previous skiing trips to Megève. The place was deserted apart from the car I told you about, the one parked directly outside the toilet block. I think there were a couple of trucks in the truck bay on the other side; there must have been at least two, the one I saw leaving and the other one, the one whose driver we spoke to after.

There was an empty bottle of water rolling around the car and we'd been eating snacks on the way up from Megève so I drove past the toilet block and down to the end of the car park where there was a rubbish bin, so that I could get rid of the wrappers. I—I should have just parked outside the toilet and walked down. If I had, then I would have been nearer. I should have been nearer.

Layla was asleep—she'd fallen asleep as soon as we'd hit the motorway, and I didn't want to wake her so I sat for a while, just to relax a bit. She woke up when I started gathering up the stuff to throw away. She didn't want to use the toilet there, she said she'd rather wait until we stopped at a proper service station, so as I got out of the car I told her to lock the doors behind me, because I didn't like leaving her there in the dark. She really hates the dark, you see.

On my way into the toilets, I passed a man coming out and a minute or so later, I heard a car drive off. He was shorter than me, maybe six foot? I think he had dark hair, he definitely had a beard. I was quick in the toilet, I didn't like being in there, I felt unnerved, as if someone was watching. Maybe it was because one of the stall doors was closed.

As I made my way back to the car, I heard a truck pull out of the parking bay and I watched it as it headed along the slip road to the motorway. He was driving fast, as if he was in a hurry, but I honestly didn't think anything of it at the time. In the distance

I could see the silhouette of our car; it was the only one left because the other one, the one that had been parked in front of the toilet block, had gone. It was only when I got closer that I realized Layla wasn't in the car and I thought she must have changed her mind about going to the toilet. I remember looking behind me, expecting to see her hurrying after me—I knew she'd be as creeped out by the whole place as I was—but she wasn't there, so I got into the car to wait. But the darkness began to get to me so I started up the engine and moved it in front of the toilet block, where there was at least a modicum of light, so that Layla wouldn't have to walk all the way back in the dark.

It must have only been a couple of minutes before I began to worry. It didn't feel right that she hadn't appeared yet so I got out of the car and went into the ladies' side of the block to look for her. There were three stalls, two were empty but the other one had the door closed so I presumed she was in there. I called to her and when there was no answer I put my hand on the door and pushed against it. It swung open easily and when I saw that Layla wasn't there I hurried back outside and began calling for her, thinking that maybe, after I left the car, she'd decided to go for a short walk to stretch her legs or get some fresh air. But even as I was thinking it, I knew she would never have wandered off, not at night, not when it was pitch-black because, as I said, she hated the dark.

I ran round to the back of the block, in case she was there, and when I couldn't find her I got a flashlight from the trunk and widened my search, taking in the whole picnic area, shouting her name. There was still one truck in the bay so I went over and called out, hoping to find someone to help me look for her. But there was no one in the driver's cabin and when I hammered on the door no one answered, so I assumed the driver was asleep in the back. I tried hammering on that door too but nobody came and when I took out my phone and realized that I didn't have a signal, I didn't know what to do. I didn't want to leave in case Layla had fallen and was lying injured somewhere, but I knew I wasn't going to be able to find her with only the light from my torch. So I got back into the car and drove as fast as I could to the next petrol station and ran in shouting for someone to help me. It wasn't easy to get them to understand me because my French isn't very good but they finally agreed to phone the local police. And then you came and you spoke good English and you took me back to the picnic area to help me look for Layla, because I really needed to find her.

That was the statement I gave to the police, sitting in the police station somewhere off the A1 in France. It was the truth. But not quite the whole truth.

PART ONE

ONE

NOW

My phone rings as I'm walking through the glass-walled foyer of Harry's impressive offices on London Wall. I turn and check the time on the digital display above the receptionist's desk; it's only four thirty, but I'm impatient to get home. It's taken months of perseverance to get Grant James, the famous business magnate, to invest fifty million pounds in Harry's new fund and I'm ready for a celebration. As a thank-you, Harry has booked dinner for me and Ellen tonight at The Hideout, the best restaurant in Cheltenham, and I know she's going to love it.

I glance impatiently at my phone, hoping it's a call I don't have to take. The caller name comes up as Tony Heddon, a police detective based in Exeter. We first met twelve years ago when I was arrested on suspicion of Layla's murder, and we've become good friends since. There's a curved steel bench to the left of the reception area so I walk over and put my briefcase down on its metallic seat.

"Tony," I say, taking the call. "Good to hear from you."

"I'm not disturbing you, am I?"

"Not at all," I say, noting that he sounds serious, the way he always does when he calls to tell me that an unidentified woman's body has been found by the French authorities. Guessing how awkward he must feel, I decide to plow straight in. "Has another body been found?"

"No, nothing like that," he says reassuringly in his soft Devonshire accent. "Thomas Winter—you know, your ex-neighbor from St. Mary's—came into the station yesterday."

"Thomas?" I say, surprised. "I didn't think he'd still be alive after all these years. How's he doing?"

"Physically he's pretty good, but he's quite elderly now. Which is why we don't want to give too much importance to what he said," he adds, pausing. I wait for him to carry on and while I wait, my mind analyzes what Thomas could have told them. But then I remember that before Layla and I left for our holiday in France, before she disappeared, Thomas only knew us as the happiest of couples.

"Why, what has he said?" I ask.

"That yesterday, he saw Layla."

My heart misses a beat. I lean my free hand on the cold metal back of the bench, trying to process what he's just told me. I know he's waiting for me to say something, but I can't, so I leave him to fill the silence.

"He said he saw her standing outside the cottage and that when he went to speak to her, she ran off," he goes on.

"Because it wasn't her," I say, my voice neutral.

"That's what I suggested. I reminded him that twelve years have passed since he last saw her but he said he'd know her after fifty. She was wearing a hood thing over her head but he was adamant it was Layla. Something about the way she was standing, apparently."

"But he didn't speak to her."

"No. He said, and I quote, "I called her name and she turned her head, but when she saw me, she ran off." He said she went toward the station but the ticket office was closed at that time and we can't find anyone who saw a woman waiting for a train. There's no CCTV so we're none the wiser."

I search for the right response. "You don't really think it was Layla, do you? Not after all these years."

Tony sighs heavily. "I'm inclined to put it down to Mr. Winter's overactive imagination. I thought you should know, that's all."

"Well, thanks, Tony." I want to hang up but it seems too soon. "When are you retiring? September, isn't it?"

"Yes, just another couple of months to go. Not too sure what I'll do with myself, though."

I grab onto this. "You can start by coming down to see us. I know Ellen would love to see you."

"I will, definitely."

Maybe he understands that I'm not up to speaking because he tells me that he has another call to make. I stand for a moment, trying to get things in perspective, wondering why Thomas thought he saw Layla. I make a quick calculation; we had celebrated his eightieth birthday just before leaving for that fateful holiday in France in 2006, which means Thomas is ninety-two now, an age at which people get easily confused, an age where it's easy to dismiss what they say, or what they think they saw. It can only be the ramblings of an old man. Confident, I take my keys from my pocket and carry on to the car park.

The journey home is unbelievably slow, which isn't unusual for a Friday afternoon. As I drive past the "Welcome to Simonsbridge. Please drive slowly" sign at the entrance to the village, my earlier excitement over the new deal starts to come back. It was good of Harry to book The Hideout; he said I should go for the venison steak, and I probably will.

A minute later I'm pulling up in front of the house, nothing much to look at from the outside maybe, but once inside it's my haven, and the garden, my sanctuary. In a normal world Ellen would be standing on the doorstep, as impatient to see me as I am to see her. More often than not, roused from whatever illustration she's working on by the sound of the tires scrunching on the gravel, she opens the door before I'm out of the car. But not now. And today, it seems ominous.

I tell myself not to be stupid, that she doesn't always open the door, that if I'd phoned ahead to tell her the good news, of course she'd be waiting. But I'd wanted to tell her face-to-face, I want to see her telling me how clever I am rather than just hearing it. I know how it sounds but it isn't that I have a huge ego, more that pulling off this deal is a career highlight. A result like Grant James is such an adrenaline rush. It even beats the high I get from outsmarting the markets.

The sound of my key in the lock doesn't bring her to the door. It doesn't bring Peggy, our red setter, either, which is even more unusual. Instead of calling out, I go in search of Ellen, a flicker of worry making itself felt. As I push open the door to the sitting room, I see her curled up in one of the armchairs, wearing my blue denim shirt, which she continually pinches from my wardrobe. I don't mind, I love to see her in it. She has her knees pulled up to her chest and the shirt pulled down over them, like a tent.

My silent sigh of relief at finding her there is checked by the way she's staring unseeingly out of the window, her eyes on a distant past. It's a look I haven't seen for a while but a look I know only too well. It explains why Peggy—always sensitive to Ellen's mood—is lying silently at her feet.

"Ellen?" I say softly.

She turns her head toward me and as her eyes come into focus, she scrambles to her feet.

"Sorry," she says ruefully, hurrying over to me, Peggy following more sedately behind her, her age showing. "I was miles away."

"I can see that."

She reaches up and kisses me. "How was your day?"

"Good," I say, putting my news about the contract on hold for a moment. "What about yours?"

"Good too." But her smile is just a little too bright.

"So what were you thinking about when I came in?"

She shakes her head. "Nothing."

I put my finger under her chin and tilt her head upward so that she can't avoid my eyes. "You know that doesn't work with me."

"It really is nothing," she insists.

"Tell me."

She gives a small shrug. "It's just that when I came back from taking Peggy for a walk this afternoon, I found this"—she puts her hand into the front pocket of the shirt and takes something out—"lying on the pavement outside the house."

I look down at the painted wooden doll sitting in her palm and a jolt of shock runs through me, quickly followed by a flash of anger, because for one mad moment I think she's been rummaging around in my office. But then I remember that Ellen would never do such a thing, and concentrate on chasing the red mist away. Anyway, hadn't she said that she found it on the pavement outside the house?

"Someone must have dropped it," I say, as casually as I'm able. "A child, on her way back from school or something."

"I know. It's just that it reminded me—" She stops.

"Yes?" I prompt, preparing myself mentally, because I know what she's going to say.

"Of Layla." As always, her name hangs suspended in the air between us. And today, because of Tony's phone call, it feels heavier than usual.

Ellen laughs suddenly, lightening the moment. "At least I have a full set now." And of course, I know what she's referring to.

It was Layla who first told me the story, of how she and Ellen both had a set of Russian dolls, the sort that stack one inside the other and how one day the smallest one from Ellen's set had gone missing. Ellen had accused Layla of taking it but Layla denied that she had, and it had never been found. Now, thirteen years after I first heard that story, the irony strikes me because, like Ellen's little Russian doll, Layla went missing and has never been found.

"Maybe you should put it on the wall outside, like people do with dropped gloves," I say. "Someone might come looking for it."

Her face falls and I feel bad, because it's only a Russian doll. But coming on the back of Tony's phone call, it feels a bit too much.

"I hadn't thought of that," she says.

"Anyway, I'll be able to buy you as many Russian dolls as you like now," I say, although we both know that isn't what this is about.

Her eyes grow wide. "Do you mean . . . ?"

"Yes," I say, lifting her into my arms and spinning her around, noting—not for the first time—how much lighter she is than Layla was. Tendrils of chestnut hair escape her short ponytail and fall around her face. Her hands grip my shoulders.

"Grant James invested?" she squeals.

"He did!" I say, pushing thoughts of Layla away. I stop spinning and lower her to the ground. Dizzy, she stumbles a little against me and I enclose her in my arms.

"That's wonderful! Harry must be over the moon!" She wriggles out of my embrace. "Stay there, I'll be back in a minute."

She disappears into the kitchen and I sit down on the sofa to wait. Peggy pushes herself between my legs and I take her head between my hands, noting with a heavy heart how gray she's getting. I pull her ears gently, as she loves me to do, and tell her how beautiful she is. It's something I often tell her, too often maybe. But the truth is, Peggy has always represented more than just Peggy to me. And now, because of the Russian doll, it seems wrong.

I feel restless, too full of kinetic energy to sit. I want to go to my office—a bespoke outhouse in the garden—and make sure that my Russian doll, the one Ellen doesn't know about, is there, in its hiding place. But I force myself to be patient, reminding myself that everything is good in my world. Still, it's difficult, and I'm about to go and find Ellen when she comes back, a bottle of champagne in one hand, two glasses in the other.

"Perfect," I say, smiling at her.

"I hid it at the back of the fridge a couple of weeks ago," she says, putting the glasses down on the table and holding the bottle out to me.

"No," I say, grasping the bottle and using it to pull her toward me. "I mean you." I hold her tight for a moment, the champagne trapped between our bodies. "Do you know how beautiful you are?" Uncomfortable with compliments, she drops her head and plants a kiss on my shoulder. "How did you know that Grant would come through?" I go on.

"I didn't. But if he hadn't, the champagne would have been to commiserate."

"See what I mean about you being perfect?" Releasing her with a kiss, I untwist the wire and ease the cork from the bottle. Champagne bubbles out and Ellen quickly grabs the glasses from the table. "Guess where I'm taking you tonight?" I say as I fill them.

"McDonald's?" she teases.

"The Hideout."

She looks at me in delight. "Really?"

"Yes. Harry booked it as a thank-you."

Later, while she's upstairs getting ready, I go out to my office in the garden, sit down at my desk and slide open the top right-hand drawer. It's a large antique walnut desk and the drawer is so deep I have to reach a long way in to find the wooden pencil box, hidden at the back. I take out the little painted doll nestling there. It looks identical to the one that Ellen found outside the house and as my fingers close around its smooth, varnished body I feel the same uncomfortable tug I always do, a mixture of longing and regret, of desolation and infinite sadness. And gratitude, because without this little wooden doll, I might have been tried for Layla's murder.

It had belonged to her. It was the smallest one from her set of Russian dolls, the one she'd had as a child, and when Ellen's had gone missing, Layla had carried this one around with her for fear that Ellen would take it and claim it as hers. She called it her talisman, and in times of stress she would hold it between her thumb and index finger and gently rub the smooth surface. She had been doing exactly that on our journey from Megève, huddled against the car door, and the next morning, when the police returned to the picnic area, they'd found it lying on the ground next to where I'd parked the car, by the rubbish bin. They also found scuff marks, which—as my lawyer pointed out—suggested she'd been dragged from the car and had dropped the doll on purpose, as some kind of clue. As there was insufficient evidence to prove this either way, I was finally allowed to leave France, and to keep the Russian doll.

I put it back in its hiding place and go and find Ellen. But later, when we're lying in bed, our hunger sated by the exquisite dinner we had at The Hideout, our bodies knotted together, I silently curse the little Russian doll she found earlier. It's another reminder that no matter how many years go by, we will never be completely free of Layla.

Barely a month goes by that we don't hear her name—someone called out to in the street, a character in a film or book, a newly opened restaurant, a cocktail, a hotel. At least we don't have to contend with supposed sightings of Layla anymore—Thomas's yesterday was the first in years. There'd been hundreds after she first disappeared; it seemed that anyone who had red hair was put forward as a possible candidate.

I look down at Ellen, snuggled in the crook of my arm, and wonder if she's thinking of Layla too. But the steady rise and fall of her chest against me tells me she's already asleep and I'm glad I didn't tell her about Tony's phone call. Everything—all this—would be much easier if Ellen and I had fallen in love with other people instead of each other. It shouldn't matter that Ellen is Layla's sister, not when twelve years have passed since Layla disappeared.

But, of course, it does.

TWO

BEFORE

It feels a lifetime ago that I first saw you, Layla. I'm not sure if you even know this but at the time I had a girlfriend, someone so unlike you, someone who was as high-flying in the world of advertising as I was in my city job. Time is an oddity when it comes to memories; I always think of you when I remember Harry and the flat in St. Katharine Docks, yet you spent much less time in that world than my ex did. You instigated the end of the life I had. Everything became "Before Layla" and "After Layla."

It must have been just after 7 p.m. on New Year's Eve 2004. You probably don't remember that but I know, because Harry had insisted we leave too much time to get to the theater. I'd felt indifferent to it being a big night but then I was indifferent to so many things back then. Until I met you.

As Harry and I went down into the underground station at Liverpool Street, I never thought I was about to fall in love. He needed to top up his Oyster card so while he queued at the machine, I watched everybody rushing to get wherever they were going to celebrate the New Year.

After a few minutes my attention was caught by a flash of color among the gray and blacks of the Londoners, the most beautiful red I'd ever seen. And of course it was you—or rather, your hair. Do you remember how you stood with your back against the opposite wall, your eyes watching in alarm at everyone surging around you? You looked scared, but back then the simplest things seemed to scare you; crowds, dogs, the dark. You were so terrified of dogs that if you saw one coming toward you, you would cross over to the other side of the street to avoid it, even if you were with me, even if it was on a lead. And that day in the underground station, as you pushed yourself further into the wall to avoid the crowds, your hair caught under the artificial lighting and it seemed to be on fire. With your tiny purple skirt, lace-up ankle boots and curvy figure, you looked so different to the stick-thin women in their smart suits and dark winter coats. Then you raised your head, and our eyes met. I felt embarrassed to be caught staring at you so intensely and tried to look away. But your eyes pulled me toward you and before I knew it, I was striding across the concourse.

"Do you need help?" I asked, looking down into your green-brown eyes. Hazel, I learned later. "You seem a little lost."

"It's just that I didn't expect London to be quite so busy," you replied, your voice lilting with a Scottish accent. "All these people!"

"It's New Year's Eve," I explained. "They're on their way out to celebrate."

"So it's not always like this?"

"Early morning and late afternoon, usually. Did you want to buy a ticket?"

"Yes."

"Where are you going?"

Do you remember your reply?

"To a youth hostel," you said.

"Where is it?" I asked.

"I'm not sure. Near Piccadilly Circus, I think."

"Do you have an address?" You shook your head. "On your reservation?" I persevered.

And then you admitted that you hadn't reserved a room.

Your naivety both appalled and charmed me. "It might be difficult to find a bed on New Year's Eve," I explained.

Your skin paled, heightening the freckles, and that's when I fell in love with you.

"Have you got a cell phone?" I asked.

You shook your head again. "No."

To meet someone so unorganized, so unaffected by modern life and the London rush was like a hit of alcohol. If it had been anybody else, I would have walked away quickly before they could ask me how to find a number for a hostel. But I was already realizing that I couldn't walk away from you.

"How old are you?" I asked, because suddenly, I needed to know everything there was to know about you.

"Eighteen. Almost nineteen." You raised your chin defiantly. "I'm not a runaway, if that's what you're thinking."

I was saved from answering by Harry appearing at my elbow.

"I've been looking for you everywhere. Didn't I leave you standing over there?"

My eyes stayed fixed on you. "This young lady is looking for a youth hostel near Piccadilly Circus. Do you know it?" I asked, safe in the knowledge that he wouldn't, because I was already counting on bringing you back to ours.

"No, I'm afraid not." He looked thoughtfully at you. "They must have given you the address when you reserved."

"She doesn't have a reservation."

His eyes widened. "I doubt you'll find a bed on New Year's Eve."

"Then what should I do?" you asked, a slight panic creeping into your voice.

Harry scratched his head as he always did when faced with a problem. "I have no idea."

"We'll have to think of something," I said, my voice low.

He turned to me with that "It isn't our problem" look in his eyes. And he was right, it wasn't our problem, it was mine. "Look, I'll help her look for a hostel, or a hotel, or something," I told him. "We can't just leave her here."

"Well, maybe somebody else can help her. We're going to the theater," he reminded me.

"Look, don't worry, I'll be fine," you said. "I've taken up enough of your time already. It's my fault, I should have planned ahead. But I never realized London would be so . . ."—you searched for a word—". . . crazy."

I reached into my jacket pocket and took out my wallet. "Here," I said, fishing out my theater ticket and handing it to Harry. "Take Samantha. She wanted to go, didn't she?"

"Yes, but—"

I pressed the ticket into his hand. "It's fine. I'll see you at the party later." He tried to catch my eye but I ignored him. "Phone Samantha. She can meet you at the theater." And before he could say another word, I took your bag and set off across the concourse. "Follow me."

I headed for the exit, my heart now hammering as it always did when I was on the verge of doing something exhilarating, or dangerous. Worried I would lose you in the crowds that thronged the streets, I reached for your hand.

“Stay with me!” I shouted above the noise of the traffic.

Your hand tightened around mine. “Don’t worry, I will!” you called back.

And I hoped that you would, forever.

THREE

NOW

It's Saturday, so Peggy and I go to get fresh bread for breakfast while Ellen has a lie-in. On Sundays, I usually lie in while Ellen makes bacon and eggs. Ellen says that one day we'll be too old to lie in and will be up at dawn, making porridge, unable to stay in bed any longer after being awake half the night with insomnia. She's probably right.

It's a short walk to the village where the bakery stands between the newsagent's and the butcher's. I buy a granary loaf and a couple of newspapers, and when I go in to say hello to Rob, the butcher, I see a nice leg of lamb for our lunch tomorrow, a little too big for just me and Ellen, but there's Peggy too.

I take Peggy for a detour along the river on the way home, hoping I won't bump into Ruby, the owner of our local pub, The Jackdaw. She often walks her Airedale in the mornings and it's still a bit awkward when we meet. I first got together with Ruby back in 2014, about a year after a small memorial ceremony we'd had for Layla, where I met Ellen for the first time. Until then, nobody in Simonsbridge knew I was the ex-partner of the young woman who'd gone missing in France. When my true identity was revealed in a newspaper article, not long after the ceremony, it didn't give anyone cause for concern, as I'd been living peacefully among them for six years. People were interested, rather than frightened, about having a possible murderer in their midst. This gave me the confidence to stop hiding myself away and I began to mix with the locals in a way I hadn't before. If people asked me about my past, I spoke truthfully—well, with as much truth as I wanted them to know.

In a strange twist of fate, the journalist who traced me to Devon and "outed" me was a cousin of Ruby's. She felt bad about the role he'd played and made it up to me in more ways than one. I enjoyed being with Ruby; she was vivacious and easygoing. When Harry persuaded me to go back to work, I would stay at the flat in London during the week and return to Simonsbridge on the weekends to see Ruby, and Peggy, who would stay at The Jackdaw while I was away. As far as I was concerned our relationship was a casual thing, something that could be dropped on a Monday morning when I left for London and picked up again when I returned to Simonsbridge on the Friday evening.

I knew from Harry, who had kept in touch with Ellen since the memorial ceremony, that she was trying to make herself a career as an illustrator. When she finally found herself an agent, and had to come to London for meetings, Harry would invite her to stay at the flat. At first, I kept my distance, leaving her and

Harry to have dinner together, wondering if there was something between them. As her career took off, she started coming to London more often and I found myself looking forward to her visits. Sometimes our eyes would meet across the table, and I would look away, determined not to get involved. But then I began inviting her to join me in Simonsbridge on weekends. And relaxing in front of a log-fire one evening, she leaned over and kissed me, and we ended up in bed.

It hadn't been my intention to lie to Ruby when she asked me about Ellen, it was more that I was uncomfortable about who Ellen was. I don't blame Ruby for feeling sore when Ellen moved in with me last year. Unfairly perhaps, I've always suspected Ruby of being behind the "Partner of Missing Woman Moves Sister In" headline which appeared in the paper shortly after. And because Ellen and I are now getting married, I'd like to delay the conversation—the one where Ruby tells me she's very happy for me while throwing me daggers—until I've had time to get used to the idea myself.

We haven't been to The Jackdaw since the wedding announcement appeared in the local paper a couple of weeks ago. Ellen insisted on placing it because she felt that everyone, especially Ruby, should know that she's here to stay. I think she was hoping to silence those who whispered that we shouldn't be in a relationship, as there are some who disapprove that I'm marrying Layla's sister. They don't come right out and say it but I can see it in their eyes and hear it in their voices as they congratulate us.

I call Peggy out from the river, and after she's shaken the water off her and onto me, I take the path back up to the road, glad that I've managed to avoid Ruby. As I approach the house, I see something standing on the stone wall that borders the front garden and recognize the little Russian doll that Ellen found last week. The fact that she kept it for so long before putting it back where she found it tells me how much it means to her and I feel guilty all over again for saying she shouldn't keep it, because I doubt the owner is going to come looking for it. But I also feel guilty for another reason. It's more proof that Ellen never goes against what I tell her, never disobeys me, and although it makes for a peaceful life, I find it perplexing.

I put the doll into my jeans pocket and go into the house. I expect to find her in the kitchen but she calls down to me from upstairs. I send Peggy to fetch her while I check the markets on my phone. A couple of minutes later Ellen comes into the kitchen, looking so desirable in her skimpy pajamas that I want to scoop her into my arms and carry her back to bed.

"I hope you didn't go outside like that," I tease.

"Outside?"

"To put the Russian doll back." I slip my hand into my pocket, intending to surprise her with it, because why shouldn't she keep it?

"I haven't put it back yet."

I look at her, thinking that she's joking. But her cheeks have flushed red.

My fingers, clasped around the Russian doll, freeze. "What do you mean, you haven't put it back yet?"

"I was going to do it after breakfast," she says, mistaking my shock for annoyance. "I wasn't going to keep it."

"Where is it?" I hate that I sound angry because I'm not, I'm rattled.

She hurries out of the room and comes back carrying the large Russian doll that has sat on top of the teak cupboard in our dining room since she moved in with me last year. She unscrews it in the middle, takes out the Russian doll inside, unscrews that one in the middle, takes out the next one, un-screws it, then takes out the next one. As she twists the last one apart, I realize that she's joking, that there'll be nothing inside and she'll smile and tell me that of course she put the doll back outside. I raise an eyebrow and begin to smile.

"Here it is." She takes a little Russian doll out and puts it down on the worktop amid its dissected relatives. "I was only going to keep it for a while."

Keeping the smile on my face, I casually remove my hand from my pocket, leaving the doll I found on the wall where it is. "Hey, it's fine, keep it if you want to."

She looks at me doubtfully. "Really?"

"Yes, nobody's going to come looking for it, are they?"

"No, I suppose not." She begins putting the Russian dolls back together but instead of stacking them one inside the other she places them side by side on the kitchen worktop, starting with the biggest and ending with the little one. It matches the rest of her set exactly. "There we are, a complete family of five. How strange that after all these years, I've finally found what's been missing."

I turn away, wondering what she would say if I told her that I just found a second Russian doll. If Layla's body had been found, she would put it down to a bizarre coincidence. But her body has never been found. And if there's one thing I don't want, it's Ellen thinking that Layla might still be alive.

I'd hate for her to have false hope.

FOUR

BEFORE

That night, it took thirty-six minutes to get from Liverpool Street Station to St. Katharine Docks. As we made our way through the crowds standing outside pubs and wine bars, already celebrating the New Year, I told myself it was the atmosphere that made me feel drunk. But I knew it was because of you.

"What's your name?" I asked.

"Layla."

"I expected something more Scottish," I admitted.

"I was lucky, my mum got to choose my name. My dad chose my sister's name and she wasn't so fortunate. He's originally from Islay so he called her Ellen, after Port Ellen."

"It's still a pretty name."

"Yes, it is. What about you? What's your name?"

"Finn."

"Irish?"

"Yes. I was born and raised in Ireland," I explained.

You couldn't get over the size of the Tower of London, proudly illuminated against the night sky, or the majesty of Tower Bridge. By the time we reached the docks, where people were partying on the various yachts and boats moored there, you were completely overwhelmed.

"This is London?" you asked.

"It is," I said, pleased at your reaction to the city I loved. I stopped in front of my apartment block. "And this is where I live."

"Where you live?" You seemed suddenly doubtful and I remembered that I was meant to be finding you a hostel or hotel.

"Yes. You'll never find somewhere to stay tonight so you can stay with me and Harry. Tomorrow, we'll find you a hostel." You still weren't convinced. "We have a little study with a sofa bed; you can sleep there. You'll be fine, I promise."

I tapped in the door code and after a moment's hesitation you followed me inside. In the lift, your unease grew—but of course, I had more or less kidnapped you. I wanted to put your mind at rest, to tell you that I hadn't been lying, that you would never have found anywhere to stay that night because every hotel, every hostel would have been booked up months ago. But we were already on the third floor and I hoped that once you saw the flat, you'd feel more comfortable.

"Oh my God, is this really yours?" you breathed as I showed you around.

"Mine and Harry's."

"It's beautiful!"

The next couple of hours passed in a blur. You were hungry, do you remember? So I made an omelette and while we ate, we exchanged information about our lives. You told me you'd lived on Lewis, a remote island in the Outer Hebrides, all your life and had been fairly happy until you were fourteen and your mother died. After, things had become difficult, you said. Your father became an alcoholic and ever since, you'd been counting the days until you could leave.

"I stayed for Christmas," you said. "Then I packed up and left. I was determined to be in London for the first of January." You paused, and the light from the massive lamp that hung above the dining room table bounced off your hair. "A new year, a new life. That's what I'm hoping for, anyway."

"What about your sister?" I asked. "Didn't she want to leave?"

Your eyes had filled with tears. "Yes. But in the end she couldn't."

"Why not?"

You took a long time answering. "My dad has cancer. He's also diabetic. Somebody has to look after him."

"I'm sorry."

You laughed suddenly, unnerving me. "Can we talk about something else? I don't want to be sad on New Year's Eve."

"I'm meant to be going to a party tonight." I pointed through the window at a building on the opposite side of the dock. "My boss lives on the top floor. We should go."

You looked doubtful. "I don't really have anything to wear to a party."

"You're fine as you are," I told you.

I don't remember much about the party except feeling as if I'd stepped into a parallel universe. You were completely out of place among the women in their dresses, their nails manicured and polished, their hair styled, and I couldn't believe it was a world I'd inhabited just a few hours before. It felt stifling and dull, and when Caroline slid her arms around my waist and asked me how I'd enjoyed the theater, I had trouble remembering she was my girlfriend. I introduced her to you and explained something of what had happened. Maybe it was the mention of a youth hostel, but the story amused her and when she turned and raised her eyebrows at me, I knew she was laughing at you. And my fists clenched, hating her for it.

FIVE

NOW

It's amazing how those two Russian dolls play on my mind. It would be easier if I'd thrown the one I found away, or at least confined it to the drawer in my desk along with the other one, the one that had belonged to Layla. But I keep it close to me, in my pocket, a reminder that I can't be complacent. Inevitably, though, it brings back memories of Layla. It doesn't help that Ellen has left her family of Russian dolls standing in a row on the kitchen worktop, instead of stacking them back together again, one inside the other, and returning them to the dining room. I don't want to ask her to move them because I don't want to give too much importance to the fact that she hasn't, or make her think that they make me uncomfortable. But the fact is, they do. Maybe it's the way Ellen's eyes are continually drawn toward them, reassuring herself that the smallest one is still there, that it's not going to suddenly disappear, like Layla did all those years ago.

I've just dropped her off at the station in Cheltenham in time for the ten o'clock train to London. She has a lunch meeting with her agent to discuss illustrations for a new book, and is going shopping in the afternoon, so she won't be home until late. I could have gone with her, gone into the office, but I tend to work from home nowadays. There's not a lot I can't do from the bank of screens I've installed in my office.

I check the markets, catch up on the news, make a couple of calls, look for new shares to invest in. I usually read the newspapers online, because it's more practical, but today I have physical copies, bought at the station earlier. So at lunchtime I return to the kitchen, make myself a pot of coffee and a sandwich and, with Peggy at my feet, spend a couple of hours reading the papers cover to cover, instead of only the financial sections, as I normally do. There's a small paragraph in the *Financial Times* about Grant James's investment in Richmond Global Equities, and I'm glad all over again that I managed to pull it off. Harry has done a lot for me in my forty-one years, so it's a relief to be able to do something in return.

If anyone has shaped my life, it's Harry. He was my brother's best friend at the LSE, and when Liam was killed in a motorbike accident not long after graduation, Harry had been there for me. Since then, he's got me out of trouble and back onto the right path more times than I care to remember. He was there twenty years ago, when I needed to get out of Ireland double-quick, inviting me to stay with him in London while I sorted myself out. A couple of months later, fed up with me mooching round his flat, filled with self-hatred, he gave me a job at Villiers, his investment firm, where I became fascinated with the workings of the markets and quickly earned a reputation for being ruthless. He was there during the nightmare of Layla's disappearance, hiring the best lawyers and whisking me back to England as soon as the French police allowed me to leave. He was there at the cottage in St. Mary's, helping me look for Layla, using his contacts and printing "Missing" posters, which he arranged to have distributed in and around the Fonches area. He was there six months later, when I could no longer stand the silent recrimination of the empty cottage, taking me back to London, to the flat I still co-owned with him. And he was there nine months after that, when I could no longer bear the London streets that echoed with Layla's presence, installing me in Simonsbridge, a little village tucked away in the Cotswolds, because he had a friend who was moving abroad and had a house to rent there.

At first, in Simonsbridge, it was no different. I lived the life of a hermit, as I had done in London, with only thoughts of Layla and playing the markets for company. I only ventured out when Harry visited and, unable to stand the stench of despair that permeated the house, dragged me along to The Jackdaw for a drink. Through the fog that clouded my brain, I was dimly aware that Ruby, the landlady, liked me. But I wasn't interested, not then.

After a few months, Harry tried to get me to go back to work. When I refused, knocking back a glass of whiskey with one hand and reaching for the bottle with the other, he told me I needed a dog. So we visited dog home after dog home where I turned down so many potential companions that Harry was bemused. I couldn't tell him what I was looking for because I didn't know myself. Then I saw Peggy and when Harry asked me why I'd chosen her, I didn't dare tell him it was because her coat was the same color as Layla's beautiful hair.

During all that time, Harry never once asked what really

happened the night Layla disappeared. Ellen has never asked me either. She's never had any reason to doubt my version of events, which were widely published in the press at the time. It's why I found myself asking her to marry me; basically, I got caught out in a lie.

When the police questioned me, in the long days and even longer nights that followed Layla's disappearance, I told them that during our holiday in Megève I'd asked her to marry me and that she had accepted. There was no truth in this, but I needed the police, and everyone else, to believe that everything had been perfect between us during those last few days. As the years passed, I presumed my lie had been laid to rest. Then, a couple of months ago, Ellen, out of the blue, said that Layla must have been very happy when I'd asked her to marry me.

"Yes, she was," I said, taken aback that she'd suddenly brought it up.

"You must have loved her very much to propose." Ellen's voice was quiet. "You hadn't been together very long." She paused, her eyes finding mine. "About the same amount of time as us, in fact."

She was right. I was with Layla for thirteen months before she disappeared and it was over a year since Ellen had moved in with me. I looked back at her, uncertain as to what she was thinking. Was she hoping for the same commitment? She'd never once asked if I loved Layla more than I loved her. But that day, I knew that if I didn't ask her to marry me, she would think I loved her less. So I ignored the feeling that I was somehow betraying Layla, and proposed.

Ellen had shaken her head. "I don't want you to feel that you have to marry me just because you proposed to Layla."

I hesitated, because I didn't want her to think less of me. But maybe it was time to come clean. "Actually, I didn't," I admitted.

"What do you mean?"

"It was something I said to the police at the time of my arrest, to make it look better."

"So you hadn't asked her to marry you?"

"No."

"But you were going to," she stated. And because I wanted her to feel that I loved her more than I'd loved Layla, I decided to lie. "No."

She looked at me in surprise. "No?"

"No." I repeated. But the truth was, I had been going to propose to Layla, on her twentieth birthday, the month after we got back from Megève. I'd had it all planned; I'd even bought the ring.

But then she spoiled everything.

SIX

BEFORE

The day after the New Year's Eve party, I told Caroline it was over. And when you tried to move out of my flat, a few days later, I did everything I could to persuade you to stay. Without asking Harry, I told you that you could have the study, at least until you found a job, saying that he wouldn't mind. But you were adamant that you wanted to move into a youth hostel, telling me that if you were to make a life for yourself in London, you needed to meet other young people. The realization that you thought of me as old was hard to take—hell, I was only twenty-seven. But in your eyes, I was nothing more than an older guy who had given you shelter for a couple of days.

In the event, you stayed a little over a week. For a man who lives in the present, I can still picture every minute of the day you moved out. I helped you move into the hostel you'd found, hoping you'd soon become disillusioned with sharing a room with five other people. Your idea was to find a job as soon as possible, which would allow you to move into a flat-share.

When it came to saying good-bye, I gave you my business card, telling you to call me if you needed help of any kind. And then I went back to my flat and drank half a bottle of whiskey, moaning at Fate for leading you to me when you weren't going to become a permanent fixture in my life.

Harry was bemused, then fascinated that I'd fallen so hard for you, Layla Gray. He pointed out that my girlfriends to date had all been smart, young city women and that you were unsophisticated in comparison. He couldn't see that that was the biggest attraction for me. Even before you, I'd become increasingly disenchanted with the uniformity of it all: the smart business suits, the killer heels, the sharp fingernails that raked my back with dreary repetition during sex. Harry tried to tell me that what I felt was infatuation and I tried to believe him. I also tried to forget you, working and partying twice as hard as before, to fill the void you'd left in my life.

I lived in hope of you phoning me, just to let me know how you were getting on. When a month passed without news, I told myself that you never would. And then, two months after you first disappeared from my life, you walked back in.

SEVEN

NOW

I look at Ellen across the table, her head bent over her bowl of muesli, Greek yogurt and blueberries, and find myself comparing it to Layla's breakfasts of toast and chocolate spread. I frown, annoyed with myself. I've been doing that a lot lately, not just thinking about Layla, but comparing Ellen to her.

Sensing my eyes on her, Ellen looks up. Although I'm staring at her, I don't see her, I see Layla, which is strange because physically, she's nothing like Layla. Maybe it's her hazel eyes. Are they what attracted me to her in the first place, because they reminded me of Layla's?

"So," she says, "any plans for today?"

I force myself away from the past and back to the present. But it leaves behind a trace of anxiety, spawned from the two Russian dolls we found, and I look over at Ellen's set suspiciously, because she still hasn't put them away.

"I'll probably go for a run. Maybe water the garden first. It's as dry as a bone." She smiles approvingly and I can't help remembering how Layla had laughed when I told her that one day, I wanted a beautiful garden in the country so that I could grow my own vegetables.

"Gardening is for old men!" she'd mocked. I'd never mentioned it again.

"Have you remembered that I'm going into Cheltenham this morning, to the beauty salon?" Ellen asks.

I hadn't, but I should have, because every three weeks Ellen subjects herself to an intense beauty regime: waxing, tweezing, a manicure and God knows what else, followed by a session with her hairdresser, who operates from the same salon. Ellen takes care of herself in a way that Layla never did. Layla never cared much how she looked.

"Maybe I'll come and meet you for lunch," I say.

"That'll be lovely," she smiles.

I stand up, take my plate and reach for hers.

"Leave it," she says, putting a hand on my arm. "I'll clear away, I've got time before I go."

Suddenly, the thought of being on my own while she's in town, with memories of Layla within easy reach, makes me claustrophobic. I run a hand over my chin, wondering if I could get my beard trimmed, or thinned, while Ellen is at the salon. But I keep it so short it doesn't really need it.

"I may as well come with you now," I say. "No point taking two cars. I'll take my laptop and have a coffee while you're at the salon."

It's not in her nature to ask why I've changed my mind, nor to question why the garden that needs water so urgently can wait.

"I'll be quite a while," she warns.

"I'll have two coffees then," I grin.

I park in the High Street and walk her to the salon, telling her to call me when she's finished. The Bookshop Café, my favorite place in Cheltenham, is further along the same street, so I head there and set up a makeshift office. I order coffee and become engrossed in my work until Ellen calls.

I go to meet her and watch as she comes out of the salon. She looks good, her angular face striking.

"Beautiful," I tell her. Unbidden, an image of Layla's long red hair, which reached almost to the small of her back, comes into my mind. "Where would you like to go for lunch?" I ask, chasing it away.

"Marco's?" she suggests, so we cross over the road to the Italian Bistro.

An hour or so later, full of truffle-stuffed pasta, we make our way back to the car, Ellen's hand on my arm. As we approach I see something lodged under the wiper. It's not flat enough to be a parking ticket, and, anyway, we haven't overstayed the four hours I paid for, so I guess someone has scrunched an advert they found on their car into a ball and stuck it on mine. But as we get nearer I find my steps slowing, until I'm not walking anymore, I'm just standing there staring. My first thought is to protect Ellen but the strangled cry that comes from her throat tells me I'm too late.

"It's all right, Ellen," I say, reaching for her hand. But she snatches it back and starts running down the street, pushing her way through a family with children. And as I run after her, I take a little Russian doll from under the wiper, shoving it deep into my pocket.

I catch up with her twenty yards or so further along. She's stopped running and is leaning pale-faced against a shop window. People pass by, looking at her with concern.

"It's all right, Ellen," I say again, my mind all over the place at finding another Russian doll. She shakes her head, unable to speak, not because running has made her breathless but because she's near to tears. So I put my arms around her and wait for her to ask me about the doll on our car.

"I know it's stupid but I'm sure it was her," she says, her voice muffled by my shirt. "Maybe it was my imagination, or someone else with red hair, but Finn—I'm certain I just saw Layla!"

Shock jolts through me. "Is that why you ran?" I ask, needing to know whether or not she saw the Russian doll, wondering if she can feel my heart hammering under my shirt.

"Yes. You saw her too, didn't you?" I shake my head, my eyes searching around us for someone who could look like Layla. "You stopped so suddenly, it's how I noticed her," she goes on.

"I only stopped because I remembered that I wanted to buy some wine for tonight and we'd just gone past the wine shop," I invent, my eyes still searching the crowd.

"Oh." She gives a self-conscious laugh. "You must have thought I'd gone mad, running off down the street like that. I was so sure it was Layla. But it couldn't have been, of course." She looks up at me, seeking reassurance.

"It was probably someone with the same color hair," I say.

"It's just that since I found that little Russian doll outside the house, I can't stop thinking about her."

"It's normal," I soothe, guiding her back down the road to where the car is parked.

"What about the wine you wanted to get?"

"It can wait. Come on, let's go home."

"Could we walk around a bit first?" she asks. "I know it probably wasn't Layla but . . ." Her voice trails off.

"Of course."

"You don't mind?"

"No," I say.

Because I know we're not going to find her.

EIGHT

BEFORE

The night you came back, I'd been at another party, half-heartedly pretending to enjoy myself. Harry had wanted me to go with him because he was fed up with me moping—as he called it—around the flat over you. I didn't like being at odds with him so I'd agreed to go. But as I looked around me at the party that night, I felt like shooting myself.

Caroline was there. She kept throwing me glances while flirting with other men and I knew she was waiting for me to admit that I'd made a mistake in breaking things off with her. A sudden rush of loneliness made me wonder if I had, and I searched inside me for something that would tell me I should take her home with me. But although I tried, I couldn't drum up the slightest bit of jealousy, or desire, so I left.

It was almost three in the morning when I walked back through St. Katharine Docks. As I approached the flat, I saw someone huddled in the doorway of the building, sheltering from the cold. I didn't realize it was you until you raised your head.

You were so cold you could barely stand. As I half-carried you into the entrance hall, I saw that your lips were blue. It took forever for the lift to arrive and while we waited, I thanked God that I hadn't stayed at the party any longer. You won't remember this but it took about an hour to get your body temperature back to normal. I wrapped you in a duvet, massaged your feet and hands to get the circulation going and gave you warm sweet tea to drink. It was as you were drinking it that you began to cry. I didn't ask you any questions and you didn't offer any explanation but I guessed it must have gone horribly wrong for you at the hostel. It was only later that you explained you hadn't been able to find a job and that, a few days previously, all your money had been stolen while you slept.

I was going to put you in your old bed in the study, where you'd slept before, but I decided to leave you on the sofa because you were warm and comfortable there. I slipped a pair of my socks over your feet and tucked the duvet tightly around you. It felt so right looking after you; for the first time in weeks I felt I had a purpose. I told you to call me if you needed anything but as I left the room you called me back, and the sound of my name on your lips made my heart start beating faster because there was something in your voice that I'd never heard before; a sort of yearning, a longing, almost. I told myself that all you wanted was a glass of water but, your voice breaking, you asked me not to leave you. So I sat down on the sofa and wrapped my arms around you while you slept.

NINE

NOW

Although we haven't mentioned Layla's name again, I know she hasn't been out of our thoughts since our shopping trip on Saturday. We'd walked around the town for over an hour, peering into shops and cafés, and I'd pretended to look for her with as much desperation as Ellen. Ever since, Ellen has that faraway look in her eyes and when I ask her if she's all right, there's a slight hesitation before she tells me that she is.

At any other time I'd insist on knowing the reason for the hesitation because it would mean that something is troubling her, and I never want Ellen to be troubled by anything. She gave me the life I live now and the love I feel for her will always be magnified by gratitude. But because I know the reason for her hesitation, I don't probe any further. Ellen wants to ask me if I think Layla could still be alive. What I need to work out is why someone is trying to provoke me, because with the appearance of a third doll, the two we found outside the house can no longer be classed as coincidence. Someone put them there deliberately and I need to find out who.

Maybe I should ask the neighbors if they saw anyone outside our house, without mentioning specifics. But our house is on one side of the road, by itself, and Mrs. Jeffries, the elderly lady who lives directly opposite us, isn't the sort of neighbor who sits in her front room looking out of the window. She's more likely to be in her conservatory out the back, or keeping an eye on the lady in the house next door to her, who's seriously ill.

She and her husband moved in some months ago but we rarely see them. I've never seen her, and apart from a quick hello if we're both out front at the same time, I've only had a conversation with Mick once, when he came round to introduce himself. He told us something of their story, probably in a preemptive attempt to stop us from inviting them around for drinks. It seems that four years ago they were involved in a car crash and lost their two young sons. His wife was badly injured and has to deal with a lot of pain and consequently suffers from depression. He didn't give any more details, about who was driving or whose fault it was, only to say that their move to Simonsbridge was an attempt to make a fresh start. He works mostly from home—he's an accountant—so that he can be on hand for his wife, and if he's out visiting clients, Mrs. Jeffries takes over.

Over two weeks have passed since I found the second Russian doll on the wall so it's a bit late to ask Mick or Mrs. Jeffries if they saw anything. I should still ask them to keep an eye out—whoever left the doll on my car has upped their game, wanting me to know that they followed me to Cheltenham. The fact that Ellen thought she saw Layla doesn't trouble me; it was unfortunate that there was someone with red hair walking along the street at the time. Or fortunate, because if Ellen hadn't run off after her, she'd have seen the doll on the car. And I need to protect her from whatever is going on.

I look at the clock; it's coming up to twelve and I haven't done any work since I came out to my office at nine. To take my mind off the Russian dolls, I play around with some shares for a bit. Ellen doesn't know about this guilty pleasure of mine. I've never told her of the wealth I've accumulated over the years by playing the markets, probably because deep down I'm slightly ashamed of it. I've tried to stop but it's become an addiction, just as Layla was all those years ago.

I push back from my desk, annoyed that I'm thinking of Layla again. I'm hungry, so I make my way across the garden to the house. I expect Ellen to be in her office but through the open kitchen door I see her standing at the worktop and as I watch, she picks the smallest of the Russian dolls up by its head and holds it in front of her eyes, turning it this way and that, a strange look on her face.

"Everything OK?" I ask, wanting to put a stop to whatever she's doing, because it's making me uncomfortable.

I expect her to jump guiltily as she usually does whenever I catch her with the Russian dolls. But she just nods vaguely and carries on examining it.

"Ellen," I say.

"It's the one I lost, I'm sure of it." Her voice is so quiet it's as if she's talking to herself. I go over to her, needing to break the spell the doll seems to have cast on her.

"What do you mean?"

"I think Layla might be alive," she says, without turning round.

"What do you mean, she might be alive?"

"Look." She holds out the doll. "See that smudge of paint there? Mine had one exactly like it."

"That doesn't prove anything," I say, peering at the black smudge near its base. "I'm sure lots of dolls have those. It's bound to happen—paint gets smudged."

She shakes her head stubbornly, something she's never done before. "I dismissed it at first, like you. But the more I look at it, the more I think it's the one that I lost. And I know Layla took it, even though she said she didn't. It's mine, I'm sure of it."

"Because you want it to be," I say gently. "Just like you want it to be Layla you saw in Cheltenham on Saturday. But it wasn't. Layla isn't alive, Ellen, not after all this time."

She nods slowly. "It's probably just as well."

I look at her curiously. "Why do you say that?"

"I'd give anything for her to be alive, of course I would." She pauses, searching for the words. "But I'm not sure she'd be happy to see us together, not when you used to be with her. It would be difficult." Her voice trails away.

I pull her into my arms. "I tried so hard not to fall in love with you," I say, my lips in her hair.

"I know," she says softly. "I remember. I kept hoping that you would make the first move. But you didn't and I realized it had to come from me."

Her words echo down the years and I let go of her abruptly.

"You do still want to get married, don't you?" she asks anxiously.

"Of course," I tell her, doing my best to make my smile reach my eyes.

But first I need to find the person who's decided to mess with my head.

TEN

BEFORE

"Promise you'll never leave me again," I murmured, about a month after you came back. I should have made you promise out loud.

You turned your face to mine, and I reached out and tucked your hair behind your ear.

"I love you," I said, glad that I could finally speak the words I'd wanted to say aloud since I first saw you. "I truly love you, Layla Gray."

"I hope so," you teased. "You've just taken my virginity."

I'm sure you'll remember that day—it was the first time we'd slept together and we were lying, our bodies entwined, listening to the pattering of the rain against the window. Even after all these years, I still remember you slipping into my bed in the middle of the night, sliding your arms around me, telling me that you loved me, that you wanted me.

"I couldn't wait any longer," you murmured. "I kept waiting for you to come to me and then I realized that you weren't going to, that you were waiting for me to make the first move."

Once you were back, you became the most important thing in my life, to the exclusion of everything and everyone else. I no longer spent any meaningful time with Harry and that made things tough. He hadn't taken to you in the way that I'd hoped he would, as he had to all the other girls that had peppered my life during the years we'd shared a flat together. Not that I think you ever noticed, because how could you believe anyone wouldn't like you? But Harry was convinced I shouldn't be with you, and when I began to draw away from him it put a further wedge between you both.

On weekends, when his disapproval chased us from the flat, I'd take you to museums and art exhibitions. I knew you found them boring, although you pretended otherwise. But you were never very good at lying. The problem was, London amplified the difference in our ages. Because of the nature of my job, I rarely got home before eleven. You'd found a job in that wine bar a minute's walk from the flat, and often worked until midnight. And when you weren't working, you wanted to go out, just as I had when I'd first arrived in London seven years before. I knew then that I needed to get us out of London. I can admit it now; I was desperate to move away before you found me boring too. I'd never felt dull, until you came along and challenged me.

It was the argument with Harry that brought things to a head. One evening, he asked if we could have a drink together, on our own, and I was immediately on edge. When he told me that he felt you were having a negative impact on me, that both my work and my relationships were suffering and that you were probably only with me for monetary reasons, I sprang from my chair, my hands clenched into fists. Harry, who knew my shameful past and had witnessed my temper firsthand, didn't flinch; it was as if he was proving himself right—that you'd sparked the side of me I'd promised to keep under control. He let me come at him, fixing me with his eyes, never letting his gaze drop, trying to shut down the red mist that was already blinding me. But I was too far gone. Not only did I knock him to the floor, I carried on hitting him while he was down, raining punches onto his face, his body, wanting to pulp him into nothing, to obliterate him. If others hadn't intervened, dragging me off him, I don't know what would have happened.

They wanted to call the police, I remember, but Harry, spitting blood from his mouth, told them not to. Guilt replaced the rage I'd felt. I couldn't bear to look at his bruised and swollen face so I left him bleeding in the bar. I knew I couldn't go back to the flat so I found a hotel for the night and asked you to meet me there. When I told you what had happened, you were horrified, and then angry, because you'd never seen that side of me before.

How I wish it could have stayed that way.

ELEVEN

NOW

I read the email again, then sit back in my chair, thinking about St. Mary's. I haven't been back to Devon since the ceremony we had for Layla, five years ago now. It was Tony who'd suggested it. It seemed to come out of the blue but the timing wasn't lost on me. It was seven years since Layla had gone missing, so around the time that she would have been declared dead had she gone missing in the UK, and I suspected that Tony, who over the years had kept Ellen and me informed of any developments, hoped a ceremony would give us some kind of closure. Except that being declared dead isn't the same as being dead.

I wasn't keen, I remember, but Tony said Ellen was, and as she was Layla's sister, I felt she had more right to decide than me. Their father had died six months previously and I guessed she wanted to put the past behind her and move on. I thought she would choose to do something on Lewis and I was looking forward to finally visiting the island where Layla had grown up. But I never got to Lewis because Ellen told Tony that Layla's happiest times had been with me, and suggested putting up a bench in a place that had some special meaning for the two of us.

I immediately thought of Pharos Hill. Layla had loved it there—the half-hour's walk from St. Mary's, the legend of the lighthouse that had once stood on top of the hill, although nothing remained of it, just a few ruins. We often climbed it for the beautiful view that stretched out over the sea for miles, sitting with our backs against the tree stump which was shaped, Layla said, like a Russian doll. So I bought a simple wooden bench in kit form and drove to Devon with Peggy, while Tony collected Ellen from Exeter Station.

I was dreading meeting Ellen that day. The only direct contact I'd had with her had been a letter I'd received a couple of months after Layla's disappearance, telling me that she knew I wouldn't have done anything to hurt her sister. It had only compounded the guilt I felt and I hoped that seven years on, it wouldn't be visible on my face. But apart from her eyes, Ellen was very different from Layla. If she'd had the same red hair, the same freckled skin, I would have found it difficult. She was slimmer than Layla, more conservatively dressed, more reserved. In short, she was the proverbial older sister and it seemed on that first meeting that she never smiled. It was still awkward though, and with my mind on Layla, I left Tony to do the talking.

Tony and I carried the box up Pharos Hill between us, Ellen following behind with a small bag of tools, Peggy at our heels. We put the bench together in near silence, and after, we'd sat side by side, each of us lost in our own thoughts, while Peggy played with the empty packaging. And sitting there in the late afternoon sun, with someone who had known Layla better than I had, and someone who hadn't known her at all, I'd felt a kind of peace.

I told myself I'd go back to Devon every year, on the anniversary of Layla's disappearance or on her birthday, or on the anniversary of the day we put up the bench, but I never have. I preferred to forget about Devon, taught myself to not even think about it. It's the email I just received that has stirred up all these memories.

It came in on my work email and was from someone claiming to be looking for a house to buy in Devon. It made me immediately suspicious. I've never sold the cottage where I lived with Layla so, technically, I do have one I could sell. But how would they know this? There aren't many people who know I still own it. Even Ellen doesn't know. She's never asked about the cottage, just as she never asked why I don't have any photos of Layla in the house. When she moved in, she didn't ask if she could put any up, which meant a lot to me, that she'd understood. Neither of us needs reminding that it's Layla who binds us together.

I look again at the email, a random message sent to addresses on a mailing list, I presume. There's no name but it's contained in the email address rudolph.hill@outlook.com. So who is Rudolph Hill and how much does he know? I decide to treat it as a genuine inquiry—which it could very well be—and send back a quick response:

Sorry I can't help

To my surprise, a reply comes straight back.

What about the cottage in St. Mary's? Surely you're not going to keep it, now that you're going to marry the sister?

My heart gives an almighty thud. I read the email again, thinking I must have misread it. But it's even more disturbing than before, because this time, there can be no mistake.

I try to be objective. Rudolph Hill, or the source behind him, has to be someone who knows my past. Ellen's announcement about our engagement will have been logged online somewhere, and knowing the relentless competitive drive in journalists to find a new story—or a new angle to an old story—there are probably Google alerts set up for my name. So this could simply be a reporter wanting to make a story out of "Partner of Missing Woman Hangs on to Cottage Despite Plans to Marry Sister" or some equally puerile headline. He must have done some digging to know that I still own the cottage in St. Mary's. Or used old knowledge. Is it the same person who left the Russian dolls? Are both these things part of some elaborate plan to make trouble for me? But who would want to? Because the Russian dolls were left with such ease, it has to be someone local.

A voice in my head hisses Ruby's name. I never found out if she was responsible for the "Partner of Missing Woman Moves Sister In" article, because it didn't really matter, even if it did stir up some animosity toward Ellen. I don't remember the name of her journalist cousin but it could be Rudolph Hill.

I find it hard to believe that Ruby would do such a thing. I understand that she's sore at me over Ellen, I understand she feels I treated her badly, and I did. But why play games, and why now, why not last year when Ellen first moved in with me? It has to be more than just to get back at me. I look at the email again, at the mention of my marriage to Ellen. And then it hits. The wedding. It changes everything—at least, in Ruby's eyes, because it makes my relationship with Ellen permanent.

I go and find Ellen. She's in the kitchen, standing in front of the open fridge, looking at its contents, Peggy sitting hopefully beside her. She turns at my arrival and her face lights up, reminding me how lucky I am to have her.

"I was wondering what to make for lunch," she says.

I go over and slide my hands around her waist.

"Wonder no longer," I tell her. "I'm taking you out." Turning up at The Jackdaw with Ellen is the best way I can think of to test Ruby, see what her reaction is when she sees me standing there so soon after her email. And safer than confronting her in private, where I might find it harder to keep hold of the anger I feel at her stupid games.

I pull Ellen toward me, and her body folds into mine. I bend my head to kiss her and when she responds passionately, we almost end up having sex, right there in front of the fridge.

"Are you sure you want to go out for lunch?" she murmurs when I begin to pull away. But I need to get this thing with Ruby sorted.

"Yes," I say. "Let's walk down to The Jackdaw." She looks questioningly at me. "We've given Ruby enough time to get used to the idea that we're getting married," I explain. "Besides, Peggy is missing Buster and I could murder a steak-and-ale pie."

I run upstairs to fetch my wallet and we walk down to the village, our fingers locked together. I walk fast because I'm impatient to get there, impatient to put an end to the uncertainty of the last three weeks, when Ellen found the first Russian doll. I want—need—to get back to how we were before, without memories of Layla intruding on us. But with Peggy stopping to explore under every hedge, it's impossible to hurry, so I content myself with imagining the look on Ruby's face when Ellen and I walk in.

The Jackdaw is packed, as it always is on a Friday lunchtime, with tourists outnumbering the locals, who know to avoid the rush and arrive later in the afternoon, once it's over. There aren't any free tables in the garden so we make our way inside. Buster is in his basket next to the bar and opens his eyes to check us out before he goes first to Peggy, then to Ellen, who bends so that he can lick her face, so different from Layla, who was too scared to touch dogs.

Peggy slopes off to drink some watered-down beer from Buster's bowl and out of the corner of my eye I see Ruby coming toward us, her dark curls held back from her face by a red bandana, a bunch of silver bracelets on her arm. She likes to pretend she has gypsy blood but the truth is that her dark skin and black hair are a legacy from her Italian grandparents.

"Long time no see!" she says, greeting us with a kiss. "I hope you haven't been avoiding me." There's amusement in her voice as she says this, as if she knows that we've been keeping out of her way since the wedding announcement appeared and I have to admire how good an actress she is. But when she insists on opening a bottle of champagne to celebrate our forthcoming wedding, doubt begins to creep in. I know Ruby well, and what you see is what you get.

We leave Peggy with Buster, and Ruby finds us a table. She fetches three glasses and pours the champagne.

"You've got yourself a good one there," she says to Ellen, raising her glass. "You too, Finn," she adds, which is generous of her because I know she thinks Ellen is wrong for me and not just because she's Layla's sister. "I hope you'll both be very happy."

After five minutes of perfectly normal small talk, all to do with the wedding, which will take place at the end of September in the little stone church in the next village along, Ruby takes our order and leaves—but not after raising her eyebrows at me when Ellen orders a small salad and no starter. There's no malice in her gesture, just a good-natured *Seriously? Is that all she's having?* I can see where she's coming from—in contrast to Ruby herself, Ellen watches her weight constantly. She's super-slim without an ounce of fat on her and no amount of encouragement will persuade her to have anything remotely caloric. I used to tease Layla about the amount she ate and also about the weight she'd started to put on once we moved to Devon. That's the thing about losing someone; you tend to remember every careless remark, even those made in jest.

While we're waiting for Ruby to bring lunch, we finish the champagne and while we're drinking it, I'm wondering why it isn't adding up, why this Ruby seems so at odds with the Ruby behind the dolls and emails. So maybe it's not Ruby, maybe it's somebody else.

The hardest thing I've had to deal with over the years is the possibility that Layla was kidnapped from the car park in France. At first, I thought she'd run away because of what happened that night, and that she would quickly turn up safe and sound. But as the days wore on, then the weeks and months, I had to consider what the police believed, which was that she'd been taken by someone, either the driver of the car I'd seen parked outside the toilet block, or the driver of the truck I'd seen taking the slip road. Despite huge efforts on the part of the French police, no trace was ever found of either driver, even though I'd been able to give them a fairly good description of the man I'd seen. The police sketch circulated to the general public had brought up no names. Like Layla, he had disappeared into thin air, so it was logical to presume that he had taken her from the picnic area.

So if Ruby isn't behind the Rudolph Hill alias, who is? And more to the point, what does he know about Layla's disappearance?

TWELVE

BEFORE

At the end of the summer, we moved from the flat I'd been renting since my argument with Harry. I hadn't seen him again. You begged me to apologize but I wasn't sure he'd forgive me. Instead, I handed in my notice behind his back and then I left, collecting our stuff from the flat while he was at work. When I think about it now, I'm so ashamed of my behavior back then. But the love I felt for you made me crazy, made me do crazy things.

I have a confession to make—do you remember that earlier that year, I took you to Devon for a week? Well, it was because I wanted to see if you liked it there. And you'd loved it. We'd toured around, staying in B&Bs, exploring the beautiful beaches and the surrounding countryside and it was all part of my plan. When I began looking in estate agents' windows, you'd been enthusiastic about me buying a property there. Then you found the cottage, only a few minutes' walk from the beach in St. Mary's. I bought it and let you choose the furniture, so that you would feel the cottage was yours too. Do you remember how we laughed when you ordered a double bed so big that it took up most of the bedroom? And still my feet hung out the end of it.

When I first suggested that we move there permanently you'd been hesitant, as I knew you'd be. So I promised that if you didn't like it, we'd move back to London. Those first months in St. Mary's were so happy. We never tired of each other's company and would walk for miles along the beach. For the first time, I felt as if I had a home. One of my greatest pleasures was seeing our shoes in the hall, your little size fives next to my enormous thirteens. I loved it when you slipped your shoes inside mine, because they easily fit. To me it was physical proof that I was carrying you through tough times. Except that when life had got tough, I hadn't carried you at all.

That winter in Devon was difficult for you, I know. Maybe it reminded you of the winters on Lewis, because it came in so suddenly and angrily; the wind whipping relentlessly against our faces as we walked on the beach, the sky heavy and gray. And whenever a postcard arrived from Ellen—a different view of Lewis each time—you became so sad I thought at first she was reprimanding you for staying away for so long. But when you read them out to me, I saw that she was only happy for you in your new life, and decided that what you felt was guilt at leaving her behind, not sadness.

Once Christmas had been and gone you became restless, and I began to worry that you would hold me to my promise and ask to return to London. In an effort to distract you I booked a ski trip in Megève. Harry and I had rented a chalet there several times, and I hoped the break would give you the space to love Devon again. All I wanted was for you to be happy, which is why I asked if you would like Ellen to join us.

I suggested that she came for a week, offering to pay for a local nurse to look after your father. But you said that Ellen wouldn't come and became angry, so that in the end I wished I'd never suggested it. In an effort to understand, I asked if you felt guilty that Ellen was stuck on Lewis while you had escaped. Do you remember your answer? "Escaped?" you said. "I escaped from Lewis and now, here I am, stuck in a backwater in Devon." You'd smiled, wanting to take the sting out of your words, but I heard the reality behind them and promised that when we came back from Megève, I'd take you anywhere that you wanted.

But I never got the chance.

THIRTEEN

NOW

I can't stop analyzing the emails. My feet pound the rough river pathway but I can't lift the pressure I feel, no matter how fast I run. I googled Rudolph Hill earlier; there are hundreds of Rudolph Hills, all of whom seem to live in the US. Not one of them lives in the UK.

I double back through the wood, and by the time I reach the house, my leg muscles are screaming from the exertion. I have a cold shower and head out to my office. I check how Villiers' investment funds are doing, then re-read the emails from Rudolph Hill. Suddenly impatient, I pull my keyboard toward me.

Who are you? I type.

A few seconds later, an email arrives in my inbox, from the Rudolph Hill address.

Who do you think I am?

I stare at the message, astounded at the rapidity of the response. It's as if the sender has been sitting at the computer since yesterday, waiting for me to get back to him.

Who are you? I ask again.

You have my email address

I sit back in my chair, thinking hard. Why "you have my email address," why not, "you have my name"? As I suspected, Rudolph Hill is an alias. I stare hard at it, puzzling it out, rearranging the letters, and find myself gasping in shock. If I need proof that Ruby is behind the emails, it's right here on the screen in front of me, the first two letters of her name followed by "dolph." Dolphin. Ruby has dolphin necklaces, dolphin bracelets, she even has a tattoo of a dolphin on her rib cage. I shake my head in disgust at her weak attempt to disguise her identity, hating that she's taken me for a fool.

My fingers slam down on the keys.

Don't play games with me, Ruby!

A reply comes back.

Who is Ruby?

I give a harsh laugh. Well, she would say that, wouldn't she? I drum my fingers on the desktop. What to do? Nothing, reason tells me, do nothing. She obviously didn't get the message yesterday so I'll carry on taking Ellen to The Jackdaw until she does.

"Again?" Ellen asks doubtfully, when I tell her we're having lunch at The Jackdaw. "I know Ruby was happy for us when we saw her yesterday but maybe we shouldn't rub her nose in it too much."

"It'll be fine," I reassure her, so at one o'clock we walk to the pub with Peggy and have a repeat of yesterday, except that Ruby doesn't open champagne and I have the spicy lamb curry instead of the pie. I watch her, waiting for a slip-up. But there's nothing, nothing at all in Ruby's behavior to show that she's less than pleased to see us, and all I can think is that she's an exceptional actress.

"I'm glad Harry's agreed to give me away," Ellen is saying as she toys with her salad. "I was afraid he might refuse."

It takes me a while to realize that she's talking about our wedding. "Why would he?"

"Well, he didn't like Layla very much."

I look at her, perplexed by her logic. "No, he didn't, not really. But he does like you."

She raises her green eyes to mine. "Do you think so? I mean, I'm never quite sure." Her voice trails away. "It's just that when you told him we were getting married, he seemed a bit shocked. I thought maybe he didn't approve because of who I am."

"I think he was shocked—in a nice way—at being asked to be best man," I say, although I had registered Harry's momentary shock too. I might not have been married to Layla but in some people's eyes, the fact that I lived with her amounts to the same thing. Therefore, I shouldn't be marrying her sister. I hadn't expected it to bother Harry, though. "Harry adores you—maybe a bit too much," I go on, reaching for Ellen's hand across the table. "It's a good job I'm not the jealous kind."

"He's coming for lunch on Sunday, isn't he?"

"Yes," I say, because Harry always comes for lunch on the first Sunday of the month.

"Good, I'll be able to show him my Russian dolls. He'll be pleased I've got a full set at last."

"Does he know the story then?" I ask curiously. "About how you lost yours as a child?"

"Yes," she says. "I remember telling him. I wonder what he'll make of it."

There's something about the way she says it that tells me she's hoping to find an ally in Harry, as if she knows he'll side with her and for some reason it annoys me. Much as I'd hoped that Harry would like Ellen more than he'd liked Layla, I sometimes wish he didn't like her quite as much. A thought pops into my head—that if Layla hadn't disappeared, we might have become a foursome, me and Layla, Harry and Ellen. Mortified, I chase it away.

"I'll give him a ring when I get back," Ellen says. "Just to check that he's coming."

We finish our lunch and I ask Ruby for the bill. The pub is busy so it takes her a while to bring it over, presented as usual on a plate, inside a card with a picture of a jackdaw on the front. Ellen goes to the toilet and I watch Ruby as she talks freely with customers. There isn't any sign of unease or tension in her body. Frustrated, I fish for my wallet and flip open the card to check the amount of the bill—and there, lying inside, is a little Russian doll.

Shock gives way to anger. But the anger I feel is not straightforward anger at someone having gone a step too far, it's an anger tinged with hatred, and its intensity shocks me almost more than the little Russian doll staring up at me with its black-painted eyes. Snatching it from the plate, I push through the throng to where Ruby is standing at the end of the bar. The smile on her face freezes when she sees the look on mine.

"That's enough, Ruby," I hiss, leaning in close to her.

She looks at me in alarm. "What do you mean?"

I reach out and grab her wrist. "Enough of the games. You've had your fun, now that's enough."

"What are you talking about?"

"Trying to split up me and Ellen."

"Look, Finn, I'm genuinely happy for you and Ellen. I wasn't being funny or anything." She tries to draw away but I hold her wrist even tighter, aware of my other hand clenching around the Russian doll. A woman pauses in her conversation and looks over at us. I take a breath, steadying myself.

"You know damn well that's not what I'm talking about," I say, my voice low. "Sending me emails, pretending to be someone else, planting little Russian dolls for me to find."

Ruby smiles reassuringly at the woman then locks her eyes with mine. "Finn," she says calmly. "I have no idea what you're talking about. Let go of me, please. You're hurting me, a lot." Realizing how tightly I've been gripping her wrist, I drop it quickly. "What on earth has got into you?" she says, rubbing the livid mark I've left.

"I mean it, Ruby, stop playing games." I open my palm so that she can see the Russian doll. "It's over, OK?"

She looks down at it, shakes her head. "I'm not following you."

"This. It's you, isn't it? You put it on the plate with the bill."

"No, I didn't! Anyway, why would I do that? I don't get it."

"Yes, you do. You get it very well. You know exactly what I would think if I saw one of these."

"Look, Finn, I have no idea what you're talking about." She

nods at the Russian doll. "I didn't put that on the plate and I have no idea what you would think when you saw it."

"You brought the bill."

"Yes."

"You prepared it and brought it over."

"I prepared it, yes, and I prepared others and I left them at the end of the counter for one of the staff to bring to you. When I saw it was still sitting there, I brought it over, and I brought others over too. I was doing my job, that's all."

"So this plate was lying on the counter?"

"Yes." She looks at me curiously. "What's this about, Finn?"

I run a hand through my hair, wondering if I've got it wrong after all. "Someone's playing games with me."

"Well, it's not me."

I'm not convinced. "What was the name of your cousin, the journalist?"

"Joe, Joe Walsh. Why?"

I thump the bar in frustration.

"Finn?" I spin round and see Ellen standing behind me, and I know from the uncertainty on her face that she saw the thump. "Is everything all right?"

I quickly relax my features. "Yes, everything's fine, just catching up with Ruby."

Ellen looks from me to Ruby and Ruby gives her a bright smile. I stuff the doll into my pocket and reach for Ellen's hand.

"Come on, let's go." I call Peggy from Buster's side and turn to Ruby. "Bye, Ruby, thanks." I don't even try to smile.

We leave the pub and walk in silence for a while. I know Ellen is waiting for me to say something but my mind is too full of my conversation with Ruby so I wait for her to begin, because maybe she won't and then I won't have any explaining to do.

"So what was all that about?" she asks.

"Just Ruby being her usual annoying self," I say casually, for Ellen's benefit.

"In what way?"

"A barb about us getting married."

"Oh." She frowns. "I thought she seemed happy for us."

"She is. But you know Ruby, she can't help herself."

"You seemed pretty angry with her."

"I was. But it's fine, I'm not anymore."

"Good. You scared me for a moment back there."

I stop and pull her into my arms. "I don't ever want you to be scared of me," I say.

Not like Layla was that night, I add silently.

FOURTEEN

BEFORE

Money never interested you, Layla, but even you were surprised when I admitted that in the seven years I'd worked in the city, I'd accumulated enough to last me a lifetime. To be really arrogant, when we left London for Devon, it wouldn't have mattered if I never worked again—which was just as well because even the thought of it left me exhausted. At not quite thirty years old I was well and truly burned out.

I knew that mentally I couldn't not work for the rest of my life. What I wanted was to take a year out, concentrate on you, on us, and worry about the future later. But you'd become restless. I could tell you were beginning to feel caged, like a beautiful, wild animal.

Sometimes you'd snap at me for no reason at all, although you were quick to apologize, as volatile in your temper as you were in your anger and frustrations.

A week before we were due to go skiing, you were invited by your ex-work colleagues at the wine bar to a girls' weekend in London. You were so excited about it; you smiled more that day than you had for a while and it got under my skin. But I was too proud to ask you not to go. Instead, I took you to the station and waved you off on the train.

It was a long two days. I went for walks along the beach and in between, I tried to be the perfect boyfriend and painted the bathroom as a surprise for you. By the time Sunday evening came, I couldn't wait for you to be back and I planned to take you straight to bed and stay there the whole of the next day. But when I met you at the station, you were so quiet, and my heart almost stopped, because I thought you were going to tell me that you wanted to go back to your old life in London. Instead, you clung to me and told me that you loved me, that you always wanted to be with me, and stay in our cottage forever. And realizing how much you'd missed me, my heartbeat smoothed out, and I was glad I'd let you go.

The following week we left for Megève but once there, your mood didn't improve. You had never skied before so I'd booked lessons for you each morning, convinced that a spirit like yours would love the mountains. But your heart wasn't in it and I couldn't hide my disappointment, or my fear, because it seemed that everything I said or did wasn't right anymore. I asked you if you were homesick or if you were missing Ellen and you dissolved into floods of tears and wouldn't let me comfort you. There was a nervousness about you and I began to worry that I'd got it wrong, that you wanted to go back to London after all, and were psyching yourself up to tell me.

On the way home, we stopped off in Paris for dinner and as we walked along the Seine, back to where I parked the car, I drew you into my arms and told you how much I loved you. A part of me wished I'd brought the ring with me, a ring I'd planned to give you on your birthday, because I could have proposed to you there and then instead of waiting. But my love seemed to make you uncomfortable, and my doubt grew.

As soon as we got back in the car, you started crying but when I asked you what the matter was, you wouldn't tell me. In the end, I couldn't stand it any longer. I pulled off the motorway into a picnic area and told you that we weren't leaving until you told me what was wrong, that I couldn't fix it if you didn't talk.

Nothing had prepared me for what you said next. You didn't tell me that you wanted to leave me and go back to London. Instead, you told me that during your weekend in London, you'd slept with somebody else.

FIFTEEN

NOW

When we get back from the pub, we go our separate ways, Ellen to her office, me to mine. I sit down at my desk and take the two Russian dolls—the one I found on the wall and the one from the car—from where I've hidden them at the back of my drawer and stand them on the edge of my desk. Then I take the one I found on the plate in The Jackdaw out of my pocket and put it next to them. Triplets. What is your purpose, I ask them silently, why are you here? What the hell is going on?

I'm still not convinced it isn't Ruby. The email address is pretty incriminating. I should have mentioned it to her, told her

I'd worked it out. Because I didn't mention it, she probably feels safe continuing her charade.

I put the doll I found at The Jackdaw back in my pocket and push the others into the drawer. Then I log on to my emails—and find another one from Rudolph Hill. I look at the time it was sent and see that it was at about the time Ellen and I left for the pub, six minutes after the previous one asking: Who is Ruby?

I open it.

I don't know who Ruby is
But I am not her

She has to be joking. I reach for the keyboard.

So who are you then?

A reply comes straight back.

What if I were to tell you that Layla is alive?

My heart thumps, then I pull myself together. It has to be some other sick bastard, Ruby could never be this vicious.

I type furiously: Then I'd call you a liar.

You don't believe me?

No. I press send and when there's no reply, I begin to relax. And then a message comes in.

You should

I want to stop but I can't.

Where is she then?

A reply comes back.

Right here

A wave of emotion slams my body. I push away from the desk and get to my feet, wanting to run, to get out into the fresh air while I can still breathe. But then, my mind in turmoil, I sit back down again, knocking a cup of cold coffee over. It smashes on the stone floor, spraying liquid everywhere. And into the mess that I've become, Ellen walks in, her phone in her hand.

"Finn," she begins. "Harry wants to talk to you." She catches sight of the smashed cup, then my face. "Harry," she says into the phone. "Finn will call you back."

I lean into my desk, my head in my hands, trying to pull myself together. Ellen's arm comes around my shoulder.

"What's the matter?" she asks urgently, crouching beside me, trying to see my face. "Are you OK?"

It's a hoax, I remind myself. It's only a hoax. "I'm fine," I say roughly.

She worms her hand through mine, trying to reach my forehead, and realizing that she thinks I'm ill, I seize on it.

"I think it must be something I ate," I say, groaning a little. "Maybe one of those prawns was off."

"Why don't you lie down for a while?"

"Yes, good idea." I get up from my desk, glad to be alone, then realize that I'm not going to be able to lie down because I'm too agitated. "Actually, I think I'll go down to the river, get some fresh air."

"Do you want me to come with you?"

"No, it's fine. You've got work to do."

"I can take half an hour," she protests.

"Really, it's fine." I can see the puzzlement in her eyes and I plant a kiss on the top of her head. "I won't be long."

"All right. By the way, Harry isn't coming this weekend, something to do with some sort of client crisis. He did explain and I listened long and hard but I didn't fully understand, which is why I wanted to pass him to you."

"OK," I say. But my mind is full of Layla, not Harry. "I'll phone him when I get back."

We walk across the garden and as I take the path round to the front of the house, I feel her eyes on me. I know she must be wondering, wondering what the thump on the bar was really about, wondering what my obvious agitation is really about. She's not stupid. Nobody who feels ill would stray very far from home, and here I am, heading to the river. Except I'm not heading to the river, I'm heading back to the pub to see Ruby.

She doesn't seem surprised to see me ducking under the doorway. It's quieter now, a couple of regulars at the bar and a few others grouped around tables close by.

"Can we talk?" I ask.

She heads to a table at the far end of the pub where we won't be disturbed and as I walk behind her, raised eyebrows and elbow nudges follow me down the room. All the locals know that Ruby and I were in a relationship and many thought we would be together long-term. Until I turned up with Ellen.

"You forgot to pay, by the way," she says, sitting down. I reach for my wallet and she puts a hand on my arm. "I'm joking. It's on the house. An early wedding present." She looks up at me. "So what was all that about earlier on?"

"I'm sorry," I say, because there are still red marks on her wrists. "I thought—"

"What?"

I sit down opposite her. "Ruby, please, tell me honestly—have you been sending me emails, pretending to be someone else?"

She shakes her head. "No," she says emphatically. "Of course I haven't. Why would I do that?"

"The email address they come from—well, it's you," I say, ignoring her question for the moment.

She frowns. "Are you telling me that someone's hacked my account?"

"No, not that. What I meant was that the address seems to be referring to you." The table has already been reset for the evening so I pull the paper napkin out from under the knife and fork, take out my pen and write rudolph.hill@outlook.com then draw a vertical line between the "u" and "d" of *rudolph*. "Ruby and dolphin. You have a dolphin tattoo."

I watch her face carefully as she considers what I've said, hoping to see something which will give her away.

"Hmm," she says. "I can sort of see why you think they might be coming from me but aren't you overthinking things a bit? I mean, why can't they be coming from someone called Rudolph Hill?"

"Because they're not. Rudolph Hill is an alias someone has used, probably to make me think they're coming from you."

"Why? What do they say?"

I hesitate, wondering how much I can trust her. But I need to speak to someone who never knew Layla, someone who can pull me back to my logical frame of mind.

"They started by mentioning a cottage in St. Mary's."

"St. Mary's?"

"Where I used to live with Layla."

"So what has that got to do with me?"

"The person who's sending them—they're trying to make me think that Layla is alive."

"Oh my God." Her eyes widen. "That's horrible, Finn!" A frown crosses her brow. "But why would I want you to think that Layla is alive?"

I look hard at her. "So that I don't marry Ellen?"

Her mouth drops open. "Seriously?" She shakes her head. "I don't know whether to be amused or outraged. Amused that you could think I'd want to stop you, outraged that you think I could be so cruel as to make you think Layla is alive." Her brown eyes search out mine. "Surely you know me better than that?"

"It's not just the email address." I take the Russian doll from my pocket and stand it on the table between us. "I found this with the bill."

"Yes, you said." She picks it up and examines it. "Cute. But what has it got to do with anything?"

And that's when I realize that Ruby couldn't have known the story of the Russian dolls because I had never told her. "Did you see anyone suspicious hanging round the bar earlier?"

She shakes her head. "No. The pub was too packed for me to notice anything much." She hands the doll back to me. "Someone must have found it on the floor and put it on the counter and it somehow found its way onto the plate with your bill on it."

"Probably," I say vaguely, because something has just occurred to me. Only Ellen, Layla, and I know the story of the Russian dolls.

And Harry, because Ellen told him.

SIXTEEN

BEFORE

You never asked me why I left Ireland and came to England. I'm not sure you really realized that I had a life over there, a life I'd rather forget about because I'm not proud of the person I was back then. People called me a gentle giant and until my mid-teens that was probably the case. At least, I never remember losing my temper before my dad told me I couldn't go out one night, and as he stood in front of the locked front door, I raised my fist and punched a hole right through it. The worst thing was, I'd been aiming for his face and if he hadn't ducked I would have done him some serious damage. Hopefully, the love I felt for him would have kicked in and I would have stopped after that first punch. The door had no love to protect it, so it got hammered into a splintered mess.

The incident terrified both my parents and me. We'd had no idea of the tinderbox that nestled deep inside me, waiting to be ignited. They impressed on me the need to recognize the warning signs and urged me to walk away from situations of conflict, citing the added danger of my size. And apart from a couple of incidents where I left people with broken noses, I managed to stay out of trouble. Until I met Siobhan.

Siobhan was my first real love. Now I know that what I felt for her was nothing to what I felt for you. But there was that same intensity, the same feeling that we were meant to be together. We didn't speak of marriage or anything like that, we were still at university. But once I started seeing her, I didn't notice any other girl, I only had eyes for her, just as I'd had for you. Then one day, when we'd been together for about a year, a week or so after graduation, she said she had something to tell me. She looked worried, scared even, and my first thought was that maybe she was ill, or someone in her family was. Instead, she told me that she was in love with my best friend and had been seeing him behind my back for months.

I actually laughed, thinking she was just playing with me, because only the day before I'd told Pat, over a couple of pints, how happy I was with Siobhan. I'd immediately felt embarrassed for confiding in him and when I saw a shadow pass over his face, I thought he was feeling the same embarrassment and blamed my emotional outburst on the drink.

Even now, all these years later, I can't bear to remember what I did, I can't bear to remember how, when I realized Siobhan was deadly serious, I yelled that I was going to kill her. I can't bear to remember how, when I clenched my hands into fists and drew my arm back, she cowered in front of me, screaming at me to stop. It was my father's words about removing myself from situations of conflict that pierced through the fog in my brain, and dropping my arms, I shoved her aside so that I could get to the door. But she fell, hitting her head on the edge of a low table. And as she lay there pale and motionless on the floor, I thought I'd done what only moments before I had threatened to do, and killed her.

She wasn't dead, but she had to have twenty stitches to the cut in her head. To my relief, she didn't press charges. Instead, her four brothers came round for a visit. I left Ireland soon after, not because of what they did to me, not because I was scared they would carry out their threat to kneecap me if they ever saw me again, but because I was worried about what I might do the next time I lost my temper. That's when I moved in with Harry.

My temper led me into two more scrapes, one of which led to me being charged with assault after I beat up a colleague who called me Paddy one time too many. After that, I managed to more or less stay out of trouble, until the night I attacked Harry.

And until the night I lost my temper with you.

SEVENTEEN

NOW

I walk into the kitchen and see Ellen standing at the worktop. At the sound of my arrival she moves away quickly, her right hand hidden guiltily behind her back. I don't have to look at the row of Russian dolls to know that the little one is missing.

"Sorry," she mumbles, as if I've caught her doing something terrible, and my heart goes out to her, hating that she feels guilty for holding a piece of her past in her hand.

"What was Layla like as a child?" I ask, wanting to give her something. Nevertheless, my question surprises me as much as it surprises her because she turns around, a frown on her face.

"That's something you've never asked me." She lets it hang in the air for a moment. "A free spirit. She loved being outside, she hated having to go to school because it meant being indoors. She loved drawing. We both did," she adds.

"It must have been hard for you both when your mother died," I say, realizing that we're having the conversation we should have had years ago.

"It was, especially for Layla. I knew how ill Mum was but I kept it from Layla to protect her. So her death affected her badly."

"In what way?"

She gives a small laugh. "She sort of became Mum."

"You mean she took on her role?"

"No, it was more than that. It was as if she was her. She spoke like her, took on all her mannerisms."

"Wasn't that uncomfortable for you and your father?"

"Yes, especially when she was both herself and Mum at the same time—you know, asking a question then replying in Mum's voice. Sometimes she had whole conversations with her."

"Weren't you worried?"

She shrugs. "I had other things to worry about. Dad tried to knock it out of her, though, and eventually she stopped, at least in his presence."

"Do you mean he was violent?" I ask, shocked.

She nods reluctantly. "He could be. It was awful that final Christmas. That's why she left. She was afraid of what might happen." Her face becomes suddenly bleak. "I miss her so much."

I want to tell her that I do too. Instead, I change the subject. "Have you seen the garden this morning? The lilies are out."

She nods. "They're beautiful. I've actually been wondering if we should have our reception in the garden," she goes on.

I look at her, then realize she's talking about our wedding.

"The garden won't look as good in September," I warn. "But we could, if that's what you'd like."

"I'll think about it," she says, smiling. "Shouldn't you be leaving? Didn't you say your meeting with Grant is at eleven?"

"I'm going now," I say, giving her a kiss. "I was waiting for rush hour to be over."

"Drive carefully," she says. "Text me when you're leaving London, then I'll know what time to expect you."

I leave the house and get in my car. I sit for a moment then type St. Mary's into the GPS. I hate that I've lied to Ellen, that she believes I'm going to see Grant James to finalize his investment. But I'm not. Today, I'm going back to my past, back to where I used to live with Layla, so that I can ask Thomas Winter why he thought it was Layla he saw standing outside the cottage.

I haven't been able to sleep for the last few nights, not after that last email from Rudolph Hill. Those two little words—*Right here*—have sent me to hell and back. If—and it's a huge if—Layla is alive and it's not some cruel hoax, then Rudolph Hill has to be Layla's kidnapper. I try not to let my mind go there, I try not to imagine her kept prisoner for the last twelve years. It's a hoax, I tell myself, it has to be.

It's hard driving along the roads that were once so familiar to me. The nearer I get to St. Mary's, the more I find myself thinking about Layla. The hardest thing over the last twelve years has been the absence of a body. I know it sounds terrible, that I should want her body to be found, but at least I'd have had closure, instead of lying awake in the dead of the night, torturing myself with images of her being held prisoner, having to endure God knows what at the hands of some maniac. It's the not knowing that's the hardest, the reason I've preferred to accept that she's dead.

I park in front of the little station, needing the walk to the cottage to calm me. As I get out of the car, I see the ghost of myself walking through the station entrance and onto the platform, waiting for the train that will bring Layla back from her weekend in London. Unable to stop myself, I follow him onto the platform and watch as Layla steps off the train, beautiful in a flowing red dress, and runs down the platform into his arms, her red hair streaming out behind her. Suddenly tearful, she clings onto him, murmuring that she missed him and when she whispers over and over again that she's sorry, he thinks, in his stupid innocence, that she regrets having gone to London and leaving him behind.

The pain of betrayal snaps me back to the present. Leaving the station, I follow the road to the cottage. I can smell the sea in the warm air, taste the salt on my lips. As I near the cottage, my heart feels suddenly heavy and my mouth goes dry. The stone wall of the cottage comes into view, then the upstairs window, then the little garden at the front, and—I come to an abrupt stop, unable to believe what I'm seeing. I expected to find the cottage unkempt and uncared-for. But the beds are full of flowers and there are red geraniums in the window boxes.

"Layla." My voice catches in my throat and for one crazy moment I think that the door is going to open and she'll be there, on the doorstep, ready to run to me and tell me that she's glad I'm home, like she used to. Even when it remains closed I can't accept that she isn't there, because in my mind the flowers prove that she is, so I run, my heart pounding as I go. I arrive at the gate, fumble with the latch, hurry to the blue wooden door and thump on it. But she doesn't open it so I thump again, and again, because I need her to be there, because I've never stopped loving her, despite trying to close my mind to her, despite loving Ellen.

A man's voice comes from behind me. "You won't get any answer, it's been empty for years."

Rage—red-hot and violent—rips through me. I stay as I am, fighting for control, trying to erase the burning anger from my face so that I can reply civilly to the person who's ruined the few seconds where I'd allowed myself to believe Layla was alive.

I gesture toward the garden. "It doesn't look empty," I snap, finding my voice but not my composure.

"That'll be Thomas."

I take a breath and turn slowly, preparing myself for the jolt of recognition that will surely appear on his face when he sees me, the words that will spring unchecked to his lips, "Are you . . . ?" before the rest of the question dies away, leaving an awkward silence in its place. But the man, some ten years or so older than me, is thankfully unfamiliar.

"Thomas?" I ask in pretend puzzlement.

"The old gentleman who lives next door. He's been tending the garden for years." He nods at my cottage. "You're not the first that's showed an interest in buying it. But it isn't for sale, never will be, according to Thomas."

I go down the path and back through the gate, closing it behind me. "He lives next door?" I ask, indicating Thomas' cottage.

"That's right. But you won't find him there. He's in hospital, been there for a couple of weeks now."

I look at the man in dismay. "Hospital?"

"Yes, in Exeter. Only to be expected really, he's in his nineties now."

I nod slowly. I want to ask him what happened, if Thomas had a heart attack, if he knows what ward he's on, but it might sound strange after I've pretended not to know him.

"Oh well, if the cottage isn't for sale," I say, wanting him gone.

"Don't think it ever will be. It's like a shrine."

"A shrine?"

The man nods. "A young couple used to live here and she disappeared during a holiday in France. The man came back for a while, apparently, waiting for her to turn up and when he realized she wasn't going to, he upped and left, leaving everything exactly as it was. Take a look through the window and you'll see what I mean."

He has a pleasant enough face but it doesn't stop me from wanting to push my fist into it.

"Do you live in St. Mary's?" I ask, tortured by images of him, and others maybe, peering ghoulishly through the windows.

"Moved here six months ago. If you're looking for something to buy, I suggest you go to one of the estate agents in Sidmouth."

I start to move away. "Right, thanks."

I feel his eyes on me as I walk back to my car. I'm gutted that I've come all this way for nothing. If I'd brought my keys with me, I could have gone back to the cottage once the man had moved on, to have a look around inside, so that I wouldn't have had a completely wasted journey. But I'd only wanted to see Thomas so I hadn't collected them from the safety deposit box at my bank in Exeter, where I'd left them twelve years ago, along with Layla's jewelry, the day I'd left St. Mary's. I could have kept them with me but I couldn't imagine ever wanting to return to the cottage. Yet I couldn't consider selling it either.

I'd like to go and see Thomas but I can't very well walk into the hospital and start asking him questions about supposedly seeing Layla. But Tony could.

I take out my phone and dial his number. He answers on the second ring.

"Finn? Everything OK?" His voice is sharp with worry, and at first I think he knows something of what's been going on.

"Yes, everything's fine," I reassure him. "Am I disturbing you?"

"No, go ahead."

"I'm phoning to ask a favor, actually. I know it's a big ask but would you pay Thomas a visit? I'm curious as to why he thought it was Layla he saw outside the cottage."

"Why, has something happened?"

I debate how much to tell him. "Just that a couple of weeks ago, Ellen thought she saw Layla in Cheltenham. It was probably only someone with the same sort of red hair but it does seem strange, coming on the back of Thomas's sighting."

"Hmm," Tony muses. "All right, leave it with me. I'll go and see him this afternoon."

"Thanks, Tony, I really appreciate it." I feel bad sending him all the way to St. Mary's when I know that Thomas is in the hospital. But I don't want him to know I've been to the cottage. And it's only a small detour; it won't take him long to get to the hospital from St. Mary's.

I don't feel like going home so I take a drive along the coast to the other side of Sidmouth, then park up and go for a walk along the beach, wishing I'd brought Peggy with me. When I'm tired of walking, I find a pub and sit nursing a beer, mulling everything over.

Tony finally phones at 5 p.m.

"Tony," I say. "Did you manage to see Thomas?"

"Bad news, I'm afraid. I went to St. Mary's only to find that Thomas was taken to hospital last week. Seems he had a nasty fall."

"I'm sorry you had a wasted journey."

"I only found out because, when he didn't come to the door, I went down to the village shop. They told me he'd been taken to the Royal Devon and Exeter so I went straight there."

"And did you see him?"

"No." He pauses. "It seems he died in the early hours of the morning."

I feel a sudden guilt. "That's so sad," I say. "I should have gone to see him, I promised I would."

"He'd been tending your garden. Full of flowers it was. I thought for a minute that you'd sold the cottage but they told me at the shop it was Thomas's work."

"Now I feel doubly bad."

"Too late for regrets," he says, not because he wants me to feel even worse but because it's the truth.

"Well, thanks, Tony. I'm sorry to have troubled you."

I hang up. All I can do now is find Rudolph Hill and draw him out. I'll let him think that I believe he has Layla, that I believe she's alive.

He'll think he's luring me, but it will be me doing the luring.

EIGHTEEN

BEFORE

"Who is he?" I yelled as we sat in the car in the picnic area at Fonches, when you told me you'd slept with someone while you were in London. "Tell me who he is!"

You shook your head numbly, terrified by my anger. So was I, and I forced myself to swallow it down. It wasn't you I was angry with anyway, I was angry with the bastard who had forced himself on you. I wanted to break every bone in his body, cut his balls off.

"I'm not angry with you, Layla," I said, taking a breath. "I just want to know who it was."

Your eyes wouldn't meet mine. "I don't know."

I didn't believe you but I let it go. "Can you tell me how it happened? Did he force himself on you? Did he hurt you?" That was how dark my mind was—I wanted to believe you'd been raped rather than that you'd chosen to have sex.

You shook your head again and I took another breath. If he hadn't forced himself on you, he must have taken advantage of you while you were drunk. I felt sick even thinking about it.

"All right." I looked encouragingly at you. "So you'd had too much to drink, is that it?"

Your eyes brimmed with tears. "No."

"But—" I tried to work it out. "If you weren't drunk, and you say that he didn't force himself on you, how did it happen?"

Your eyes were pleading with me, begging me not to dig any further and as I watched the tears spill from your eyes, dread wormed its way into my heart. But still I couldn't stop myself. I had to know, even though the truth was staring at me from your tear-streaked face.

"Tell me, Layla. Tell me how it happened."

"I c-can't."

"Why not?"

"You wouldn't understand."

"Try me."

You bowed your head. "I wanted to know what it was like."

I frowned, not understanding. "What it was like?" My voice echoed hollowly around the car.

And then you told me. "Nobody forced me. I wanted to know what it would be like to have sex with someone else, that's all."

My mind was slow putting it together. Wanted to know what it was like. With someone else. It. Sex. You had slept with someone, a stranger, because you had wanted to know what sex was like with someone else. First Siobhan, now you.

I don't remember much about what happened next. I know I

leaped out of the car, tore round to your side, wrenched your door open and dragged you out. I remember shaking you, shouting at you. I remember your voice as you screamed at me to stop, I remember the fear in your eyes as I raised my arm. And then I remember being in the toilet block, trying desperately to control the terrible rage that had consumed me. And after—how long after, I don't know—I remember going back to where I'd parked the car and finding you gone.

At first I thought that you were hiding from me, because I could remember dragging you out of the car and shaking you. But I couldn't remember what had happened between the moment I had raised my arm, and finding myself in the toilet block. I started calling you, telling you I was sorry and when you didn't come, I took a torch from the trunk and went looking for you, terrified that I'd come across your body, that I'd killed you and hidden your body in the trees that circled the picnic area before blanking the whole thing from my memory. But I couldn't find you, dead or alive.

I had no idea what to do. I knew I'd have to report you missing but that I'd have to have a story, otherwise they'd see my history and if you didn't turn up, I'd be arrested for your murder. So that's what I did; I drove to the nearest service station, because I couldn't get a phone signal, and made up a story.

NINETEEN

NOW

“Shall we take the afternoon off?” I ask Ellen over lunch, needing some sort of distraction, because I’ve spent the whole morning wondering if I should phone Tony back. But I know how ridiculous it will sound. If there were only the emails, it would be more believable. But the fact that someone is leaving little wooden dolls around for me to find proves it’s some sort of sick game and I prefer to find out who’s behind it myself.

Ellen stretches her arms above her head, flexing them. “Good idea, I could do with a break.”

“I thought we could go for a walk in the hills.”

“Not with Peggy, then. It’ll be too far for her.”

"I'll take her out when we get back."

We leave Peggy asleep under the table, put a couple of bottles of water in a rucksack, and make our way to the end of the village and up into the hills beyond.

"So," I say, as we walk along hand in hand. "How are your illustrations coming along?"

"Fine. I just hope Stan likes them."

"How old did you say he was?"

"Eighty-three."

"Just shows you're never too old to write," I muse.

It's a beautiful day, perfect for walking because the sun isn't too hot and there's a gentle breeze blowing off the hills. After an hour or so we find a flat stone to sit on and stop for a drink of water. And all the while I'm wondering if an email has come in from Rudolph Hill.

Impatient of sitting still, I stand up and pull Ellen to her feet. "Come on, time to go."

Our pace picks up on the way back. As we approach the house we see Mick in his front garden.

"Hello, Mick," I say, going over. "How's your wife?"

"Not well," he says. He shakes his head wearily. "Depression is a terrible thing."

"Perhaps I could go and see her," Ellen offers. "Have a chat with her."

"She doesn't really like to chat."

"Read to her, then. Would she like that, do you think?"

"It's very kind of you but she isn't comfortable around people. She doesn't even like family visiting. She's all right with Mrs. Jeffries, though."

"Well, if you ever feel like you need a break or a beer, you know where we are," I tell him.

"Thanks." There's an awkward pause. "I better go and see if she wants anything," he says, turning toward his front door.

We cross over the road to our house.

"I just thought she might like some younger company than Mrs. Jeffries," Ellen says.

"Unfortunately, when you're depressed, you end up cutting yourself off from the entire world," I reply, and because she knows something of what I went through in the years following Layla's disappearance, she gives my hand a sympathetic squeeze. In comparison to Mick's wife—I realize that we don't even know her name—who lost her two sons and her health, I feel slightly ashamed that Layla's disappearance affected me so badly.

Peggy is awake so I take her for her walk and when we get back, she heads for her basket and I head to my office. The first thing I do is check my emails. There are plenty of new ones and I run my eye down them quickly. But there isn't one from Rudolph Hill and I feel frustrated by his silence.

I decide to take the bull by the horns.

I think we should meet, I write, knowing he'll never agree. And unbelievably, a reply comes straight back.

So do I

I stare at the screen, my skin prickling at the image of a faceless person sitting patiently in front of a computer for the last four days, waiting for me to get back to them. I pull my mind together. Time to reel him in.

Where?

You have the address

My heart thuds dully. The cottage. Had there been someone there yesterday, secretly watching me? Would they have shown themselves if that man hadn't come along? Had they watched me leave, happy to have lured me there for nothing?

When? I write.

Tomorrow

What time?

4 p.m.

Should I mention Layla, see what he says when I ask him to bring her with him, as if I believe he's genuine? In the end, I simply tell him that I'll be there.

After dinner, I tell Ellen I've had Grant on the phone and need to go back and see him.

"Tomorrow," I add. "You don't mind, do you?"

"Of course I don't," she says. "He's your client, you need to keep him happy."

"I need to keep you happy too," I say, going over and putting my arms around her.

"Then how about we go up to bed?" she murmurs.

I nuzzle her neck, about to agree, when my eyes fall on the family of Russian dolls standing on the side behind her.

"I wish I could," I sigh, removing my arms and stepping away from her. "But I need to go back out to the office and prepare a couple of things for the meeting." Her face falls with disappointment. "I'll try not to be too long," I promise, eyeing the Russian dolls balefully, wondering how it's possible for them to emasculate me just by being there. Tomorrow, I tell myself, tomorrow I'll know who wants me to think that Layla is alive.

TWENTY

BEFORE

I told the police so many lies. I hadn't wanted to use the toilet, we hadn't been eating in the car, we had no rubbish to throw away. I didn't tell you to lock the doors as I got out of the car, I didn't promise to hurry and, after, I didn't drive the car back up to the toilet block so that you wouldn't have to walk all the way back in the dark.

Some things came back to me. I remembered that when I went into the toilet block, I passed a man coming out, that was never a lie. I remembered hearing the car drive off, the one that had been parked outside, and seeing the truck drive down the slip road, those weren't lies either. But I couldn't recall those vital minutes before walking into the toilet block.

Under interrogation, I told the police that we'd been blissfully happy the whole time we were in Megève, I told them that I'd asked you to marry me and that you had accepted, because I needed to get them to stop looking at me as a suspect. Sometimes we lie for the greater good, don't we? I wish that's what you had done, I wish you hadn't told me that you'd slept with someone else. If you hadn't, we'd still be together, you'd be here with me right now. But it wasn't a total lie. I had been going to ask you to marry me, on your birthday in April. It's important that you know that.

I was allowed to make a phone call so I called Harry. I hadn't seen or heard from him since the night I'd beaten him up seven months before. His calm "What's up, buddy?" reduced me to tears, because he automatically knew that if I was phoning in the middle of the night, it was because I needed him to get me out of a shitload of trouble again. Within an hour I had a lawyer, within five Harry himself was with me.

I owe him so much.

TWENTY-ONE

NOW

On my way to St. Mary's, I stop off at my bank in Exeter and access my safety deposit box to get the keys to the cottage. It's hard opening the wooden casket because Layla's jewelry is there and a thousand images rush through my mind, of her slipping the silver bracelet onto her wrist, of her arms around my neck when I gave her the gold watch, of the sudden glimpses I'd get of her earrings when she threw back her head in laughter. I close the box on my memories, and with the keys safely in my pocket, I leave the bank and drive to Sidmouth, where I sit with a pint and a sandwich in a café on the seafront, trying to calm myself. I check my phone for any new emails, but there's nothing from Rudolph Hill, so I take a look at the markets and when I see that the stocks I bought yesterday have plummeted, it seems like an omen.

I have no idea how the next few hours are going to play out. A lot depends on whether Rudolph Hill is waiting for me outside the house, or inside. If he's outside, it means that he's just some sick bastard who has never met Layla. If he's inside, it means he has her keys, because there have only ever been two sets, mine and Layla's—which means that Rudolph Hill is probably the person who took her from the car park that night. Or at least knows who did.

For the first time, it occurs to me that this could be about money. If Rudolph Hill is Layla's kidnapper, maybe he knows I am wealthy, maybe Layla told him when he first took her that I would pay him if he let her go. But why wait twelve years, why not make his demand sooner? Nothing makes sense. Unless he kept her alive all this time and she really is with him. I chase the thought away, before hope can set in. But it comes straight back. What if he brings her to the cottage?

I close my eyes and see myself walking through the gate of the cottage at four o'clock, going into the house and seeing Layla standing there, looking just as beautiful as she did twelve years ago. I open my eyes and do a quick reality check. She wouldn't, though, would she? Twelve years would have changed her, especially if she's been kept prisoner. She probably wouldn't look anything like I expect. And what would she think when she saw me? I look every one of my forty-one years. Although I still have my hair, I also have a beard, and my hair is streaked with gray at the sides, a legacy of her disappearance and my subsequent depression. And despite all the running, I'm a little heavier. I shake my head impatiently, because it's a wasted exercise. Layla won't be there. Rudolph Hill, whoever he is, is just using her as bait.

Checking the time, I finish my sandwich and leave for St. Mary's. When I arrive, I park outside the cottage. There isn't anyone waiting for me in the road. I get out of the car; nobody comes out of the house. My feet are heavy as I open the gate and walk down the path, my heart hammering so hard I'm sure whoever is inside can hear it. Inside. So he has Layla's keys. I feel such a rush of violence toward him that I hammer on the door with the full force of my fist, as if I'm driving it into his face. He doesn't appear, so I take my keys from my pocket and look for the right one. It jams in the lock, but eventually it turns. I push the door open and, ducking my head automatically, step into the hall.

The smell of mustiness and neglect hits me straightaway. I'm assailed by so many memories that my legs are almost pulled out from under me—of Layla standing here in the hall, of her sitting on the stairs to pull her boots on, of her running down them and into my arms. I wait for the images to fade, listening for the sound of somebody's presence, a movement from one of the rooms, a floorboard creaking upstairs. But there is only silence, and the dust of hopes never fulfilled, taunting me with what could have been, if only I'd acted differently.

The front door is still open and as I turn to close it, I notice a large pile of musty letters, leaflets and free newspapers pushed back against the wall behind it. Another couple of leaflets lie by themselves on the mat, newer, cleaner. Realizing what it means, sweat prickles my spine. The only way the mail could have become squashed up against the wall is by somebody opening the front door wide enough to let themselves in. The leaflets on the mat have come in since, maybe earlier this morning. Which means that someone was here, might still be here.

I reach out and push open the door on my left, which leads to the kitchen. There are so many familiar things—the pottery mugs that hang from hooks beneath a rack where we stored our plates, the row of eggcups sitting on the windowsill, the low armchair where Layla would sit curled up in front of the wood-burning stove. They are all there—but they are almost unrecognizable. Twelve years of dust has obliterated all color from the room and the pervading air of neglect and abandonment shocks me to the core. I remember how I had wanted to keep everything as it was, in case Layla came back. But if she had, how would she have felt to see the cottage unloved and uncared for?

I take a quiet step back into the hall and push open the door to the right. The sitting room is also empty. I think about calling out, but if there is anyone there and they had wanted to be seen, they would have shown themselves by now. But why would they hide? They've brought me here, so it must be for a reason.

I should have called Tony, asked him to come with me. It's too late now. I'd been so sure it was just some elaborate hoax. But what if it wasn't? I look up the stairs to the landing above, remembering the *Right here* message I received. Is Layla up there, bound, gagged, Rudolph Hill standing over her, waiting for me to come and find her? The urge to tear up the stairs is overwhelming. But I need to be careful, I can't afford to put Layla in danger. I check myself; Layla can't really be up there, can she?

I put my foot on the first step, testing it. It doesn't creak so I start going up as quietly as I can, bending my head to avoid the low ceiling. The bathroom is on the left, the door ajar, which explains the smell that sours the air, from stagnant water in the toilet bowl. On the right is the bedroom that Layla and I used to share. I go in; it's empty. Her dressing gown, barely distinguishable under its cover of gray, lies across the chair where she draped it the morning we left for Megève. The smaller bedroom, along the corridor from the bathroom, yields no secrets, no Layla tied to the bedpost waiting to be rescued, no Rudolph Hill waiting to blackmail me. Emotionally drained, I sit at the top of the stairs, looking down into the hall below, trying to absorb the knowledge that my journey here today has come to nothing. I'd left home thinking that by this evening, I'd know the truth behind the trail of Russian dolls and the emails. But I'm just as far away as ever.

I take out my phone to check the time. It's 4.30. Time to send a message to Rudolph Hill to find out what the hell is going on.

I'm here. Where are you?

A reply comes straight back.

Where I'd said I'd be

I feel a wave of fury that he's continuing to play with me.

No, you're not. I'm at the cottage but you aren't
I can't believe you've forgotten

I type angrily: Forgotten what?

I thought you would understand

I pause, suddenly aware of the shift in the tone of the messages. There's something that seems off about them.

What do you mean? I ask.

The address

I sit for a moment, wondering if I should stop the whole thing now. But I've come this far, so I may as well carry on.

What address?
The email address

The urge to hurl my phone down the stairs is terrifying. Instead, I stab out a message, my fingers fumbling on the tiny keys.

Who are you, why are you doing this?
You know who I am
Yeah, Rudolph fucking Hill!
I can't believe you haven't understood
What—that you're some sick psycho trying to make me think that you have Layla?
I chose it especially so that you would know it was me
If you still loved me, you would have understood
Goodbye Finn

I stare at the message, completely thrown at the mention of love, and the use of my name. I read the message again, more slowly this time. A chill runs down my spine—the bastard wants me to think the message is coming from Layla. Unless—no, it's a trick, another step in his game. But my fingers are already picking out her name.

Layla?

I wait, my heart in my mouth. But there's no reply and I give a roar of frustration, hating that I've fallen into his trap again. He never had any intention of being here today, all he wanted was to lure me to the cottage. But why? Just to prove he's the one calling the shots?

I go downstairs, weary from all the mind games, and push open the door to the kitchen, planning to shake the dust from a chair and sit for a minute. I pull one out from the table and stop, my hand on its back, remembering the last time I'd sat on this chair, the day I wrote the letter to Layla, the letter I left for her to find in case she came back. Suddenly my ghost is there, and I watch as he takes a ring from his pocket, the ring he'd been planning to give Layla on her twentieth birthday, and puts it in the envelope along with the letter. I watch as he seals the envelope and places it in the center of the table, ready for Layla to find. But—my ghost disappears as suddenly as he came—the letter is no longer there, all that remains is a rectangle of brown oak where the envelope once lay. Yet the rest of the table is barely discernible, covered by a thick layer of dust. I reach out, run my finger over the rectangle and find it almost dust-free. Which means that, fairly recently, someone took the letter.

I shake the dust from the chair and sink heavily onto it. For all I know, the letter could already have been gone when I came here two days ago, to see Thomas. Is that why Rudolph Hill knows so much about me, from my letter? Is that why there was something so real about his last messages, why I thought for one crazy moment that they were actually coming from Layla? I'm gutted I fell into his trap—how he must have laughed at my desperate *Layla?* But what had that been about, the one that said the email address had been chosen so that I would know who was sending the messages? Wasn't I meant to think they were coming from Ruby? If that wasn't the sender's intention, the address must signify something else, something I should know. If it isn't a person, what else could it be? A place? I know lots of hills but none of them are called Rudolph. So some other hill?

With infinite slowness it dawns on me. Not Ruby and dolphin but Russian doll. Russian doll, Pharos Hill. The Russian doll on Pharos Hill. I feel momentarily stunned, as if I've just witnessed a miracle. Other than me, only one person knows that Layla likened the tree stump on Pharos Hill to a Russian doll and that's Layla. Tears flood my eyes and I dash them away fiercely. It isn't true, it can't be. The emails can't be coming from Layla. And yet, they must be.

I don't remember leaving the cottage but suddenly I'm back in the car. Pharos Hill is thirty minutes away on foot but only ten by car. Please don't let her be gone, I pray, as I ram the car into gear and drive off. Please don't let her be gone.

It takes me eight minutes to get there. I pull to a stop near the foot of the hill and start sprinting up it. By the time I get to the top my breath is coming in ragged gasps and my lungs feel as if they're about to burst. I look around wildly. I can't see anyone, but the stump, the one shaped like a Russian doll, isn't visible from here. I run past the bench we put up all those years ago, its struts etched with the names of friends and lovers, and disappear over the brow of the hill, my leg muscles trembling from the demands I've just made on them. The stump comes into sight and I run toward it, even though I can see no one's there, and there's nowhere for anyone to hide. Just as I'm wondering if it's all some hideous joke, and that she was never here,

I see a little Russian doll, perched meticulously on top of the stump.

"Layla!" Her name tears out of me, half-sob, half-cry. "Layla!" I snatch up the doll and turn in a circle, calling her name over and over again, *Layla! Layla! Layla!* willing the breeze to carry it to wherever she is. I call until my voice is hoarse, but she doesn't come.

TWENTY-TWO

I'm going to have to finish this letter, Layla, because Harry is coming to pick me up to take me to the flat in London. I'm leaving the cottage, you see. You've been gone for six months now. I'm not giving up on you, please don't think that. It's just too hard being here without you.

Now that you've read my letter, I hope you'll understand how sorry I am for what happened that night and find it in your heart to forgive me. I'll be close by, waiting for you. If I move on from London, Harry will always know where I am. So come and find me, Layla, and when you do, we'll get married.

I'm leaving you a ring, the ring I was going to give you on your twentieth birthday, when I asked you to marry me. I love you. I always have, I always will. No matter how long you are gone, I'll never stop loving you.

Finn

PART TWO

TWENTY-THREE

LAYLA

I should never have gone back to St. Mary's. If I hadn't, it wouldn't have come to this. I blame Finn. If he hadn't decided to marry Ellen, I would have stayed away.

The truth is, I could have returned to the cottage any number of times over the years; I had the keys. But I hadn't, because it had been enough to know that Finn had never sold it. In my mind—and I'm the first to admit that my mind isn't what it used to be—it meant that he wanted to hang on to a vestige of our life together. But about to embark on a new life with Ellen, the thought that he might sell the cottage without me ever seeing it again was unbearable.

After, as I sat on the station platform, my heart beating crazily from the near-miss with Thomas, it seemed incredible that I had just risked everything for a fleeting look at the place where I'd spent a relatively short amount of time. But I had been happy there. That's not to say I'm not happy now, because I am, happier than I deserve to be. All I'd wanted was a glimpse of a past long gone. But Fate had been waiting for me in the form of Thomas. It was only when he'd come hobbling toward me, saying "Layla, is that you?" his rheumy eyes wide with surprise, that I realized my mistake. How could I have known he would still be around? He'd already seemed ancient all those years ago.

Even then, I could have saved the situation. I could have bluffed my way out of it, told Thomas that he was mistaken. But lost in the past, I forgot that I no longer look like I used to. So what had given me away? As I'd stared, mesmerized, at the cottage, had I reverted to my old way of standing, my left hand grasping my right elbow? Or, as I remembered the life I used to have, had the look on my face betrayed me? Whichever it was, Thomas seemed to know it was me.

Stupidly, I turned and ran, no doubt confirming his suspicions. I found myself back at the station, my heart pounding with fear at the thought that Finn might find out I was alive. I tried to calm the agitation I felt. Even if Thomas were to tell the police that he'd seen me, they probably wouldn't believe him. Even if he somehow managed to contact Finn, he would probably dismiss it as the ramblings of an old man. I was glad he would never know. I tried to imagine how he would feel. Happy in his new life with Ellen, it would surely be the worst possible news.

But then I remembered the way the cottage had looked. I'd expected to find it neglected, abandoned, yet there had been flowers in the garden and geraniums at the windows. If Finn had been tending it for all these years, maybe it was because he harbored a hope that one day, I'd come back. I knew that he loved Ellen—how could he fail to when she was perfect? But if I were to suddenly reappear, what then? Was it possible that after all these years, Finn still loved me? If it came down to it, would he choose me over Ellen? Surely he wouldn't—but what if he did?

In that instant, everything changed. Suddenly, my greatest fear wasn't that Finn would find out I was alive, but that he wouldn't. If my return was what he had been hoping for all these years, didn't I owe it to him to let him know I was alive? Before he went ahead and married Ellen? Before it was too late? Recognizing the danger of false hope, I reminded myself of all I'd achieved and everything I'd be risking if I chose to come back now. But the need for Finn to know I was alive wouldn't go away.

I needed to be careful. I couldn't just walk back into his life, not without being sure that he wanted me to. My reappearance needed to be a gradual thing, a possibility before it became a reality. And it would only become a reality if he wanted it to.

But how could I let him know I was alive without anyone else knowing? Agitated, I rubbed my thumb backward and forward over the smooth contours of my little Russian doll, the one that had belonged to Ellen, seeking solace. For the first time, it didn't bring me comfort. Instead, it gave me an idea.

The train for Cheltenham came in and without a moment's hesitation, I got on it.

TWENTY-FOUR

FINN

It's a while before I'm able to make my way back down Pharos Hill to where I left the car. I feel disorientated, as if I've been taken from a life I knew and plunged into an alien, parallel world. When I finally accepted that Layla—because it had to be her—had been, and gone, that I might only have missed her by a matter of minutes, I'd gone back to the wooden bench, remembering the last time I'd been there, the day of her ceremony, and how I'd pleaded with her—*Look, Layla, we have put up a bench in your memory so if you aren't dead, please give me some sort of sign that you're still alive.* But she never had. Until now.

There's no way I can drive back to Simonsbridge, to Ellen, not in this state, so I find a small hotel and check in. Then, from my room, I phone Ellen to tell her I won't be coming home tonight.

"Are you all right?" she asks. "Your voice is all over the place."

"Migraine starting. Which is why I'd rather not drive."

"Poor you," she says, sympathetically. "How did it go with Grant?"

"Fine. Problem solved."

"Good. Have you taken painkillers?"

"Yes."

"Maybe you should go to bed, lie down at least."

"I'm going to. I'll see you in the morning."

I hang up, already knowing I'm not going to tell her that Layla is alive, not yet. I can't add "not until I'm sure" because I am sure, 100 percent sure. I can't think of anyone Layla would have told about the tree stump shaped like a Russian doll on Pharos Hill. Layla is definitely alive. And I feel terrified—for her, for Ellen, for myself.

I check my emails, hoping there'll be one from the Rudolph Hill address, from Layla. There isn't. Which means the ball is squarely in my court. Because it's still a game—the only thing that's changed is that it's Layla who's playing it. Why? Why is she hiding? And where has she been for all these years?

Unable to sit, I pace up and down the hotel room. I think about phoning Tony, telling him everything. At first, he'll probably think as I had, that somebody is playing me. But once he adds it all up, including Thomas's sighting of her, he'll come to the same conclusion as me, that Layla is alive. What then? Well, he'll close the net on her and she'll eventually be found. But I can't let that happen without knowing what the implications will be. Will Tony be able to protect her, at least for a while? Once it gets out that she's back, the media will be all over her, hounding her, wanting to know her story. Could she be charged with something, perverting the course of justice, maybe? Unless she was being held against her will for all these years, she must have heard the appeals for her to get in contact, to let someone know she was safe. What if she's sent to prison? Maybe that's what she's scared of, why she is hiding. If she is back, what will happen to her?

In the end, I decide to send an email, not to Tony but to Layla, just to let her know that I finally understood what she meant.

> I worked it out, Layla. I went to Pharos Hill, I found the Russian doll.
>
> You should have waited.

But she doesn't reply and eventually, I fall into an exhausted sleep.

I'm reluctant to leave the next morning. I feel close to Layla here in Devon. Yet reason tells me this isn't where she's hiding. The Russian dolls that she's been able to leave with such ease mean she's more likely to be somewhere nearer to Simonsbridge, Cheltenham maybe. The fact that Ellen saw her there lends weight to this, and I wonder about stopping off on my way home and spending a couple of hours walking around the town. But I doubt I'd see her in the street, or through a shop window, or sitting in a café.

I don't remember much about the drive home. I must have driven to Exeter and got onto the M5 because I suddenly find myself driving down the road toward the house. I slam the brakes on. It's too soon, I'm not ready to face Ellen, pretend it's just another ordinary day. But much as I want to, I can't sit here. If I don't go in, it will seem strange.

I shift the car into gear and drive through the gate. I'm still not ready so I take out my phone and pretend I'm on a call. I hear Peggy barking and out of the corner of my eye, I see Ellen at the window. I turn my head, showing her my phone, and understanding, she gives me a little wave and disappears.

I sit with the phone clamped to my ear until I can't delay any longer. I get slowly out of the car and make my way to the front door. As I open it, Peggy wraps herself around my legs, and I crouch down and bury my face in her neck, telling her how beautiful she is.

"If I didn't love her as much as you do, I'd be jealous," Ellen says, and for a moment, I wonder who she's talking about. I feel a sudden rush of guilt. This is my life, I tell myself fiercely. Ellen is my life now, not Layla.

"You're my life," I tell Ellen, taking her in my arms. Surprised by the urgency in my voice, she laughs softly and tells me that I should go away more often. Peggy scrambles up onto her hind legs, trying to get between us. "I'll take her for a walk," I say. "I need to stretch my legs after all that driving."

"How's the migraine?"

"Gone."

"Good. I don't suppose you could pick up some milk, could you? And something for tonight?"

I set off, Peggy at my heels, and as I walk I wonder how Layla traced me to Simonsbridge, and when. Maybe she's been looking for me for years, maybe it was the article in the newspaper about Ellen moving in with me that finally led her to me. How must that have made her feel, to know I was with Ellen?

I buy milk at the village store then go to the butcher's to get some steak, and some homemade pâté for lunch. Suddenly hungry, I ask Rob to cut me a few slices of German sausage, realizing I haven't eaten since lunchtime yesterday. A lifetime ago. I almost ask him if he's seen anyone hanging around the village. But the newspaper article last year had been accompanied by a photograph of Layla, her distinctive red hair flashing like a warning sign. If I give a description, he might guess I'm talking about Layla. I can't risk it.

At the river, I share the sausage with Peggy, and allow my mind to wander. If Layla turns up, what will happen? Ellen is her family, we couldn't turn our backs on her. And I wouldn't want to. So where would that leave me and Ellen?

I call Peggy from where she's rooting under a bush and head home. As I walk past The Jackdaw, Ruby comes out.

"You look as if you could do with a coffee," she says, so I follow her inside and sit at the bar while she pours me a mug from the glass jug that sits on the counter.

"Thanks," I say, closing my hands around the mug, appreciating the warmth.

"Rough night?"

"You could say that." The need to confide in someone is overwhelming and anyway, Ruby already knows most of it. "I misunderstood the email address—"

"No kidding," she says dryly.

"Layla is alive, Ruby." The words sound strange on my tongue.

"What?" She looks at me, stunned.

"Did you see anybody with red hair in the pub last Friday, at the bar?"

She shakes her head, still trying to process what I've just told her. "Not that I noticed. Finn, are you sure?"

"Yes. I went to St. Mary's to meet her."

Ruby's eyes grow wide. "You've seen her?"

"No." I shake my head. "She wasn't there."

"So how do you know she's alive?"

I take the little Russian doll from my pocket. "I found this on a tree stump on Pharos Hill."

"Pharos Hill?"

"It's near where we used to live in Devon, not far from St. Mary's. Doll number five." I stand it on the table between us. "This, coupled with the email address, can only mean she's alive. Rudolph Hill. Russian doll, Pharos Hill." She frowns, not getting it. "I found the doll on Pharos Hill, standing on a tree stump Layla used to say looked like a Russian doll," I explain. "Nobody else would know its significance."

"It could be somebody pretending to be her," she points out carefully.

"No. She was there, Ruby, I know she was." Something must show on my face, maybe the frustration I feel at having arrived too late to see Layla, because she lays a hand on my arm.

"I think you'd better start at the beginning," she says, giving me the benefit of the doubt.

So I tell her everything, even what I've never told her before, the truth behind the holiday in France when it all went so drastically wrong, right up to the letter I left for Layla asking her to marry me, the letter that has now gone.

"If what you say is true," she says slowly when I get to the end, "it's horribly creepy."

It isn't the reaction I expected and I open my mouth to defend Layla, then realize that Ruby's right. Just because Layla is behind the trail of Russian dolls, it doesn't mean that there isn't something sinister about it.

"I think the Russian dolls were a way of getting my attention," I say, making excuses for her anyway. "Now that she's got it, I don't think I'll be finding any more. What I'm trying to do is piece everything together. What made her come back now, what prompted her to leave that first Russian doll? What prompted her to start sending emails, luring me to St. Mary's?"

She thinks for a moment. "Because of the timing, I'd say she—if it is Layla—isn't happy about you marrying Ellen. Maybe she saw the wedding announcement." She pauses, calculating backward. "She started to leave the Russian dolls not long after it appeared in the newspaper, didn't she? If she's been keeping tabs on you all these years from wherever she's been hiding, she must have been pretty shocked to learn that you were with Ellen. Maybe, at first, she thought the only reason you were with Ellen was because she's her sister, that you were trying to find her—Layla—in Ellen. But to go as far as marrying her means something different altogether. It means you love Ellen for who she is, not because she reminds you of Layla. I know, because that's how I felt." She looks at me ruefully. "I thought your relationship with Ellen was because you needed to get Layla out of your system and that once she was, you'd come back to me. It was quite a shock when I heard you were going to marry her. So I kind of get where Layla is coming from."

"But I was free for years! She could have come back anytime! Why didn't she?"

"Maybe she was scared of you—you know, after that night."

"But to stay away for twelve years?"

"Maybe she couldn't come back before."

"Why not? I doubt she was being kept prisoner. I used to think that she was, I used to torture myself imagining that she was being kept against her will. But I don't think that now."

Ruby shrugs. "Maybe she was ill."

"For twelve years? So what does she think will happen now? What is she expecting?"

"Maybe she isn't expecting anything." She pauses. "On the other hand—"

"What?"

"You said that the letter had gone from the cottage, and only recently."

"That's right."

"And that in it you told her to come and find you, that you would always love her. Isn't that what you told me you wrote?"

"Yes."

"Well, maybe, in her mind, she thinks it still holds true."

"What—that if she comes back, I'll fall in love with her all over again?"

"Perhaps."

"And leave Ellen?" I pick up on something she said. "What did you mean, 'in her mind'?"

"She's disturbed, Finn."

"Disturbed?"

"Fragile. And maybe a little unbalanced." I stare at her. "Balanced people do not go round leaving little Russian dolls for people to find," she goes on.

I sigh, knowing she's right. "What am I going to do?"

"I think you're going to have to be cruel to be kind. Send her an email, refer to the letter if you want, but tell her that twelve years is a very long time and that you've moved on."

"With her sister."

"She probably knows that already. The thing is, are you going to tell Ellen?"

"I don't know."

"You should. You can't keep something like this from her. If I were Ellen, I'd want to know."

"I'd want to know what?" Turning, I see Ellen standing in the doorway behind me. She's smiling, but there's worry in her eyes.

"Where he's planning on taking you for your honeymoon," Ruby says, without missing a beat, while, with as much casualness as I can muster, I sweep the little Russian doll that I'd left standing on the counter into my pocket. "He's planning to surprise you, but I was saying that in your place, I would want to know. I mean, how's a girl to know what sort of clothes to take with her?" Ellen laughs at this. "Are you coming in for coffee?" Ruby goes on.

I pull out the stool beside me. "Come on, come and rescue me from Ruby. She keeps telling me I'm doing everything wrong. Would you really prefer to know where I'm taking you?"

"Well, I'd like to know if we're going somewhere hot or cold," Ellen says, sitting down. "And whether it's a lying on the beach type of honeymoon or a sightseeing one."

Ruby pours a coffee and puts it on the bar in front of her. "Exactly. He's been asking my advice on possible destinations so maybe you'd like to drop me a discreet hint or two."

"The Seychelles. Mexico." Ellen leans over and kisses me. "I never thought you were the type of man to prepare a surprise honeymoon."

"I have hidden depths," I tell her.

We stay a while longer, Ruby and Ellen chatting about possible places to go on honeymoon, while I nurse my coffee, unable to let Ruby's comments about Layla go.

"I wasn't checking up on you," Ellen says as we walk back home.

"I know," I say, kissing the top of her head.

"I was worried that you'd been away so long, that's all. Rob said you'd been in to see him so I thought I'd see if you were in The Jackdaw."

"Sorry," I say, giving her another kiss. "Ruby called me in for a coffee."

She nods at my bag. "So what did you buy?"

"Steak for tonight and pâté for lunch."

"Perfect," she smiles.

TWENTY-FIVE

LAYLA

It was right that Ellen should find the first Russian doll. After all, it was hers, the one that had gone missing from her set when we were children. I hadn't stolen it, as she'd thought, but when it eventually turned up a few years later, at the bottom of our old toy chest, I kept it. I'm not sure why I didn't just give it back to her. Maybe I was worried she would say I must have stolen it after all, maybe I thought it no longer held any importance for her. But now that it was back in Ellen's possession, I felt bereft. I hadn't realized how much I relied on it, how often my right hand strayed to it in times of stress. Without it, I felt vulnerable, unprotected. I no longer had mine—I'd lost it in the picnic area in Fonches. So I searched the Internet for Russian dolls, in order to replace it.

I hadn't realized there were so many different sets, comprising any number of dolls, and I flew through the images, panic-stricken that I wouldn't find the one Ellen and I had had, because it had to be exactly the same, painted in the exact shades of yellow and red, with exactly the same face. And like a mother who recognizes her child in a photo of hundreds, I found it, its little eyes staring back at me from the screen. I had to buy the full set to have it, but it didn't matter.

I kept trying to work out how Finn must have felt when Ellen showed him the doll she'd found. Maybe he hadn't felt anything, maybe he'd forgotten the story I'd told him. If he had, the Russian doll wouldn't have held any significance for him. Even if he hadn't forgotten, he might have dismissed its appearance as a coincidence. Unless he knew that Thomas had seen me. But did he? I had no way of knowing. Maybe Thomas hadn't bothered to tell the police, maybe he had but they hadn't bothered to tell Finn.

The thought that despite leaving my precious Russian doll outside the house, Finn still might not know I was back, itched away at me. Instead of ignoring it, I scratched at it until it became a wound. And instead of leaving it to scab over, I picked at it until it began to fester. I couldn't let it go. If Finn didn't know I'd been at the cottage, if nobody had told him, the Russian doll wouldn't mean anything.

In a panic, I went back to the Internet and ordered ten more sets of Russian dolls. When they arrived, I went a bit mad, unscrewing the wooden corpses as fast as I could to get to the smallest ones, leaving dissected bodies littering the floor around me. As I cradled the ten little Russian dolls in my hands, I felt all-powerful.

Once I started leaving them for Finn to find, he wouldn't doubt that I was back.

TWENTY-SIX

FINN

I know I should do as Ruby suggested and send Layla an email making things clear, telling her that I've moved on, that I'm going to marry Ellen in September. But it's not what I want.

I take the Russian doll out of my pocket, the one from the tree stump on Pharos Hill, and stand it on my desk. Knowing I was so near to Layla is hard. If only I'd understood sooner. Now, if she doesn't get back in contact, I'll never find her. She must be living under a new identity because how could she have a bank account, a job, without one? And she must have a job, because how would she manage for money otherwise? Unless she isn't alone.

Unsettled, I take out my phone and open my emails. I scan them quickly and see that one has come in from Rudolph Hill. Taking a breath, I open it.

Do you believe that it's me now?

I reply quickly: Yes

I went to the cottage

I found your letter, Finn

You told me to come and find you

I have no idea what to respond. I should ask her where she is, if she's all right, if she needs help. But now that she's mentioned the letter, I'm wary of continuing the conversation, worried where it might lead. So I wait, hoping she'll send another email. But she doesn't.

Feeling restless, I take the three Russian dolls that I found from my drawer and stand them alongside the one from the tree stump. Quadruplets. Ruby's right, I think, scooping them up and putting them away again. This isn't the work of someone who is sound of mind. I should phone Tony, ask his advice. But not yet, not until I know what Layla wants.

It's hard to get down to work but despite having one eye out for an email coming in, I manage to cast an eye over some new Requests For Proposal. Ellen comes to get me for lunch and we listen to some jazz while we eat the pâté I bought earlier, Peggy at our feet. Is that why I fell in love with Ellen, I wonder, because she loves the things that I love, dogs, jazz, cooking? Because she's a better match for me than Layla was?

"I can't believe how high our water bill is," Ellen is saying.

"It's the price we have to pay for a beautiful garden," I say, aware that my phone has just beeped, a sign that an email has come in. But I'm not going to look at it here, in front of Ellen, in case it's from Layla.

"Dessert?" Ellen asks. "I've poached some apricots from the garden."

"Lovely."

I rush through the apricots and with a quick kiss to Ellen, head out to my office.

The email is from Layla. I open it quickly.

AND NOW I HAVE

TWENTY-SEVEN

LAYLA

The trouble was, I couldn't see inside Finn's head. Despite the two Russian dolls that I'd left for him to find—one on the wall outside the house, another on his car—despite letting Ellen catch a glimpse of me in Cheltenham, which personally, I thought was a stroke of genius—maybe he was still refusing to believe I was back. Perhaps he didn't want to believe it. He was going to marry Ellen and no amount of Russian dolls was going to change that. Anyway, didn't she deserve him after all the sacrifices she'd made?

So I tried to let go. And I might have managed to if I hadn't returned to the cottage, this time to go inside to take a keepsake of our time together there. The keys to the cottage were the only thing

I'd had with me the night I'd disappeared, because they were in the pocket of my jeans, the jeans I'd been wearing the day we left St. Mary's.

I chose to arrive at lunchtime when there was less chance of being seen by Thomas. Like the previous time, I passed unnoticed out of the station. My steps quickened as I walked toward the cottage and as I approached, the past dug its claws in deeper, dragging me back to before, so that when I arrived at the gate, I fully expected Finn to fling open the blue front door, worried that I'd taken so long to come back from my walk to the village. When he didn't, I thought he must be in the garden, so I let myself in. Lost in the past, I was surprised to find the key hard to turn in the lock, the door difficult to open, as if something was holding it shut. Maybe Finn had put a bag of rubbish there, to take out to the bin later.

I pushed the door harder, shoving whatever was behind it out of the way, and stepped into the hall. And the past, having had its fun with me, tossed me right back into the present. Disorientated, I stared at the mail piled up behind the door, yellow with age, trying to understand, because it seemed so at odds with the flowers in the garden. Even if Finn only came by once a month to keep the cottage up to scratch, surely there shouldn't be this much mail?

Unwilling to accept what my eyes and nose were telling me—the stench of neglect was everywhere—I reached out and pushed open the kitchen door. A shower of dust fell from it and as I stood on the threshold looking in, it was hard to make sense of what I was seeing. Inch-thick dust covered every available surface and cobwebs hung from the beamed ceiling in shrouds. It eventually sunk in. Finn hadn't been looking after the cottage, waiting for my return. How could I have ever thought that he would? He hadn't been hoping that I would come back. I could stop leaving little Russian dolls for him to find. I wasn't going to get the past back, I wasn't going to be able to come out of the darkness and into the light. I was going to have to spend the rest of my life in subterfuge, hiding my true self away from the world.

Devastated, my eyes swept around the kitchen. Something caught my eye: a slightly raised rectangular shape on the table, something there under the dust. As if in a trance, I walked over and picked it up, exposing the brown wood surface of the table beneath. It was a letter, the envelope covered in the dust of a thousand years. I studied it for a moment, wondering why it wasn't lying in the hall with the rest of the mail. I ran my finger across the front of it, dislodging the powdery film, and saw that the envelope had been handwritten, not typed, the ink so faded I could barely make out what it said. I held it up to the light streaming in through the window. There was just one word—Layla.

I don't know how long I stood there, staring at the letter Finn had left for me, because I recognized his handwriting. Eventually, the terrible shaking that had taken hold of me when I first saw my name on the envelope drove me to put it into my bag, terrified that the letter, fragile with age, would disintegrate in my hands before I'd had a chance to read it. What did it say, this letter that Finn had left me all those years ago? Was it a letter of warning, never to go near him again, to not seek him out, in the event that I did turn up? Or was it a letter of a different kind?

Aware of time passing, I left the cottage quickly, pulling the door closed behind me, then locking it, glad there was no sign of Thomas. As I hurried toward the station, I slipped my hand into my pocket and closed my fingers around the little Russian doll, one of the new ones, trying to calm my racing heart. When I arrived, I walked to the end of the platform, where there was less chance of somebody trying to strike up a conversation with me. Not only was I incapable of talking, I didn't want a friendly local asking me why I'd come to St. Mary's, or a tourist telling me where I should go to next. But the family of four I walked past were too wrapped up in themselves to take any notice of me, as were the young couple sitting on the only bench, his arm around her shoulders, reminding me painfully of how Finn and I used to be.

Eventually, the train came in. The end carriage was mercifully empty and I chose a seat at the back, where I was less likely to be disturbed at subsequent stations. And then, as carefully as my trembling fingers would allow, I unsealed the envelope and gently pulled out the sheets of paper. My heart was in my mouth as I unfolded the pages, and as I did, something slid out and onto my lap. Looking down, I found myself staring at a ring.

I picked it up. It was gold, with a solitary diamond, like an engagement ring. My breath caught in my chest. I felt dizzy, sick. My vision blurred, and fearing I was going to pass out, I forced air into my lungs. The breath that escaped was huge. It shook the whole of my body so violently that the letter slid to the floor. Scared that the ring would too, and that I would never find it, I tried to slide it onto my finger. It was too big for my ring finger so I jammed it onto the middle one. It fit perfectly. And then I stooped down, rescued the letter from the floor and unfolded it.

The words danced before my eyes. It was a while before I could focus on them and as I read, my whole world, the one I had created for myself, came crashing down around me.

TWENTY-EIGHT

FINN

Since the email from Layla yesterday, I haven't been able to relax, which is why I'm out for a run. It was the capital letters that did it. They creeped me out. I'd felt threatened, which is stupid, I know. And now I keep wondering what will happen if Layla suddenly appears on the doorstep.

Maybe it wouldn't be so bad if she did. Sometimes I go as far as imagining it—hearing the ring of the doorbell, going into the hall, opening the door, seeing her standing there. But I can't imagine giving her a hug, ushering into the hall, then into the kitchen where Ellen is waiting. What I can imagine is taking her in my arms and never letting her go. Or taking her by the hand

and leading her far, far away from everyone and everything. That's what makes me afraid.

I arrive at the fence that borders the back of our garden and jump over it onto the lawn. I stand for a moment, breathing heavily, stretching my calf muscles, then take out my phone to check my emails. There's nothing from Layla, probably because I haven't replied to her last message, the one where she said she'd found me. I feel I owe her a reply, even if it's only to tell her to stay away from me, from us, from Ellen and me. But that seems a bit harsh considering we're her family. So I reply: I'm glad you have.

I don't want to bump into Ellen so I decide to delay my shower and go to my office instead. I log on to my computer and sit there, waiting. A few minutes later, an email comes in.

Have you told Ellen I'm alive?

Truth or lie? Because I'm on uncharted territory, I go for the truth.

No, not yet.
Why not?
Because I want to know where you've been for all these years first.
I shouldn't have come back
What do you mean?
You're going to marry Ellen

My fingers pick out letters of their own accord so it's only when I'm about to press SEND that I realize what I've written. Snatching my hands away, I push my chair back abruptly, putting distance between me and the keyboard. I take a moment, then reach down with one finger and press the delete button until the three little words—No, I'm not—disappear. I need to reply something, but what? Something benign.

How are you? Are you OK?
Maybe we should meet

I feel a prickle of something like danger. Or maybe it's excitement.

When?
I'll let you know

I stare at the screen in frustration. Maybe it's the fact that she suggested we meet but suddenly I miss her, I miss the Layla I knew twelve years ago. I miss the way we were together. It's so different from the way I am with Ellen. With Layla, there were highs and lows; with Ellen, everything is constant. There are no ups and downs. We never argue—but we don't laugh either, not like I laughed with Layla. I tell myself it's because we're older but I know that it isn't. Ellen is more—I search for the word and when I realize I was going to use "boring," I quickly substitute it for serious, ashamed at myself. I'll be all right once I've seen Layla, I tell myself. When I see her, I'll explain that I'm now with Ellen, that it's Ellen I love, and everything will be all right.

Another email comes in. I open it, thinking she's going to tell me when we can meet.

I'M WEARING YOUR RING, FINN

TWENTY-NINE

LAYLA

The words went round and round in my head and the train picked them up, taunting me with them as it trundled along—there'd been no need to run that night, there'd been no need to run. If I hadn't disappeared, it would have been all right. But I'd thought he was going to kill me.

I should never have told him that I'd slept with someone else. But he knew something was wrong and he kept trying to find out why I'd been so quiet since my return from London. At first he thought I was homesick, or missing Ellen, and the mention of Ellen had made me cry, because of course I was missing her. But it compounded the guilt I felt, because Ellen would have been horrified at what I'd done. If she'd met someone like Finn, she would never have betrayed him, she would have loved him and cherished him and thanked God every waking moment that she'd found a good, kind, and decent man, as different as possible from our father in every single way. At least that's what I'd thought, until I saw a side of him I hadn't known existed.

I knew that he'd had a fight with Harry, that he'd beaten Harry quite badly, but I had no idea how explosive his temper could actually be until that night. It all happened so fast. One minute I was sitting next to him in the car at Fonches, a little scared at what I'd just told him but proud that I'd been honest with him, the next I thought I was about to die. I didn't recognize the man who dragged me out of the car and shook me until my teeth rattled. The look in his eyes as he yelled he would never forgive me, and my inability to reach him, to break through his rage, was terrifying. I didn't see him, I saw my father, and when he drew back his arm and I saw his clenched fist, I felt myself being dragged into some dark and sinister place. Maybe I passed out through sheer terror because the next thing I knew, I was lying on the ground next to the car. There was no sign of Finn, and I was so convinced he was going to kill me that I thought he'd gone to look for a weapon—a branch from a tree, a discarded iron bar—to finish me off with. And so I ran.

I know the reason for his anger now. I know what happened with Siobhan, his girlfriend in Ireland, he explained it in his letter. I also know that he would have forgiven me for what I did. The desolation I felt was terrible. If I hadn't run away, we would be together. No matter how hard I tried, I couldn't get past the fact that the last twelve years had been for nothing. NOTHING!!! Scared that the despair I felt would take me back to where I'd been before, I tried to rein it in. I took deep breaths, told myself that everything would be all right. But how could it be when Finn was with Ellen now?

It had never occurred to me that he would marry Ellen. I didn't doubt that he loved her but I didn't believe he loved her as much as he'd loved me. I felt betrayed. I reminded myself that I had betrayed him first. Finn had moved on and I needed to accept it. But I couldn't; memories of the life I used to have wouldn't leave me alone. I wanted that life, not the one I had now. By rights, Finn was mine. MINE! Layla's, not Ellen's. Not Ellen's, Layla's. I felt feverish, sick. Now, more than ever, I needed Finn to know I was back.

I started sending him emails. I didn't use my name because if I had, Finn would have thought they were coming from someone pretending to be me. He did anyway. I was stunned that he hadn't understood the significance of the email address—I'd chosen it especially so that he would know my true identity. The Russian doll that I managed to leave, at huge risk, on the plate at The Jackdaw, only compounded his belief that someone was pretending to be me. And I realized that the only way he would believe I was back was if I lured him to the cottage and he saw that the letter had gone.

I could have told him that I'd found it, and saved him a trip. But then I realized that he still wouldn't know it was me, because sometime over the past twelve years, anyone could have got hold of my keys and taken the letter. It was imperative that he worked out the email address by himself, that he got to the truth by himself. I made a pact; if he couldn't work out what Rudolph Hill referred to, I would disappear again and let him get on with his life with Ellen. But if he worked it out—well, it would be the start of a whole new chapter.

THIRTY

FINN

I sit on the edge of the bed, staring at Ellen's clothes through the open wardrobe door, noticing for the first time that almost everything is gray—different shades of gray, maybe, but gray nonetheless. There are a few items in other pastels but nothing like the vibrant colors Layla used to wear. My eyes drop to Ellen's shoes, neatly arranged in two rows at the bottom of the wardrobe, all of them with the same-sized heel, and I feel suddenly stifled at the uniformity of it all.

Ellen is downstairs so I take out my phone and look at the latest email I received from Layla. I haven't replied to it yet. It's a tough one. I mean, what am I meant to reply when she asks if I'm happy she's wearing my ring?

The truth is, I feel a bit emotional at the thought of her wearing it. But I can't tell her that.

It's yours, I bought it for you, I reply.

Did you buy one for Ellen?

I think of the little silver knot ring I gave to Ellen after I asked her to marry me. I hadn't bought her a traditional engagement ring because that wasn't who she was, unlike Layla, who'd loved anything that glittered. Nevertheless, I decide to sidestep her question.

Do you still want to meet?

Is Ellen wearing your ring?

Yes. Do you still want to meet?

I shouldn't have come back

What do you mean?

It's too late

No, it isn't. It's never too late.

It is. You're with Ellen now

We need to talk, Layla.

But she's gone, leaving me as she's left me before, hoping she'll be back, not knowing if she will be.

I go down to the kitchen.

"I've made porridge," Ellen says, looking up from the saucepan she's stirring.

"No, thanks," I say shortly. "I'll make myself some bacon."

"I'll do it."

"It's fine." I move to the oven, take the grill pan out and clatter it onto the side.

"Is everything alright?" Ellen asks.

"Everything's fine."

"It's just—"

"What?" I snap.

"You seem on edge."

"Just because I don't want to eat your damn porridge?" She looks at me, hurt. "Sorry," I say, hating that I'm taking my frustration out on her, hating that Layla is coming between us.

"Is it Grant?" Ellen asks.

"Another client. I'm just a bit under pressure, that's all."

"Maybe you can talk to Harry when he comes for lunch tomorrow."

We eat our breakfast in near-silence. I can't stop thinking about Layla, about where she might be, if she's somewhere close by, and I realize she's consuming me just as she consumed me all those years ago.

"I thought I'd do pork," Ellen is saying. "If you could get me some apples, I'll make a sauce to go with it."

It takes me a moment to realize she's still talking about lunch with Harry. "I'll get them now," I say, getting to my feet.

"There's no rush." Ellen's voice follows me anxiously out of the back door. "Pork is all right, isn't it?"

"It's fine," I call back. But I can't bring myself to turn around and smile at her.

When Harry arrives the next day, he seems pretty pleased with himself and when he tells Ellen that he has a surprise for her, I wonder what he's bought as well as the huge bouquet of flowers he's already holding.

"I've got something to show you first," Ellen says excitedly, taking his hand and drawing him into the kitchen. She stands back and throws her arm out, showing him the worktop where her set of Russian dolls stand. "Look!"

Harry looks so bemused that I feel almost sorry for Ellen, although I don't know why she's making such a thing of it. He doesn't seem to have the slightest idea why he should be impressed.

"She has a full set, Harry," I prompt.

"Right," he says. "Yes, I can see that. Amazing."

Ellen picks up the littlest doll. "I found this lying outside the gate," she explains. "I couldn't believe it had turned up after all these years."

"Not the same one, surely," Harry says.

"Finn doesn't think so, but I do." She holds out the doll to him. "See this smudge of paint? Mine had that too."

"I've told her that lots of them probably do," I tell Harry. What I don't tell him is that none of the four that are lying at the back of my drawer do.

"But why would it suddenly turn up after all these years?" Harry asks. "And how?"

Ellen hesitates, and before she can tell him that she thinks she saw Layla in Cheltenham a few weeks back, I jump in quickly. "Let's have a drink," I suggest, because if Harry knows there's a possibility that Layla is alive, he's not going to let it go after everything he did twelve years ago to find her.

After lunch, we go out to the garden for coffee. Ellen asks me if I'd mind clearing away while she shows Harry her latest illustrations, and it's only when I'm stacking the dishwasher that I realize she'll use this time alone with him to tell him that she saw Layla anyway. She won't be able to help herself. So when he comes to find me in the kitchen half an hour later, and suggests taking Peggy for a walk, I know I'm in for a grilling.

He waits until we're heading down to the river, then launches his attack.

"Is everything all right, Finn?"

"Everything's fine."

"It's just that you seem a bit restless."

"What has Ellen said?"

"That she thought she saw Layla in Cheltenham a couple of weeks back."

"Yes, but it was only someone with the same color hair."

"So you don't think it was her, then?"

"No, and Ellen doesn't either. We agreed she was probably mistaken."

He raises his eyebrows at my choice of words and a part of me wishes I could confide in him. But he'll tell me to tell Tony and I don't want to do that before I know what Layla wants, and why she's chosen to come back now.

"What about the Russian doll?" he says. "Strange that it should turn up after all these years."

"It's not the one that Ellen lost all those years ago."

"She thinks it is."

"It's wishful thinking. She wants Layla to be back, which is why she's managed to convince herself that she saw Layla in Cheltenham."

"What about you? Do you want Layla to be back?"

I keep my voice calm but my irritation is mounting. "Layla's been missing for years. She isn't going to come back, not now."

"Hm." He slows his pace, reaches into his pocket and draws something out. I look down and see a little Russian doll lying in the palm of his hand. "I found this standing on the wall when I arrived earlier and I couldn't wait to give it to Ellen because I remembered her telling me that she'd lost hers years ago." He pauses. "But she already had one."

So that's why he was acting so strangely. I want to grab the stupid doll and throw it as hard as I can into the water. Luckily, Harry presumes that I've gone into some kind of shock at the implications of what he thinks is a second Russian doll turning up.

"Too much of a coincidence, don't you think?" he goes on.

"What are you suggesting, Harry?" I ask, my voice thick with anger at Layla. Yesterday, she refused to meet up with me, yet she's willing to risk coming to the house and being seen. Unless she came during the night.

"That maybe it *was* Layla that Ellen saw in Cheltenham."

I sit down on the grassy bank. Harry picks up a stick and throws it into the water for Peggy. She retrieves it and brings it back to him and he throws it for her a couple more times. I stay silent. I know he'll be assuming all sorts of things about what I'm thinking and I feel an odd sense of power that he has no idea what I know about Layla.

"Did you show the doll to Ellen?" I ask, when he finally sits down beside me.

"No, not yet."

"I'd rather you didn't. I don't want her getting her hopes up." And the last thing I need is Ellen getting involved in a search for Layla. For the moment, she only knows about the Russian doll that she found, and that's the way I want it to stay.

"What about you?"

"What do you mean?"

"What about your hopes?"

"I want Layla to be alive, of course I do," I say.

"Well, it certainly looks as if she might be."

I give a short laugh. "On the basis of two Russian dolls and a possible sighting? Isn't that a bit weak?"

"Perhaps. But I always thought she might turn up one day."

I find myself frowning. "Really?"

"Yes. I've never thought she was dead. Or that she was kidnapped."

He's never told me this before. "So where has she been all these years? And if you're right, why has she turned up now? Why not last year, or five years ago, or five months after she first disappeared."

"I don't know." He shrugs. "Maybe it's all about timing."

"What do you mean?"

"Well, with you about to marry Ellen. Maybe she's been keeping up with your life from wherever she's been living and doesn't like the fact that you're about to marry her sister." He turns his eyes on me. "You do still want to marry Ellen, don't you?"

I stretch my legs out and move to stand up. "Yes, of course."

"Even if Layla is back?"

I want to give him another "Yes, of course" but I feel strangely bereft. Maybe Harry senses this because he puts a hand on my arm, as if in apology for asking the question in the first place.

"Come on, let's head back. Didn't Ellen say she would make scones?"

I ask him if he managed to sort out the problem that prevented him from coming down the previous weekend and he tells me about one of his notoriously difficult investors.

"Sometimes I'd like to get out of it," he finishes. "I reckon I'm getting too old for this game."

"You're forty-five."

"And I've been doing it for twenty-five years. It's been my life. But sometimes I can't help wishing I'd got married, had a family."

I laugh. "You'd be bored out of your mind tied to one woman."

He gives a wry grin. "Maybe."

"Anyway, if that's what you want—marriage, a family—it's not too late. What about the current lady in your life? Would you consider making an honest woman of her?"

"Absolutely not."

"Then don't waste your time—or hers," I advise.

We arrive at the house and I pause, my hand on the gate.

"Would you mind giving me the Russian doll you found?" I ask. And Harry, being Harry, hands it over without question, putting it down to my need to have a tangible reminder of Layla.

Later, after he's left, I go out to my office and open the drawer in my desk. I take out the four little dolls one by one and stand them in a line, then add Harry's onto the end. Five pairs of unblinking eyes stare straight ahead, five painted mouths smile benignly. Or mockingly. Once again, I find myself asking—what is Layla playing at?

I get a clue when I check my emails and find one from Rudolph Hill.

I STILL LOVE YOU

THIRTY-ONE

LAYLA

Finn did exactly what I thought he would. He automatically presumed I was talking about the cottage and went straight there, which was good, because I wanted him to know I'd found his letter. But I also needed to get him to Pharos Hill, so that he would know, without a doubt, that I was back, because I intended to leave a Russian doll on top of the tree stump, the one I used to tell him was shaped like a Russian doll. So I was glad when he finally worked out the significance of the email address I'd chosen. I doubted he'd been back to Pharos Hill since the day he put up a bench in my memory. What had it been like for him to realize that I'd been there earlier, and had gone? Had it reminded him of the night I'd disappeared from his life?

I'm not really wearing his ring. But sometimes I take it from where I've hidden it and slide it onto my ring finger, pretending it fits. And the bitterness comes, at twelve wasted years. It brings me so low I'm afraid I'll go back to being what I was before, a nothing being, secret and soulless. It took me years of courage to move out of the shadows and into the light. I'm still a lesser being than I was before I disappeared. But at least I exist.

I suppose it's unfair to blame Finn. But the way I see it, if I hadn't thought he was going to kill me that night, I wouldn't have disappeared. Hence my aggressive email, telling him I'd found him. I wanted him to be afraid of me, as I was once afraid of him. I'm not sure why that is. But my emotions have always been volatile. Anyway, Finn replied that he was glad I'd found him. Now why would he say that if he truly loved Ellen?

It brought me back to my original question, the one I asked myself as I sat on the platform at St. Mary's, the day Thomas saw me. If it came down to it, would Finn choose Ellen over me? Or was it possible that he would choose me, and I would get my old life back?

It was time to find out.

THIRTY-TWO

FINN

I push back my chair and put my bare feet up on the desk. They're wet with dew from where I walked across the lawn ten minutes ago. It's only six thirty but I couldn't sleep. I feel as if I've reached some sort of crossroads with Layla; her declaration of love has thrown me.

I look around my office, at the paintings on the walls. They are all of the sea in some shape or form. Layla chose the one that hangs on the wall behind the door. Because of its positioning, no one really sees it except me. I pull my feet from the desk and go over to it. There's an anger to the sea that I've never been aware of before. My mind goes back to what Ruby said, about the trail of Russian dolls being the work of someone unbalanced. Did Layla manage to disappear for so long because she had some sort of breakdown? Her mother died when she was just a young girl, her father was violent. To have experienced violence from me might have tipped her over the edge.

And as always, not knowing is worse than knowing.

I can't stand it any longer. Going back to my desk, I send Layla an email.

I really need to see you, Layla.

The minutes tick by without a reply so an hour later, I send another.

Please don't disappear from my life again.

Two hours later, just when I've given up all hope of ever hearing from her again, an email drops into my inbox. Thank you, thank you, God, I breathe, when I see the name Rudolph Hill. I open it quickly.

Do you still love me?

I stare at the screen. Of all the questions she could have asked, it's the one I wouldn't have wanted her to. It's impossible to answer. If I say no, I'll never hear from her again. Anyway, it would be a lie. I've never stopped loving her. But if I tell her that, what then? The pressure to reply is terrible. I take a gamble.

Yes, of course I do. You were a huge part of my life.

More than you love Ellen?

Christ.

The love I have for Ellen is different.

I think you should tell her I'm back

I want to see you first.

There's no immediate reply so I presume she's mulling it over. Come on, just give me a time and a place, that's all I want, just a time and a place. An email arrives.

Tell Ellen that I'm back first

I reply stubbornly: No, not until I've seen you.

It's the wrong thing to say. There's no answering email granting me my wish, no negotiating. Only silence.

I leave my office and walk across to the house, breathing in the morning air. Ellen isn't in the kitchen but the door to her office is open, so I move toward it, not to do as Layla asked but to reassure myself that if it came down to it, I would choose her over Layla. Engrossed in her work, she doesn't realize I'm there so I watch her for a moment, absorbing her, reminding myself how lucky I am to have her. Sensing me there, she looks up and smiles.

"To what do I owe this honor?" she teases, and I realize it's usually her that comes to find me.

"I wondered if you wanted breakfast."

"What time is it?"

"Around ten, I suppose."

She puts down her pencil. "You were up early. I guessed you were in your office so I thought I'd get some work in until you surfaced."

"I couldn't sleep." I go over. "How are you getting on?"

"Not too bad. Come and see my fairy glen." She moves back from her drawing board, making room for me.

"Ellen, this is beautiful," I say, genuinely awed by her talent, because her attention to detail is incredible. "How many of these little creatures are there?"

"Thirty-seven at last count but I still need to draw a few more."

"Not now," I say, firmly. "We're having breakfast first."

"I'll make some eggs."

"Or we could go to The Jackdaw for a fry-up," I say, suddenly hungry from being awake all night. "Ruby always does them during the holiday season."

"Good idea," Ellen says. "It'll make a nice change."

We're quiet during our walk to the pub but it's a comfortable silence. Ellen links her fingers in mine and as I turn to smile at her I feel a sudden rush of love. It's not love, it's gratitude, a voice tells me. You've never felt true love for Ellen, not like you felt for Layla. Admit it, Finn, you've never been in love with Ellen. You've grown to love her out of gratitude, that's all.

"Come on," I say abruptly, tugging her along faster, "I'm hungry."

The Jackdaw is nicely empty.

"Any more Russian dolls?" Ruby asks, while I'm ordering breakfast at the bar.

I glance at Ellen, who's making a fuss of Buster. "Harry came to lunch the other day and found one standing on the wall outside the house. Ellen doesn't know," I add, warning her.

"You should have brought him in for a drink," she says, pouring me a coffee. "How is he?"

"Fine. He wants to get married."

She laughs. “Harry? Married? Two words I never thought I’d hear together.”

“Don’t worry, it’s just a phase,” I grin.

She takes another mug from under the counter and pours a coffee for Ellen. “Does Harry know that Layla is back?”

“Apparently, he never believed she was dead. Like you, he thinks she’s reappeared because I’m going to marry Ellen. And now, because of the ring I left Layla, in the letter, everything has become even more complicated.”

“Why?”

“Because she’s wearing it, apparently.”

“Oh, Finn,” Ruby says softly. She looks at me. “You really need to tell Ellen, you know. It’s not fair on her.”

Aware that Ellen has moved to a table and is waiting for me to join her, I pick up the mugs of coffee.

“Thanks, Ruby, see you later.”

“Anytime,” she says.

The huge breakfast takes the edge off the frustration I feel, and with Ellen reaching for my hand across the table, everything is soon all right in my world again. Breakfast over, we wander back to the house and get down to work. I spend a lot of time on the phone making introductory calls to possible investors, and even more time checking how competitors’ funds are doing. Later, as Ellen and I move around the kitchen making dinner, chatting about our day, a quiet contentment comes over me, making me determined not to let Layla destroy what I have.

While Ellen’s getting ready for bed, I take out my phone to quickly check my emails, acknowledging that for the first time, I don’t want there to be one from Rudolph Hill. But there is. Heart in mouth, I open it.

TELL ELLEN, OR I WILL

THIRTY-THREE

LAYLA

I know I should stop what I'm doing. I need to accept that Finn is with Ellen now. But something won't let me.

After my mother died, I used to hear her voice in my head. It was as if, in dying, she had left something of herself behind in me. Or maybe I couldn't bear for her to be gone. I began to adopt some of her mannerisms and say things she would have said, which infuriated my father to no end and Ellen would have to protect me from his wrath. Our mother died from pneumonia, brought on by living in our freezing stone house in the most desolate part of Lewis and never seeing a doctor. But sometimes I dream that he murdered her and buried her body in a peaty bog where it would never be found. I know it's not true, though. It's just my mind getting mixed up.

It got mixed up a lot after I disappeared. But once I arrived at my place of refuge, I quickly adapted. I had to, for survival. I did what I had to do—I hid my true self, banished my true voice from my head and became the person I needed to be. Eventually, it led to a happiness I'd never imagined finding again. It wasn't the same kind of happiness I had known in my previous life—how could it be when I wasn't the same person, when I had to live in secret? But it was good, solid happiness, one I could have lived with for the rest of my life. Then Finn decided to marry Ellen and everything changed. My true voice started to come back. "You're never going to get your old life back," it taunted. "Finn loves Ellen now."

The other day I asked Finn if he loved me and he said that he did. "That may be," said the voice. "But while Ellen is around, you'll never get him back." And I realized that the voice was right.

I thought about what I could do. If Ellen left Finn of her own accord, it would make things easier. If she knew I was back, surely she would understand that Finn was rightfully mine and disappear from his life, as I had done all those years ago? It was a long shot, because I knew how hard she had worked to make Finn love her. But if I had to fight her for him, so be it.

THIRTY-FOUR

FINN

Layla's last message made me jumpy, like I was losing control. She'd made it sound like some kind of test. What was she thinking—that if I told Ellen she was back, Ellen would move out so that she could move in? Or that Ellen, sure of my love for her, would ask me to choose between them? But how could I? I feel terrible, because it should be simple.

Looking over at Ellen as she gets dressed, I feel a stab of shame. I should have told her about Layla—but there's no point now. A week has gone by since that last email and I haven't heard anything since. I tell myself that it's for the best. But how can I forget everything that has happened, go back to how I was before? It will be the not-knowing all over again—not knowing where Layla is, not knowing where she was, not knowing why she came back, only to disappear again.

"Is everything all right?" Ellen asks, and I realize I've been staring at her, except that I wasn't seeing her, I was seeing Layla.

"Yes, sorry. I was miles away."

"Well, now that I've got your attention, can I talk to you about something?" She pauses, pulls a gray vest top on and picks up a pair of pale gray jeans, and I guess she's going to ask me about plans for our wedding, because with it less than three months away, we need to get down to the technicalities, who we're inviting and where we're holding the reception. I had thought of holding it at The Jackdaw but something tells me Ellen is expecting more than steak and chips, and that the wedding isn't going to be the simple affair I'd hoped it would be.

"Go ahead," I tell her, determined to give her my fullest attention.

She finishes pulling on her jeans, takes something from the pocket and holds out her hand. "This came through the door yesterday." Looking down, I see a little Russian doll lying in her palm. Hiding my shock, I pick it up and make a show of examining it, giving myself time. Doll number seven—I have five and Ellen now has two. "I should have told you straightaway, I know, but . . ." her voice trails off.

I want to ask her why she didn't but then I remember all that I've been keeping from her.

"When you say it came through the door, do you mean it was pushed through the letterbox?" I say, handing the doll back to her.

"No, it came in an envelope."

"Who was it addressed to?"

She frowns at this. "Me, of course. I wouldn't have opened it otherwise."

I'm angry that Layla has done this, that she's gone ahead and done what she threatened to do. "Was it typewritten or handwritten?"

"Typewritten. The thing is . . ." She hesitates.

"Yes?"

"I guessed what it was before I even opened it. It wasn't just the shape, it's more that I've been expecting something like this." She looks at me defiantly. "I know you said it wasn't Layla that I saw in Cheltenham that day but it was. I'd recognize her anywhere."

"Even after twelve years?"

"Even after fourteen," she corrects, because she hasn't seen Layla since she left Lewis for London. "She is my sister." There's a fierceness in her voice. "OK, so I didn't see her face. But there was something about the way she was moving through the crowd that told me it was her. And her hair. She can't hide that—well, not unless she cut it off and dyed it. But she would never do that, she was always so proud of her hair. And now there's this second Russian doll."

"Maybe you shouldn't read too much into it," I warn gently. "It could just be someone having a joke. A sick one, maybe, but nevertheless, a joke."

She shakes her head. "I don't believe anyone would be so cruel. Anyway, nobody knows about the Russian dolls except you, me and Layla."

"And Harry," I remind her. "You told him about them, remember."

"Yes, of course, and Harry," she says impatiently. "But nobody else." She turns her green eyes on me. "You didn't tell Ruby, did you?"

"No," I say firmly.

"It's just that when I came looking for you at The Jackdaw the day you got back from seeing Grant, I saw a little Russian doll on the counter, before you put it in your pocket. I thought you'd been showing her the one that I found outside the house. But when we got home it was still there, standing on the side with the rest of the set. Which means the one you showed Ruby came from somewhere else."

"I'm sorry," I say, annoyed that she hasn't asked me about it before, wondering why she didn't mention it. "You're right, it was a different Russian doll."

"But where did you get it?"

My mind goes into overdrive, wondering what to say because I can't tell her the truth, that it was the one I found on Pharos Hill. "You know the time that we went to The Jackdaw for lunch? I found it on the plate along with the bill and I thought Ruby had put it there. She denied it at the time but I wanted to make sure. That's what we were arguing about that day."

"On the plate?" I hear the excitement in her voice. "But that means Layla was there, in the pub, when we were there!" Bewilderment creeps in. "But she can't have been—we would have seen her, surely?"

"That's why I thought Ruby had put it there. I thought I must have told her the story of the Russian dolls and she decided to plant a couple to make me think that Layla was back so that I wouldn't marry you." Ellen frowns. "But she didn't know what I was talking about and then I remembered that I had never told her the story about the dolls."

"So why didn't you tell me that you found a doll on the plate?"

"Because I didn't want to worry you."

"Worry me?" Now she looks puzzled and there's a rare flash of anger. "Why would I be worried?"

"Sorry, wrong word. I meant disappointed. I didn't want you to be disappointed if it was just a joke."

"But it isn't, is it? It isn't a joke, Finn. Layla is alive, I'm sure of it!" She looks how I felt when I first realized that Layla was back: half-excited, half-scared.

"I don't think so," I say.

"Well, she must be! What I don't understand is why she sent this doll specifically to me." She thinks for a moment. "Maybe she was hoping I'd find the one outside the house, and the one on the plate in The Jackdaw. Maybe she doesn't want you to know that she's back." I'd like to tell her that she's wrong, that Layla wants very much for me to know she's back but I can't bear to admit to all the other dolls I've found, the emails, my secret trips to Devon. "Does she really think I wouldn't tell you something so important?"

I feel so bad that I have to turn away. Why am I so reluctant to tell Ellen that her sister is alive? I can't believe I'm keeping something so momentous from her. The truth—that I want to keep Layla to myself—fills me with guilt. But only until I've found out what her intentions are, I tell myself. Once I know, then I'll tell Ellen.

"Finn, what's the matter?" When I don't reply she comes to stand in front of me, forcing me to look at her. "Is it because you regret asking me to marry you now that there's a possibility that Layla is back?" she asks, her voice faltering.

"Never," I say, putting my arms around her. "How could I regret that?"

"So if it is Layla who sent me the doll, if she is alive, you wouldn't want to be with her?"

"Not in that way, no. I'd be glad to see her, of course I would. But twelve years have gone by. We're not the same people, we're not in the same place."

"Thank you," she says softly. "Thank you for that. When the doll arrived yesterday, I was so happy. But then I was worried,

worried that Layla being back would change things. That's why I couldn't bring myself to tell you about it. Because she is back, Finn, surely you must see that? Between us we've found three Russian dolls."

"But why is she leaving the dolls in the first place?" I ask, hoping she might have a different insight. "Why not just come to the house and tell us she's back? She obviously knows where we live."

"I don't know. I've been thinking about it all morning. Maybe she's scared." She raises her head and looks up at me. "We should tell Tony. He'll know what to do."

"Not yet," I say quickly, needing more time. "We don't know for sure that it is Layla behind the dolls." She opens her mouth to protest but I carry on. "Let's wait a few days, see if anything else happens. You never know, she might turn up on the doorstep," I add, hoping that she won't, because how could I choose between them if they asked me to? "Maybe the Russian dolls are a way of preparing us for her arrival."

"I never thought of that," Ellen says. She thinks for a moment. "But it's a bit odd, isn't it?"

"We don't know where's she's been or what she's been through, if she has come back. Her mind might not be as stable as it was."

Ellen frowns at this. I take her hand. "Have you got the envelope the doll came in?"

"Yes, it's in the kitchen."

"I'd like to have a look at it."

"Come on, then."

The envelope is brown, the sticker with our typed address, white. Even though Ellen had said it came in the post, I'd presumed it had been put through the door, because the other Russian dolls had all been hand-delivered. But there are stamps, and a postmark. I bring it up to eye level.

"Cheltenham," says Ellen. "It was the first thing I checked when I saw what was inside." Again her voice has that mixture of excitement and fear. "She's here, Finn, close by. After all these years. It's incredible." She hesitates. "But also a bit scary. I mean, it's wonderful that she's alive, but it's not going to be easy, is it?"

"No, probably not," I say, acknowledging the understatement.

By the time I go out to my office three hours later I feel mentally exhausted from trying to keep up with Ellen's continual speculation about where Layla has been for the past twelve years and what will happen now that she's back. It had been hard to find reasons as to why I shouldn't phone Tony to ask his advice, or Harry to tell him the good news. When she asked me if I would be willing for Layla to stay with us if she needed to, just until she had sorted herself out, I began to realize something of the nightmare I could soon be in and I felt real anger toward Layla for sending the doll to Ellen. How much longer was I going to be able to stall before Ellen insisted that I speak to Tony? Did Layla understand what she had set in motion? I take out my phone, determined to spell it out to her. But she's beaten me to it.

Did Ellen receive the Russian doll I sent her?

Yes

Does she know we're in contact?

No. Can we meet now?

Soon

What is it you want, Layla?

The answer is so long in coming that I think she's going to leave me hanging again. But then a message comes in, no text, just attachments. I open the first one and find myself looking at a photo of the two of us, taken on Tower Bridge by one of Layla's friends from the wine bar. Then other photos, set up by Layla on a delayed timer so that she could run and join me in front of the camera, her arms round my neck, her lips on my cheek. It's painful to remember how much in love we were. I continue to scroll through photo after photo, evidence of how happy we were together, and the pain intensifies. And at the end, a one-word answer to my question.

YOU

THIRTY-FIVE

LAYLA

I asked Finn to tell Ellen I was back as a kind of test. He'd said he wanted to see me but I didn't want us to meet, not yet.

The voice rejoiced when he didn't do as I asked. "You see," it said. "He doesn't want to see you that much. If he did, he would tell Ellen." I didn't care. The way I saw it, the fact that Finn wouldn't tell her meant he wanted to keep me to himself. More important, it meant he was keeping secrets from her.

I gave him a week, then sent a doll to Ellen so that she and Finn could have that conversation, the one where they both acknowledged I was back. I worried that I'd played my hand too soon but Finn and I had reached an impasse and I was eager to move things forward. Now it was up to Ellen. I loved her and didn't want to hurt her but I needed her to do the right thing, and leave me and Finn to get on with the rest of our lives together. I knew it was naïve to expect her to walk out so that I could walk back in again but it was only the reverse of what had happened before, when I had walked out and she had walked in. At the time, I'd been happy for her to have Finn. But now it was time to give him back.

I knew Finn would be annoyed that I'd sent a doll to Ellen. He wasn't able to see beyond the complications to the endgame. It was also about control, or lack of it. I was unpredictable. He didn't know what I was going to do next. He didn't know that it depended on Ellen.

Because Ellen had her secrets too.

THIRTY-SIX

FINN

It's three in the morning and I'm driving round Cheltenham. I know I'm not going to find Layla but I had to get out of the house. I couldn't sleep, not after seeing the photos. I didn't want to lie there and think about the life I'm living now, and be confronted with the truth, that it's a pretend life, a second-best life, a life I chose only because being with Ellen makes me feel closer to Layla. I didn't want to see Ellen lying next to me and wish it was Layla, as I had so many times before. Ellen deserved better than that. She deserved better than me. I wasn't with her because I truly loved her. If she hadn't been Layla's sister, I would never have fallen for her in the first place. Ruby was right when she said that I'd been hoping to find Layla in Ellen.

I can't believe that I'm thinking like this but it's the truth. When Ellen and I had first begun spending time together, the thing I'd been most afraid of was that she would talk about Layla nonstop, or ask about my relationship with her. I didn't want to discuss Layla with anyone and, sensing my reticence, Ellen hadn't asked any questions at all. If she did mention Layla—in relation to something from their childhood, for example—she did so hesitantly, in a testing-the-water kind of way. It's the same now. Since her three-hour onslaught yesterday, when she told me about the Russian doll that came through the post, she's hardly mentioned Layla at all. Sometimes, though, I catch her looking at me curiously, and I don't know if it's because she's wondering why I'm not mentioning Layla or if it's because she's wondering if there are other things I've kept from her. Although I explained why I didn't tell her about the Russian doll I found, I'm not sure she believed it. And because we agreed to wait and see what Layla does next, we're living in a sort of no-man's land.

"Where did you go last night?" Ellen asks over breakfast. She hadn't moved when I'd climbed into bed beside her at four thirty, so I thought she hadn't noticed I'd gone out.

"For a drive. I couldn't sleep. It's this new client. He's even harder work than Grant was." She looks at me sympathetically and, feeling guilty for lying yet again, I get to my feet. "I think I'll go for a run."

It's the waiting that's driving me mad, I realize as I pound the river footpath back toward the house. The urge to contact Layla and push her into some sort of action is unbearable. I slow down as The Jackdaw comes into sight. It isn't open yet but when I knock on the door, Ruby unlocks it.

"You're ten minutes too early for breakfast," Ruby remarks, pouring me a mug of coffee.

"Ellen knows," I say. "She knows that Layla is back."

"Well, at least it's out in the open. That's a good thing, surely?"

"You would have thought so." I sigh heavily. "But now things are awkward between me and Ellen, especially as she saw you and me discussing the Russian doll I found. She wanted to know why I didn't tell her about it. I hate to think what she'd say if she knew about all the others that have turned up."

"Does she know Layla's been emailing you?"

I shift uncomfortably on my barstool. "No. Nor that I've been to the cottage, or about the letter I left for Layla asking her to marry me, the letter that Layla now has."

Ruby raises her eyebrows. "That's a lot of secrets, Finn."

"I know."

"So how does Ellen feel about Layla being back?"

"Excited. Scared. She asked me if, now that I know Layla is back, I regretted asking her to marry me and of course I told her I didn't."

"Hmm," Ruby says.

"We've decided to wait and see what Layla does next," I go on, ignoring her vote of no-confidence. "It might be that she'll suddenly turn up on the doorstep and put us all out of our misery. It's these games she's playing that are so frustrating."

"What do you think she wants?"

"I know what she wants," I say grimly. "I asked her and she said she wanted me."

"And how do you feel about that?"

"It doesn't matter how I feel because it's impossible. I'm with Ellen now. I can't just ask her to leave because Layla has decided to come back. And I wouldn't want to. I love her." Even to my ears the words sound hollow.

"Then you need to make that clear to Layla."

"I've tried."

"Try harder. And if she still doesn't get it, go to the police." She looks thoughtfully at me. "I'm surprised you haven't already."

"I need to find out where she's been for the last twelve years first."

"Hasn't she told you?"

"No, not yet. That's why I need to see her before I involve the police."

"Be careful, Finn," Ruby says softly.

Her words echo in my ears as I walk back to the house. Be careful of who, I want to ask her. Layla? Or myself?

When another day passes without news from Layla, I do what I didn't want to do and send her an email.

We need to talk, Layla, face-to-face

You don't know how much I want to

But I can't, not while you're with Ellen

Why not?

Because it would be too hard for me

I love you, Finn

No, you love who I was twelve years ago

I'm not that person anymore

I'm with Ellen now

Exactly. And while you're with her, you can't be with me

So what do you want me to do?

Do you truly love Ellen?

If you do, I'll leave you in peace

That's not what I want!

So what is it you want?

I've told you, to see you

And I've told you it's not possible, not while you're with Ellen
I don't understand what you expect me to do

And of course, there's no reply, because she knows there's nothing I can do. I can't ask Ellen to leave, I can't tell her that I've changed my mind about marrying her, not now that she knows Layla is back. I should have told her before, I realize bitterly, I should have told her I'd changed my mind the moment I knew that Layla had found my letter. I'd had the perfect opportunity; I'd stayed away that night, pretended I'd had a migraine. When I came back the next day, I should have told Ellen that the reason I hadn't come home was because I'd been thinking about us, about our forthcoming marriage, and had realized I'd made a mistake. She would have been upset, tried to get me to change my mind perhaps. But if I'd stood firm, what could she have done except pack her bags and leave?

An email comes in, from Layla, and I cross my fingers, hoping she's relented.

GET RID OF ELLEN

THIRTY-SEVEN

LAYLA

Deep down, I knew that Ellen wouldn't relinquish Finn just because I was back. Why would she when she was happy with what she had? She knew Finn didn't love her as much as he had loved me but second-best was enough for her because it was better than what she'd had before. But it worried her that I was back; I could feel her digging her claws in, determined not to let me have him and that surprised me because I had never known her to be tenacious before. But the steely determination she'd had to cultivate over the years to get where she was must have had something to do with it.

When I sent Finn the message, spelling out to him what he would have to do if he wanted to see me, I felt for him, I really did.

But there isn't room for both Ellen and me. Once upon a time, there had been. Once upon a time, we had shared everything. After our mother's death, we'd been inseparable, standing firm against our father. And unable to rule us, he had divided us. It was the only thing I ever learned from my father. Divide and conquer.

That's what I'm planning to do to Ellen and Finn, divide them. And once I've managed to pry them apart, Finn will be exactly where I want him to be.

And this time, it will be Ellen who will disappear.

THIRTY-EIGHT

FINN

I've taken to watching Ellen as she stands by the cooker stirring something in a pan, or sits at the table, her head bent over a magazine, and try to imagine what would happen if I were to say the words aloud, the words that would rid me of her, the words that would buy me the freedom to see Layla. Sometimes I go as far as mouthing, "Ellen, I'm sorry but I can't marry you," trying the words for size, testing the weight of them in my mouth. And then I imagine her reaction, first the shock, then the bewilderment, followed by a dawning realization that I've never truly loved her. And finally, a quiet acceptance that I am no longer hers, now that Layla is back.

Except it wouldn't be like that. There would be tears, which I couldn't stand, and recriminations, which I couldn't stomach. So the words remain trapped inside me until I feel as if I'm going to break under the strain of leaving them unsaid. Sometimes, when I'm watching Ellen, I wonder how it has come to this, how I can be contemplating life without her. But then I think of Layla, and Ellen fades into nothing. I remember Harry saying, all those years ago, that Layla had bewitched me. Well, now she's bewitching me all over again.

As the days go on, I become desperate. I email Layla, asking her again if we can meet, telling her that we need to talk, that I need to see her. But as I make no mention of having done as she asked, she doesn't reply.

"How much longer are we going to give Layla?" Ellen asks one evening. We're in the sitting room listening to music and supposedly reading but, like me, I'm not sure she's actually turned any pages.

I lift my head from my book and look across to where she's curled up on the sofa, acknowledging that I would never normally sit so far away from her. Before Layla, I would have been next to her, her head on my shoulder, my arm around her.

"What do you mean?" I ask, playing for time, because I know very well what she means. It's six days since Layla's last message, seven since the Russian doll came through the post.

"Before we tell Tony, or someone, that she's alive." I hear the nervousness in her voice. "We can't keep it a secret. The police need to know."

"Not yet," I say, for the third time. "We agreed that we'd wait."

"We said a few days. It's been a week now," she persists. "If she was going to turn up of her own accord, surely she would have by now."

"She was missing for twelve years. We need to give her more time."

"Then can we at least tell Harry about the Russian doll that came through the post?"

"Why?" I say, perplexed. "What good would that do?"

"I want him to know that I was right when I said that Layla was back. I could tell that he didn't know what to think, despite the Russian doll I found." Something occurs to her. "Did you tell him about the one you found on the plate in The Jackdaw, the one you showed Ruby?" she asks.

"No," I admit.

Now she looks perplexed. "But it would have backed up my theory."

"As I said, I didn't want to get anyone's hopes up until I was sure."

"But you're sure now," she says emphatically, making it impossible for me to stall any longer.

"All right, I'll give Tony a ring."

Ellen looks relieved. "Three heads are better than two. He'll know what to do. What about Ruby? How much does she know?"

Her question takes me by surprise. I make a quick calculation. I can't tell her that Ruby knows ten times more than she does, that she knows as much as I do, so how much is it feasible that Ruby would know?

"She knows why I was upset to find the Russian doll on the plate," I say slowly, trying to work it out as I go along. "She knows I thought it came from Layla. When I accused her, I mentioned the story from your childhood, so she knows that now."

"Does she know that I thought I saw Layla in Cheltenham?"

"No, I don't think I mentioned it to her," I say, keeping it vague.

She's quiet for a moment and I hope it's a sign that she's going to leave it alone for the moment. "But what if—" She stops.

"What?" I prompt.

"You said that you didn't want to get my hopes up until you were sure it wasn't some kind of sick joke," she says slowly. "But what if it is? What if it's just someone who wants us to think that Layla is back?"

"But as you rightly said, who would do such a thing? And nobody really knows the story of the Russian dolls except us."

"And Harry."

I frown. "You don't seriously think that Harry has anything to do with it?"

She bursts out laughing. "No, of course not, not Harry! I was thinking more of Ruby."

"Ruby? But—"

"Yes, I know, she didn't know the story of the Russian dolls until you told her in The Jackdaw." She leans forward urgently. "But what if you had told her before? I mean, you thought you had, which was why you thought she was behind them. So maybe you had and she just pretended that you hadn't."

My head feels as if it's going to explode with trying to keep up. "But what about you seeing Layla in Cheltenham?"

She shrugs. "Maybe you were right all along, maybe it was only someone who had the same sort of hair as Layla." She pauses. "Ruby has the same sort of hair, long and curly."

"But not the same color," I say.

"Maybe she wore a wig."

"Anybody could have worn a wig. Anyway, Ruby didn't know we were going to be in Cheltenham that day."

"She could have seen us leave and followed us."

"So are you telling me that you don't think Layla is back anymore, that you think Ruby is behind it?" I ask, frustrated.

"But isn't that what you thought at first? That Ruby put the Russian doll outside the house and then one on the plate so you would think Layla was back and change your mind about marrying me?"

"Yes, but I don't anymore."

"So what changed your mind about Ruby? The only thing that has happened since then is that I received a Russian doll through the post. Is that what convinced you that Layla is back? Because if it is, it could easily have been sent by Ruby."

But I'm not thinking about Ruby, I'm thinking about something else she said, something so shocking that a strange weariness comes over me, as if I'm finally having to accept something I've suspected all along, but have hidden from. The air around me suddenly feels heavy. It presses on my chest, making it tight and I realize I can barely breathe. Ellen jumps to her feet and the look of alarm on her face as she hurries over to me makes me wonder if I'm having some kind of heart attack. Craving fresh air, I push her out of the way, go through to the hall and wrench open the front door, gulping in the cool night air.

"Are you all right?" Ellen's voice comes from the hallway behind me.

"I'm fine," I say. "I just need some air—it was hot in there."

She hovers for a moment but when I don't say anything more, she disappears into the kitchen.

I sit down on the step and wait for normality to return. It's a long time coming. I know what did it, why I felt suddenly ill. I push the thought away but it bounces straight back, forcing me to look at it, examine it, consider it. Is it possible that this whole thing with Layla is a hoax after all? Is it possible that I've been betrayed by the one person I would trust with my life—Harry, the person I love like a brother?

It was something Ellen said—no, the way she had laughed

when I'd thought she was pointing the finger at Harry when in fact she'd been pointing it at Ruby. "No, of course not!" she'd said, "Not Harry!" because it was unthinkable that Harry would do such a thing. But I know better than anyone that love makes us behave out of character, that it drives us to do things we never thought we'd do. Hadn't Harry told me only the other day that he wished he had married, settled down?

I hate where my mind is going but I can't stop myself. Maybe he's in love with Ellen, has been from the very start. Was that why he used to invite her to stay at the flat during her trips to London? When I asked Ellen, at the beginning of our relationship, if there'd ever been anything between her and Harry, she'd assured me there hadn't been. But what if there had been, on Harry's part? He himself had said the appearance of the first Russian doll was all about timing, because I was going to marry Ellen. What if it had been him who had left it, and when neither Ellen nor I mentioned finding it, he had brought one to lunch with him so that he could pretend he'd found it standing on the wall outside the house, hoping to provoke us into admitting that we'd found one too. I remember the look on his face when Ellen had showed him she now had a full set. Had that been a look of relief, that the seed he'd wanted to sow—that Layla had returned—had already taken root? There'd been no need for him to show us the Russian doll he had in his pocket—until I told him I didn't believe that Layla was back. I hadn't confided in him about all the other dolls I'd found, as perhaps he was expecting me to, so he had shown me the Russian doll he'd supposedly found on the wall, hoping maybe to prompt me into telling him about the others. But I hadn't. What about the one I found on the plate in The Jackdaw? How could he have put it there without Ruby or Ellen or me seeing him? Unless he asked someone to do it for him. Someone who worked in the pub? Ruby?

Were Harry and Ruby in this together? My mind feels as if it's spiraling out of control.

Wanting to put an end to it, I drag myself off the doorstep. Ellen comes out of the kitchen, worry furrowing her brow.

"Are you all right?" she asks.

"Fine." I head for the stairs. "I'll be as right as rain after a shower and a sleep."

"If you need anything, call me."

But all I need are answers, and she can't give me those.

With so much going round in my mind, I dread not being able to sleep. But I fall asleep quickly and when I wake up the next morning, I wonder where the turmoil of the evening before had come from. How can Harry be behind the emails? They're so obviously from Layla, as are the photos I received. There's no way that Harry could have got his hands on them, or known that Layla and I referred to the tree stump on Pharos Hill as a Russian doll.

It's strange what he said, though, about never believing that Layla was dead, or that she'd been kidnapped, that he'd always thought she'd turn up one day. He'd never told me that, although he may not have wanted to get my hopes up. I give my head an angry shake, hating that other theories, even more terrible than those that had tortured me last night, have begun to crowd my brain, demanding attention. What if Layla had turned to Harry after she disappeared from the picnic area in Fonches? Is that why he never believed she was dead, because he knew that she wasn't? Is it possible that he gave her shelter, helped her to hide? But why would he have done that? He didn't even like Layla. Unless his dislike of her had been a smokescreen. Maybe he'd been in love with her all along, maybe he was the guy she'd slept with in London that weekend. I shake my head, annoyed at myself. First I think Harry's in love with Ellen, now with Layla.

I turn and look at Ellen, asleep beside me, one arm behind her head on the pillow, the other lying across her chest. Not so very long ago, I would have gently lifted her arm out of the way and gathered her to me, I would have started kissing her while she was still half-asleep. But that was before Layla. The guilt I feel drives me out of bed and down the stairs to the kitchen. The post is lying on the mat and as I stoop to pick it up, I see a brown envelope with the same white sticker on the front, except that this time it's addressed to me, not Ellen. I don't have to open it to know that it contains a Russian doll. I take it through to the kitchen, slit it open with a knife and shake the contents into the palm of my hand. As I thought, it's a Russian doll. Except that this one has had its head smashed in.

THIRTY-NINE

LAYLA

I knew Finn wouldn't understand the *GET RID OF ELLEN* message, at least not fully. Since receiving it, he'll have been trying to think of ways to tell Ellen that it's over between them, he'll be wishing he'd never asked her to marry him in the first place. He'll have opened his mouth a hundred times, ready to say the words that will bring me back. Yet he'll never say them, not because he lacks the courage but because he's too kind to break Ellen's heart. Which sort of annoys me, because he hadn't been too worried about breaking my heart all those years ago. I put aside my annoyance because it isn't important. What is important is that Finn understands what I meant.

It still surprises me that I want to hurt Finn when I love him so much. But there's something in me that needs him broken, so that I can put him together again just as I want. My disappearance all those years ago hadn't broken him, not really. His descent into hell had been self-indulgent. Financially stable and without dependants, he could allow himself to wallow in depression. If he'd had to work for a living, or had a child or children, he would have given himself the proverbial kick up the backside; he would have had to, just as I'd had to, in order to survive.

It's why I'm not letting him off lightly. He must have reached the point where he's beginning to doubt everything he thought was true and everyone he thought he could trust. Which is exactly what I want.

FORTY

FINN

The doll with the smashed head sends my mind to places it's never been before. I should have thrown it straight in the bin but, afraid that Ellen might find it, I took it out to my office and put it at the back of my drawer with the others. But its image has burned itself into my brain, taunting me. What is my purpose, it asks, why have I been sent to you? What does my smashed head signify? Who do I represent? The only answers I come up with are dark and terrifying. The doll represents Ellen, and whoever sent it—because I've gone back to thinking that they might not be from Layla—wishes her harm. Not only that, they are expecting me to do it. The *GET RID OF ELLEN* message has taken on a whole new meaning. Harry or Ruby—yes, because since Ellen mentioned her, Ruby has crept back onto my list of possible suspects—both know I'm capable of violence. Are they using that knowledge against me? Are they trying to provoke me?

Because sometimes, when Ellen comes and puts her arms around me, when her head is against my shoulder, I find myself wondering what it would be like to move my hands slowly upward until they reach her neck, and squeeze the life out of her. Sometimes, when she's asleep next to me, I find myself wondering what it would be like to place my pillow over her face and gently press the life out of her. Sometimes, when we walk along a path with a sheer drop only a few feet away from us, I find myself wondering what it would be like to push her onto the ground below, crushing the life out of her. I can no longer sleep the untroubled sleep of the innocent. Just as I used to have nightmares about having killed Layla, I now have nightmares about killing Ellen.

She hasn't mentioned phoning Tony again. Since the other night, she's been giving me space. I enjoy the reprieve, but it doesn't last long.

"You look tired," she says one morning, after another nightmarish night. She comes over and cups my face with her hands. "Maybe we could go away for a few days."

"I'd been thinking the same thing," I tell her, because suddenly, getting away seems like the best idea in the world.

She searches my face. "But first we need to decide what to do about Layla. You said you'd phone Tony."

"I will," I tell her.

"If you don't, I'll phone him." There's an edge to her voice that I haven't heard before. "It's making you ill, Finn."

"I'm tired, that's all," I say irritably. "Anyway, I thought you had doubts about the dolls being from Layla."

"I know I said that it could be Ruby but only because I wanted you to be aware that it was possible," she says. "Ruby is what she is, but she's not malicious." She gives a short laugh. "I just wish I knew what Layla wanted."

Unbidden, the image of the doll with the smashed head comes to mind and I tighten my arms round her. It would be so easy, a voice whispers. All you have to do is move one hand to the back of her head and press it into your chest so that her nose and mouth are covered, and slowly tighten your other arm around her. At one point, when she realizes that she can't breathe, she'll struggle. But not for long; your height and weight will ensure that it's over quickly. Then, when the police ask, you'll lie to them as you lied to them before and tell them that she suddenly collapsed, that she must have had a heart attack.

"Finn, I can't breathe." Ellen twists her head to the side, freeing it from my grip. She takes a gulp of air, a laugh in her voice. "I know you love me but you don't have to hold me so tightly!"

Shocked, I drop my arms, take a step back. "Sorry," I mutter, raking a hand through my hair.

"Will you have a think about where we can go for a few days?" she says.

I stare at her. Had I really been about to smother her? "Yes, of course. I'll look for something now."

I go out to my office, my heart pounding. Get a grip, I tell myself, Ellen wasn't in danger, you weren't going to do anything.

But there's a darkness in my mind that won't go away.

The next day, five days after I received the doll with the smashed head, the office door opens. Expecting it to be Ellen, I fix a smile on my face. But it's Harry and my smile fades as fast as it came.

"Hey, don't look at me like that," he reproaches and I realize he must have seen the mistrust in my eyes. "Ellen asked me to come."

I can't bring myself to get to my feet and hug him as I usually do. "Why?" I ask.

"Because she's worried about you." He looks around for something to sit on and pulls out the stool I keep under my desk. "What's up, buddy?"

I have to find out, I have to know if he's behind the dolls and the emails. I can't stand not knowing who I can trust.

"Are you in love with Ellen?" I say, trying not to sound accusatory.

His eyes widen in surprise and he opens his mouth, about to say something, and I find myself hoping that he's going to tell me he is, because then, if Ellen loved him back, it would leave me free for Layla. But he closes his mouth and swallows hard and, because I know him well, I know he's just bitten back an angry retort.

"No, Finn," he says, looking back at me steadily, realizing maybe how important his answer is. "Lovely though she is, I am not in love with Ellen, nor have I ever been." He gives a short laugh. "You must have realized by now that we don't have the same taste in women? All those girlfriends you had in London, they weren't your type. Think about it, Finn—they were all carbon copies of mine because you thought they were the sort of girls you should be going out with. But you were never very interested in them. Then you met Layla, as different from those girls as chalk is from cheese. And as you realized quite early on, I couldn't see what you saw in her." He pauses a moment and I wonder what he would say if I told him that only a few days ago, I'd questioned if he was the man Layla had slept with in London. "But here's the thing," he goes on. "I've never experienced true love, I'm not sure it even exists. But if it does, it was what you and Layla had."

I wait, giving him time to add "and what you and Ellen have" but he doesn't. The silence stretches out between us. He's waiting for me to say something and when I don't, he takes pity on me.

"Why did you think I was in love with Ellen?"

I can't tell him that, in a moment of madness, I suspected he was sending me emails and planting Russian dolls, pretending to be Layla so that I wouldn't marry Ellen.

"Someone's messing with my head," I say instead.

"Layla?"

"Maybe."

"Ellen told me she got a Russian doll in the post and that even though it would seem to confirm that Layla is back, you're reluctant to go to the police."

"We agreed to give her a few days." I decide to open up to him. "I've found a couple of dolls that I haven't told Ellen about."

"Right." He nods thoughtfully. "Where did you find them?"

"One was outside the house, one on the car, in Cheltenham." I don't mention the others because the list is getting too long. "The latest one came through the post. It was postmarked Cheltenham—its head was smashed in," I add.

"They're not very careful at the post office," he says. "Probably the machinery."

It never occurred to me that it could be anything but deliberate. Have I been sending myself to hell and back for nothing?

"I wondered if it was damaged on purpose."

He frowns. "What, you think there was some kind of message behind it? A threat, or something?"

"I don't know."

"Boy, Layla must be really angry that you're with Ellen."

"So you think the dolls are definitely from Layla?"

"Who else could they be from? But she must be seriously disturbed. I mean, to go as far as wishing you actual harm—that's kind of worrying."

For a wonderful moment, I feel better—the doll with the smashed head represents me, not Ellen. But then I remember the *GET RID OF ELLEN* message.

"You need to tell the police," Harry goes on. "You look dreadful, so does Ellen. She's worried about you." He pauses. "And she's worried about what will happen when Layla turns up."

"I've told her it won't change anything," I say curtly, annoyed with Ellen for not only doubting me, but for telling Harry that she does.

"Well, maybe the way you are at the moment isn't filling her with confidence."

I shift uneasily on my chair. Has she somehow sensed the dark thoughts I've had about killing her? I run my hands through my hair, haunted by the nightmares I've been having. Harry claps me on the back. "Come on, let's go and see Ruby."

Ellen encourages us to go to The Jackdaw on our own but Harry persuades her to come with us. Ruby is delighted to see Harry and we arrange to have a late lunch, once the rush is over, so that she can join us. The four of us sit with a couple of bottles of wine, laughing and talking, and I feel better than I have for a long time. I catch Ellen throwing me anxious glances and, understanding that she's worried I'm annoyed with her for inviting Harry down to talk to me, I reach for her hand across the table. Harry notices, and when it's time to leave, he says he wants to stay and talk to Ruby for a bit, giving me and Ellen a chance to be on our own.

"You didn't mind me inviting Harry?" Ellen asks, as we stroll back to the house.

"No, it was good to talk to him. He made me see things more clearly." And at least I can eliminate him from my list of suspects, I think silently. Which only leaves Ruby and Layla and I'm pretty sure that Ruby isn't involved. The relief I feel, that it must be Layla, tells me that the darkness I've felt over the past few days wasn't only about not knowing who I could trust, but from the fear she hadn't come back after all.

"So will you phone Tony?"

"Yes," I say, realizing that was her aim in getting Harry down. "I'll give him a ring on Monday."

Harry doesn't stay long when he comes back to the house because he has a dinner in London. After he's left, I spend a bit of time in my office. I still haven't received an email from Layla. Is she seriously waiting for me to harm Ellen, to kill her? I slide open my drawer and reach inside, searching for the Russian dolls. I run my fingers over them, drawing a strange comfort from the feel of them. It's almost as if they're telling me not to lose faith, that everything will work out in the end. Then my fingers fall on the one with the smashed head and I withdraw my hand quickly. It's strange that Ellen never asked me for the one she saw me with in The Jackdaw, has never asked if she can add it to her set of Russian dolls, like the one she received in the post. It stands next to the one she found on the wall, two twin sisters staring blank-eyed at me from the worktop.

By the time night falls, I can't bear the silence any longer. I encourage Ellen to go up to bed, and I take out my phone.

When can we meet? I ask. I don't really expect her to reply because she didn't to the last ones I sent her asking the same thing. But this time, a reply comes straight back.

Did you get the doll?

I ignore her and ask again: When can we meet?

Did you get the doll?
Yes

There's no point in going around in circles.

When can we meet?
When you've done what you have to do

What do you mean? I ask, remembering Harry's theory that the doll got damaged in the post.

You've seen the doll

A wave of fury takes hold of me.

It's not going to happen, never! Goodbye Layla.

I throw my phone down on the sofa as if it's become toxic. Somewhere along the way, Layla has lost her mind. What she's suggesting, what she wants me to do, is madness.

I wait a while, then go quietly upstairs, hoping Ellen will be asleep. She's in her usual sleep mode, one arm behind her head on the pillow, beautiful, desirable. Go on, a voice taunts. Get in beside her, prove that you love her more than Layla. After all, you've just chosen her over Layla. She stirs, half-opens her eyes, holds out her arms to me, smiling sleepily.

"I'm going for a shower." I speak in a whisper, an encouragement to her to go back to sleep. Disappointment shadows her face and she drops her arms.

In the shower, I try to wash some of my shame away. But when I get out its stain is still there, making it impossible for me to get into bed beside Ellen.

I wander the house restlessly. My body aches with fatigue; I've barely slept in three days. In the sitting room, I lie down on the sofa, hoping sleep will take me. Something digs me in the back and I realize it's my phone, from when I threw it down. I don't want to check my emails, I don't want to find one from Layla, I'm not ready for another of her ultimatums. But maybe it will be the message you've been waiting for, says a voice, the one that will give you a time and a place, the one that will tell you the Russian doll with the smashed head was a joke. So I check my emails and find one from Layla.

YOU HAVE TEN DAYS

FORTY-ONE

LAYLA

There was something about smashing the little doll's head that was strangely satisfying. My own head felt better after, and I wondered if maybe I'd smashed the voice out of it, the one that kept dragging me back to the past, taunting me with visions of how things could have been. But I'd only quietened it because, after a few days of relative calm, it came back, driving me on, propelling me forward to an end I didn't yet know.

Finn's reaction to the Russian doll was predictable. Disbelief, anger, blunt refusal. I almost laughed at his last message, at the implication that he had any choice in the matter, as if his "goodbye Layla" actually meant something, actually meant that he was never going to contact me again, or read any more emails from me. Didn't he realize that he was dancing to my tune and still had a lot of steps to learn?

I couldn't keep him dancing forever though. The strain of keeping it together was beginning to tell on me. The voice began to intrude more and more and the effort of blocking it out made my head tired. I needed to impose a deadline. I couldn't let Finn prevaricate indefinitely. It wasn't good for him.

And it certainly wasn't good for me.

FORTY-TWO

FINN

Reading Layla's message, I prepare myself mentally for ten days of silence. I doubt she'll be emailing me unless I tell her what she wants to hear and as I won't ever be able to, I won't be emailing her. At first, I feel lost—how am I going to last ten days without some sort of contact with her when a day without news is already difficult? But then disquiet sets in at what might happen once the ten days are up. Surely Ellen won't be in danger from Layla? But what if she is? I feel torn between my desire for Layla and my desire to protect Ellen. Now, more than ever, I need to tell Tony. But I feel stuck in an impasse, unable to move. Maybe a ten-day silence will be a good thing. I'll have time to clear my head, devote myself to Ellen, work out a strategy. We'll go away for a few days and I might even begin to forget about Layla.

I go up to bed and when the sun wakes me early the next morning, I feel calmer than I've felt for ages. With the prospect of ten days' respite from Layla's increasingly erratic demands, I feel almost optimistic. I look at Ellen asleep beside me and feel a twinge of guilt at the way I turned my back on her last night. I wish I could make it up to her, take her in my arms, show her that I love her. But I can't. And the thought that she might wake up and expect me to propels me out of bed.

I dress quietly and go downstairs.

"Shall we go for a walk?" I ask Peggy, giving her a morning cuddle.

It's one of those beautiful, still Sunday mornings when everyone is in bed and the only sound comes from the birds chirruping in the trees and the chickens clucking in the garden of a nearby house. I glance across at Mick's house and see him standing at the window. I raise my hand in acknowledgment and when he waves back, I feel guilty that I haven't made more of an effort to get to know him.

As I walk along the river, I think about where Ellen and I could go. I've never lost my desire to visit Lewis but when I suggested it to Ellen last year, she said it was the last place she wanted to go. I can understand why. It's where she lost her mother, where she lost her father—even if that wasn't such a great loss. It's also where she saw Layla for the last time. Anyway, it's too far. Perhaps we should just stay here; Simonsbridge is so beautiful at this time of the year. Why sit in a car for hours only to end up somewhere equivalent?

My sudden reluctance to go away niggles at me, urging me to be honest with myself instead of hiding behind a long car journey. The truth is shameful; in a hotel, I won't be able to wait until

Ellen is asleep before joining her in bed. My mood plummets. I call Peggy from the river, hating the person I've become, the person Layla has made me become.

The village shop opens at eight on a Sunday so I buy bacon and eggs along with the papers before heading home. As I approach the house, I'm struck by a terrible sense of déjà vu. Because there, standing on the wall, is a little Russian doll.

I cover the last few yards in a couple of seconds and snatch it up, putting it quickly in my pocket. I look up and down the road but there's no one around. Remembering how I saw Mick standing at his window, I go over and knock on his front door, forgetting that it's only quarter past eight in the morning.

He takes a while opening it.

"Sorry," he says. There's a bowl of porridge in his hand. "I'm in the middle of giving my wife her breakfast."

"No, I'm sorry," I say, taking in his disheveled appearance. "I'll come back later. I just wanted to ask you something."

I wait for him to ask me what it is I want to know but he's already shutting the door.

"Sorry," he says again. "I have to go." He raises the bowl of porridge, reminding me of his task in hand. "Come back in about an hour, I should have finished by then."

I cross back over, looking up and down the road again, knowing that I'm not going to see Layla because she'll be long gone by now. Gone where? Back to Cheltenham? My ears pick out the sound of a car engine turning over, then the sound of it driving off. It sounded as if the driver was in a hurry. Was it Layla? She hadn't yet learned to drive when I knew her, but twelve years is enough time for that to have changed.

In the hall, I hear the sound of the shower running, which means I have a few minutes before Ellen comes down. I take the shopping through to the kitchen, intending to make a start on breakfast. But I feel too agitated so I go out to the garden, hoping its tranquility will work its magic on me. A window opens upstairs and looking up, I see Ellen smiling down at me.

"Did you go for bread or have you been in your office?" she asks and I want to yell at her to leave me alone.

"Bread," I say. "I got some bacon and eggs too," I add, making an effort.

"Not for me, thanks," she says. "I'll have muesli." Words rush into my mouth—why can't you be more like Layla!—and I bite them back quickly.

Over breakfast, I feel her eyes on me as I work my way through my bacon and egg sandwich.

"Finn," she says, after a moment.

"What?"

"Please phone Tony."

"It's Sunday."

"He won't mind."

I know she's right. Besides, Layla has gone too far now with the doll with the smashed head. At least the one I just found on the wall was intact.

"All right, I'll phone him after breakfast."

I don't particularly want to phone Tony in front of her but she'll think it strange if I disappear into my office to do it, and I don't want her to think I have anything to hide. Even though I do. Which is why I draw the line at putting Tony on loudspeaker, as Ellen perhaps expects. But the risk of him mentioning that Thomas saw Layla standing outside the cottage is too great.

"I'm afraid this isn't just a social call," I say, once we've established that we're both fine.

"Go on," he says, and I suddenly realize that Ellen doesn't know I told Tony that she thought she saw Layla in Cheltenham.

"It's about Layla," I begin. "A couple of things have happened that have made Ellen and I wonder if she might still be alive."

"Has something else happened?" he asks.

"Some weeks ago, Ellen found a little Russian doll on the wall outside the house. Then a few days later she thought she saw her in Cheltenham," I add for Ellen's benefit.

"Yes, you told me about that. But what has a Russian doll got to do with it?"

"When they were young, Ellen and Layla had a set each of Russian dolls and one of the dolls went missing. Since the one that Ellen found, another has turned up—two, in fact," I amend quickly, remembering the one Ellen saw me with in The Jackdaw. "Ellen received one in the post and we found the other one in the local pub, along with our bill. The thing is, they—Russian dolls—have a significance for both Ellen and Layla, a significance nobody else knows about." And I go on to explain the story from their childhood.

"And nobody else knows the story?" he asks when I've finished.

"Only Harry—Ellen told him."

"And you're sure you didn't mention it to anyone else? Someone who would want to get back at you? An ex-girlfriend, maybe?"

"No," I say firmly. "I've never told anyone."

"Hm. The one that came through the post—do you know where it was sent from?"

"Cheltenham—which is where Ellen thought she saw her."

"That lends a lot more weight to Thomas's assertion that he saw her outside the cottage," he says. There's a silence while he mulls it over. "Leave it with me, Finn. I'll have a think, speak to a few people and get back to you."

"Thanks, Tony, I appreciate it." I hang up and turn to Ellen. "He'll get back to us."

"But does he think that Layla has come back, that she's alive?"

"I think he thinks it's worth looking into."

She gives a small smile. "It seems a lot more real now that we've told somebody official. I began to wonder if we were mad to think that Layla had come back. What I don't understand is why she's hiding. I can't stop wondering what she actually wants."

"We'll have to wait and see." I get to my feet. "I need to do a couple of things. See you for lunch?"

In the office, I think about phoning Tony back and telling him about all the other dolls I've found, including the one with the smashed head. But if I'm going to go that far, I'll have to tell him about the emails, as there's no point in him only having half the story. In the end, I decide to wait until he phones me back. If he says that what they've got to go on isn't enough to spend time looking for Layla, then I'll tell him the rest.

It's a long morning. I take a look at the markets but I need to be in a good place to trade and today isn't one of those days. I look for something to distract me and remember that I'm meant to be going to see Mick.

"Just popping to see Mick," I tell Ellen. "See if he wants to come over for a drink."

"That's nice of you," Ellen says approvingly.

He doesn't take as long answering the door this time and I'm relieved to see that his hands are free.

"Sorry about this morning," I begin. "I didn't realize it was quite so early. I was just wondering if you saw anybody hanging round outside the house this morning, you know, when you were standing at the window."

He shakes his head. "Can't say I did but I wasn't there long.

I'd just opened the curtains when I saw you, and then Fiona called me. A couple walked past but they didn't stop."

"Past your house or mine?" I ask.

"Yours."

"I don't suppose you saw them leave something on the wall, did you?"

"Not to my knowledge. Unless they came back once I'd gone. You could always ask Mrs. Jeffries, although she tends to sit in her conservatory out the back."

I nod. "Well, thanks, Mick. How's your wife doing?"

He shrugs. "No change."

"Well, if you ever feel like having a drink, just pop over. We're usually in."

"Thanks." He gives a rueful smile. "You never know, I might take you up on your offer one day."

As I cross back over the road, I think about the couple who walked past our house, wondering why I had dismissed them without a second thought. I should at least have asked Mick if the girl—woman, I remind myself—had red hair. But I don't want to believe that Layla has someone in her life. If she did, why would she be playing these games?

The rest of the day passes unbelievably slowly. Then just before I go to bed, I check my emails and see that one has come in from Layla. I think about not opening it but as always, curiosity gets the better of me. There's just one word.

TEN

FORTY-THREE

LAYLA

The day I gave Finn his ten-day ultimatum, I picked up my next consignment of Russian dolls from the post office in Cheltenham. As I carefully unwrapped each of the ten dolls, a pleasing image came to mind. Ten little Russian dolls, lined up on the wall. It reminded me of the song Ellen and I used to sing when we were young, about ten green bottles hanging on a wall. And how, if one green bottle should accidentally fall, there'd be nine green bottles hanging on the wall. I felt a surge of excitement. What if I did a countdown? The more I thought about it, the more I liked the idea.

The voice liked it even more.

FORTY-FOUR

FINN

We're almost into August so business is slow. I spend the morning on the phone to Harry, talking about investments, looking at what our competitors are doing, which funds are working and which ones aren't. Later, feeling hungry, I wander back to the house and as I go into the kitchen, I see a note on the table.

> *I've gone to do some shopping. If you'd like to join me for lunch, give me a call*
> *xx*

I glance at the clock on the oven and see that it's already two thirty, which means Ellen must have left sometime in the morning. I don't know when the last time was that I actually came out of my office to have lunch with Ellen. The days of meeting in the kitchen at one o'clock have long gone. Ellen used to come and fetch me but she doesn't anymore and it bothers me less than it should.

At first, I thought the email Layla sent last Sunday saying ten, coupled with the Russian doll she left on the wall, was her way of reminding me that I had ten days to do whatever it was she was expecting me to do, even though I'd told her it would never happen. But the next morning, when I went downstairs to give Peggy her breakfast, I found another brown envelope lying on the mat along with the rest of the mail. Realizing what it was, I stooped to pick it up. Like the last one, it was addressed to me.

I could hear Ellen moving about upstairs, so I stuffed the envelope under my shirt and went through to the kitchen. I knew it contained a Russian doll but I didn't know if it had its head smashed in, like the last one I received. I didn't want to risk opening it where Ellen might see me, so I went to my office, tore open the envelope quickly and shook the contents onto my desk—one Russian doll, its head mercifully intact. Breathing a sigh of relief, I pushed it quickly into the back of my drawer. It was only when I received an email that evening that said *NINE*, that I realized I was caught up in a macabre countdown.

The next day—Tuesday—there was another envelope in the post, containing another doll, and another email in the evening—*EIGHT*. Layla's subsequent emails, on Wednesday evening—*SEVEN*—on Thursday—*SIX*—and again last night—*FIVE*—only add to the sense of helplessness I feel, at being unable to stop the wheels of fate from turning. Bizarrely, the overriding emotion I feel is shame, that at forty-one years old, and six foot four, a few little dolls can unsettle me so much.

The pressure of the countdown is beginning to take its toll. Exhaustion has set in. I only go to bed when I'm dropping with tiredness and I lie there, my mind going round in circles, wondering where it will end, how it will end, while Ellen sleeps the sleep of the dead next to me. Each morning, I'm up early so that I can hide the latest Russian doll in the drawer in my office before she gets up.

Tony got back to me the day after my phone call—the ninth day of the countdown—to say that he and a couple of officers, armed with the photo of Layla they'd used in the initial search, plus a computer-enhanced photo of what she might look like now, were going to make discreet inquiries at hotels, B&Bs, and hostels in Cheltenham. I used this news to persuade Ellen that going away wouldn't be a good idea even though a part of me was tempted to jet off somewhere exotic just to get away from the relentlessness of the countdown, only coming back once the ten days were up.

"Imagine they find Layla and we're at the other end of the country," I said, and Ellen had agreed it would be better to stay in Simonsbridge.

Sometimes, I can't believe I'm still keeping things from her. But if I tell her about this latest series of Russian dolls, she'll urge me to tell Tony about them and Tony, with this added proof that Layla is back, will double his efforts to close the net on her. And I don't want that. I don't want her arrested like a common criminal. What I want is to be able to see her first, to talk to her by myself. Which is why I sent her an email on Wednesday warning her that she's currently the object of a search.

I shouldn't have, I know. I only sent one line: The police are looking for you in Cheltenham

If I'm honest, it isn't just about not wanting her to be found until I have a chance to see her. Stupidly, I thought she might be so grateful for the tip-off that she would put aside her countdown and agree to see me. But she never replied.

I look at Ellen's note again, wondering what I should do. She'll have had lunch by now, so there's no point in driving into Cheltenham just to come home again. The thought of her having a solitary lunch in a café makes me feel guilty all over again. When had I become so careless with Ellen's feelings, when had I stopped making an effort? If only I'd been honest with her five weeks ago, when I found the doll on the wall. If only I'd shared the dolls, the emails with her. If I truly loved her, I would have, I acknowledge. If I truly loved her, I wouldn't have let anything come between us. Now the distance between us seems huge—her note is evidence of that. Normally she would have come and told me that she was going shopping. Maybe I should phone her and suggest meeting for coffee.

The sound of the car coming in the drive makes the decision for me. I go into the hall and open the front door.

"Sorry," I say, as she takes a couple of bags of shopping from the car. "I've only just seen your note."

"It's fine," she says, but I know that it's not by the way she pushes past me into the house without letting me take the bags from her, as she usually would.

I follow her into the kitchen.

"I'm sorry," I say again.

"Don't worry, I'm used to it," she says, dumping the bags on the side.

Something in her voice, a slight bitterness, makes me look at her properly. Her face is drawn, unhappy, and when I think about it, I realize she's looked drawn and unhappy for a while. I can't remember the last time she laughed. I can't remember the last time I laughed.

"What do you mean?" I ask.

"Having lunch on my own. I left you the same note on Tuesday and it was still on the table when I got back." She stops unpacking the bags and looks at me, a bunch of bananas in her hand. "You didn't even notice I'd gone."

"What's with the note anyway?" I ask, getting angry. "Why didn't you just tell me you were going out?"

"Why should I always be the one to come and find you? You never leave your office anymore, you don't even bother to have lunch unless I fetch you."

"That's not true," I protest.

"The last three days I've had lunch here in the kitchen on my own. So, as I said, I'm used to it."

Hating that I'm the cause of the hurt in her voice, I take the bananas from her and put my arms around her.

"If I tell you I'm sorry a third time, will you forgive me?" I ask. "It won't happen again, I promise. It's holiday time, so I'm not going to be so busy now," I add, knowing she'll think that the reason I've been staying in my office is because of my workload.

"I thought you were avoiding me."

"No," I say softly. And as she sinks her body into mine, I feel real hate for Layla for coming between us, for upsetting the equilibrium of our relationship.

Late in the evening, my usual email arrives—*FOUR*—a reminder that I have four days left to get rid of Ellen before—what? Layla takes matters into her own hands? What will she do, turn up at the house and confront us? Or get rid of Ellen herself? I shake my head, knowing it's just exhaustion speaking. Layla would never harm Ellen. But my mind keeps going back to the doll with the smashed head and the When You've Done What You Have To Do email. Given that twelve years have passed, I might not know Layla as well as I once did.

Despite everything, I manage to sleep solidly for the first time in weeks, maybe because I've sorted things with Ellen. When I wake, I feel stronger, refreshed. I stretch out my arm and realize Ellen isn't beside me, that she must already be up, and I leap out of bed, hoping she hasn't got to the post before me. As I'm throwing my clothes on, I realize that it's Sunday, which means there won't be any post. The relief I feel is short-lived; I can't imagine Layla letting me off for the day, especially when I remember that last Sunday, she left me a Russian doll on the wall.

I go down to the kitchen and find Ellen sitting at the table, a cup of coffee in front of her.

"I'll go and get some fresh bread for breakfast," I say, planting a kiss on the top of her head.

"I'll come with you," she offers.

"No need, it's fine. Stay and finish your coffee."

"I have. Anyway, I could do with a walk." She reaches under the table. "Come on, Peggy."

There's nothing I can do except grab the Russian doll—if there is one—off the wall before she sees it. But as we walk down the path there's no sign of a doll and I don't know if I should be grateful or worried. Maybe Layla has left it somewhere else this morning, in which case I'm going to have to hunt for it surreptitiously when we get back.

We buy the bread and walk back to the house hand in hand. As we approach the house, Ellen stops suddenly, dragging me to a standstill, and my senses immediately go on alert.

"Oh my God," she says, pointing toward the house, and she sounds so incredulous that for a moment, I think Layla has turned up. "Look, Finn, on the wall!"

"Oh my God," I echo, glad it's only a doll, not Layla, because I'm not ready to see her, not now, not like this. I'm about to say something more but Ellen is already running, past the house, down the road, all the way to the corner. Ignoring the doll, I run after her, wondering what she's seen, wondering if she saw Layla.

I catch up with her in the next road. "Did you see anything?" I ask.

She shakes her head, out of breath. "We must have just missed her." She looks up at me, the all-too-familiar fear and excitement on her face. "She was here, Finn, Layla was here! She left a doll on the wall!" Her eyes fill with sudden tears. "We might have seen her if we'd walked back a little faster."

"She doesn't want us to see her," I say gently, putting my arms around her.

"Why hasn't Tony found her?" she says, her voice wobbling, angry now. "How much longer are we going to have to wait?"

"I don't know," I soothe.

"Can you phone Tony? Ask him if they've found anything. She must be in Cheltenham, she has to be."

"If there was any news, he'd have told us. And I don't want to phone him on Sunday again. I'll phone him tomorrow, all right?"

She nods mutely and I curse Layla for leaving the doll on the wall. Where the hell is she anyway? I'm not so sure that she is in Cheltenham. Just because Ellen saw her there and the envelopes have a Cheltenham postmark, it doesn't mean she's living there. She could have dropped them into a mailbox in any of the outlying villages and they would automatically go to the main post office at Cheltenham to be sorted.

"Can we go to Cheltenham?" Ellen asks. "We were only gone about half an hour. She can't be that far ahead."

"We don't know that she's in Cheltenham," I say.

"She is," Ellen says fiercely. "I know it."

"I really don't think—"

"I don't mind going on my own. I'll get the car keys." She heads toward the house, taking the Russian doll from the wall as she passes.

So we go to Cheltenham on what I know is a wild-goose chase because we're not going to find Layla sitting in a café or walking along the road any more than I would have if I'd stopped on the way back from St. Mary's that time. We traipse the streets anyway, and when Ellen eventually concedes defeat, we stop for lunch. It's not a huge success. Neither of us is in a talkative mood, so we sit largely in silence, each of us lost in our own thoughts.

We get home and Ellen disappears into her study for the rest of the afternoon. In the evening, we watch a film which neither of us really follows. After Ellen has gone up to bed I sit down at the kitchen table and check my phone for emails. There's one from Layla. I already know what it will say.

THREE

I don't usually write back but after the near-miss this morning, I do.

Where are you?

A reply comes straight back and I can't believe that at last, she's actually going to tell me. I take a breath and open it.

CLOSER THAN YOU THINK

FORTY-FIVE

LAYLA

I wanted to stop the countdown. I was so sure I'd been caught when I left the first of the ten dolls on the wall last week. But the voice reassured me. You can post the others, it said. You don't have to take any more risks. Except that yesterday, I had to leave another on the wall, because it was Sunday again.

Last week, I ordered more Russian dolls. The voice told me to. I ordered twenty this time. They were delivered the next day and it gave me a real rush to open the box and see them lying there, waiting for me to perform caesarean after caesarean after caesarean and release all the little babies. I don't know what the voice has planned for this newest lot. It's getting harder for me to ignore it, to shut it out. Maybe it thinks that I'm going to have to extend the countdown. But I have faith in Finn, in his love for me. He will get rid of Ellen.

There are only two days left. If I could, I'd end it all now. It's why I replied to Finn's email, asking where I was. Don't tell him, the voice said, don't tell him where you are. I couldn't defy the voice but I gave Finn a clue, hoping he would understand.

And bring me back, before it's too late.

FORTY-SIX

FINN

I start awake, my heart pounding, my body sleek with sweat. Disorientated, I look around me and find I'm lying on the sofa in the sitting room. It was a nightmare, I tell myself, that's all. If I go upstairs, Ellen will be safe and sound in bed, not lying crumpled at the bottom of a cliff, her body bloodied and broken. It was only a dream.

It had been so vivid though. I was standing close to a clifftop edge with Ellen while Layla urged me to push her onto the rocks below. I couldn't see Layla, there was only her voice, but I understood the choice I had to make—if I wanted to see Layla, I had to kill Ellen otherwise Layla would disappear again, this time forever. And Ellen, sensing what I was about to do, grabbed hold of me, dragging me off the cliff with her. And as we hurtled to the ground below, my voice was one long scream of *Laaaaaaay-laaaaaa!*

Had I screamed her name out loud? Is that what woke me? I wait for the drumming in my ears to stop and establish that the house is silent, that if I had been calling out in my sleep, it hadn't woken Ellen. Dawn is filtering its way through the night sky and I get groggily to my feet, feeling more exhausted than before I fell asleep. Coffee, I need coffee.

The *CLOSER THAN YOU THINK* message has been going round and round in my head, like a stuck recording. Because of the message I sent, warning that the police were looking for her, Layla knows I think she's in Cheltenham, so if she's closer than Cheltenham she could be in any of the nearby villages—or even in Simonsbridge itself. It would explain how she's been able to leave the dolls so easily.

I told Ellen that I'd spoken to Tony, as she had asked me to do, and that he'd said they hadn't found Layla yet but that they were still looking. None of it was true but it put her mind at rest.

It's almost over anyway. Yesterday, I got another doll in the post, and the subsequent email—*TWO*. Today I'll get the last Russian doll and tomorrow—well, tomorrow I have no idea, only that my time has run out. Ellen is still here, I haven't got rid of her as Layla asked me to do. So what next? Is she going to carry on with her game, extend the countdown? God, I hope not. But what if it becomes something worse, what if she hasn't been bluffing? It's disturbing to know I have no idea what Layla is capable of doing.

I hear Ellen's footsteps on the stairs and realize with a start that I haven't checked if the envelope has arrived. I get to my feet then sit back down again. It's the last one, so it hardly matters if Ellen gets to it before I do.

The mail only arrives as we're having breakfast. I go out to the hall but Ellen follows me.

"Anything for me?" she asks.

"I don't know, I haven't looked yet." I wait for her to walk back to the kitchen ahead of me so that I can stuff the envelope under my shirt but she reaches round and takes the post from my hands.

"It's just that I'm waiting for my new contract," she explains, rifling through it. "Cathy put it in the post two days ago." She picks out the brown envelope. "This must be it." She turns it over. "Oh, it's for you." A sudden frown creases her brow. "It looks like the one I received a couple of weeks ago. Do you think . . ." Her voice trails away.

"Let's open it and see," I say, because there's no use pretending I don't know what she's thinking. "Maybe there'll be a letter or something."

"I think it's another doll," she says, feeling the envelope with her fingers. She hands it to me and because there's nothing else I can do, I carry it through to the kitchen and open it. I shake it onto the worktop, not thinking for one second that it will have its head smashed in. But it does.

Ellen looks at it in dismay. "What a shame!" She picks it up. "Poor little doll. I feel like complaining to the post office—they must have dropped a box on it or something. Where was it posted?"

I look at the postmark. "Cheltenham, the same as yours."

"Is there a letter?"

"No, nothing."

"How strange."

We carry on with our breakfast but Ellen's eyes flit constantly to the broken Russian doll lying on the worktop and I can almost see her mind whirring with theories and suppositions.

"You don't think . . ."

"What?" I prompt.

"That the doll was damaged on purpose."

"What do you mean?"

"Well, that Layla damaged it on purpose, you know, as a kind of message."

"A message?"

"It's just that this one was sent to you, not me."

"You mean Layla wishes me harm?"

"It's just a theory," she says hastily. "It's just that if this *is* about you marrying me, it kind of makes sense."

"Let's hope Tony finds her quickly then," I say, attempting a smile.

"If it is Layla," she says.

"You've changed your mind again?"

"I don't know," she says helplessly. "But if it isn't Layla, I'm going to be really mad with whoever it is for getting our hopes up." She thinks for a moment. "Can we go to The Jackdaw for lunch?"

I look at her curiously. "If you like."

"It's just that the more I think about it, the more I can't believe that Layla would do this kind of thing—you know, come right up to the house and leave a doll on the wall without coming in to see us. I know Layla, it's not in her nature to be cruel, and sending these Russian dolls is cruel, especially when they have a smashed head. So if it is someone else, the most likely candidate is Ruby, hoping to break us up. Remember that Partner of Missing Woman Moves Sister In article? She must have been behind it."

What if she's right, I think feverishly, what if it really is some kind of hideous joke and Layla hasn't come back? I catch myself—when did I become this man, doubting myself, doubting my mind? The man who pulled off the Grant James deal six weeks ago feels like someone I can't remember being.

"You do still want to marry me, don't you?" Ellen goes on.

I feel suddenly furious. "You asked me that before and I told you that I did!"

"That was weeks ago."

"So, nothing has changed."

"Everything has changed."

I push my chair back abruptly. "Let's go out for lunch, then." I get to my feet, throw my bowl in the sink. "I'm taking Peggy for a walk."

I'm not proud of walking away. I know Ellen wanted more from me, wanted some sort of reassurance but I can't give her what she wants, not at the moment. I go down to the river, wishing Ellen hadn't brought Ruby back into the equation, wondering what I'll do if it does turn out to be her. I rub the corners of my eyes, wishing I wasn't so damn tired, wondering why I'm doubting Ruby all over again. If there's one thing I'm sure of, it's that all this—Layla—has nothing to do with Ruby. I know very well that Layla is back. What I should be asking is why am I letting her do this to me, instead of taking control? When did I become so passive?

The need to do something physical is overwhelming. If I could numb my mind for just a moment, rid it of all confusion, I'd feel better. If I hadn't brought Peggy with me I could have gone for a run. The cool water of the river, the early morning sunshine playing on its surface pulls me toward it. Pulling my sweatshirt over my head, I strip down to my boxers and plunge into the river. The shock of the deceptively freezing water invigorates me and fills me with renewed energy. I power up and down the river, scattering ducks, focusing only on one thing, emptying my brain.

Later, on the way to The Jackdaw, Ellen links her arm through mine, determined to show Ruby our unified front. The intention irritates me and I feel almost vindicated when we arrive, because there's no sign of Ruby behind the bar and when we ask, we learn she's been away for the last week and that she isn't due back until the weekend. I've never known Ruby to go away for any length of time, just an occasional day off to visit her mum but never—I make a quick calculation—around ten days. Ten. I close my mind to the implications. Where has she gone? When I ask, nobody seems to know. The general feeling is that she's gone to her mum's in Cheltenham. Or is she closer than I think?

"Well, that's that, then," says Ellen despondently. "We're no nearer finding the truth."

That evening, the final email comes in.

ONE

FORTY-SEVEN

LAYLA

I knew even before I sent that last doll that I'd lost. When I smashed its head in, it was my head I was smashing and I hoped Finn would understand, I hoped he would realize that this time, the doll represented me, not Ellen, and that in not choosing me, he may as well have killed me. The voice was right. Finn wasn't going to give Ellen up for me. I'd always known he wouldn't harm her—although I was happy to put the idea into his head—because he wasn't that sort of man, not unless he was in a tearing rage. And why would he lose his temper with Ellen, who never did anything to upset him?

I did think he would tell Ellen it was over, though, especially as they'd grown so far apart. I could see it every time I saw them together, the widening of the gap between them, getting larger and larger until it was almost a chasm. How could they ever recover from that? It would never be the same. He may as well have chosen me.

He would realize, of course, that he'd made the wrong choice and ultimately, he would regret it. But it would be too late. By then, I'll have disappeared again, never to come back. Tomorrow, I'm leaving.

The voice is not impressed. I can't believe you're giving up that easily, it scorns. If you really want something you have to fight for it, surely you know that by now. I did fight, I reply. I fought and I lost. Finn doesn't want me. That's because you fought the wrong person, replies the voice. It's Ellen you should be fighting, not Finn. If you want Finn, you'll have to fight Ellen. Properly. To the death.

The thought terrifies me. What you're asking me to do is impossible, I tell the voice. I can't kill Ellen. You'll have to if you want to survive, it says. You said yourself that there wasn't room for both of you. I can't, I say again. Of course you can, says the voice. Who do you want Finn to have? You, or Ellen. It's your choice.

But I don't want to make the choice. I think about what I can do and I decide to give the choice to Ellen. The countdown is over. It's up to her now. She has one day. If she can get Finn to prove that he loves her, to the exclusion of all else, to the exclusion of me, she can have him. If she can't—well, Finn will be mine. And I'll be able to get rid of Ellen once and for all.

FORTY-EIGHT

FINN

I'm tempted to reply to Layla's email and ask her what happens now that I've received the last doll. What has she planned for tomorrow, now that time has run out? What I hope is that she'll concede defeat and give me a time and a place where we can meet. But her inferred threat against Ellen plays heavily on my mind. It seems inevitable that there'll be a confrontation of some kind.

If she turns up at the house, how will it feel to see her again? Will I fall instantly in love with her, regret that I hadn't chosen her over Ellen? Probably. There might still be a chance for us. There's such a distance between Ellen and me that I'm not sure we'll ever recover. We didn't speak at all on our way back from The Jackdaw. Come to think of it, we didn't speak while we were at The Jackdaw either. We ate our meal in almost total silence. Well, I ate and Ellen pushed her food around on the plate. She's become so thin, thinner than she's ever been. Why hadn't I noticed?

At least the terrible pressure of the last ten days is off. Each day seemed so long and yet, as each day came to a close, as each email came in, reminding me that I was one step nearer the end, reminding me that I had let another day slip by without taking action of any kind, I wanted to snatch it back again.

I feel I could sleep tonight, a proper sleep, a dreamless sleep. I haven't slept in my bed for a week now—I've taken to falling asleep on the sofa—so I'm longing to climb into it. Ellen is moving around up there so I'll have to wait until she's asleep. I fish a bottle of whiskey out of the cupboard and pour myself a glass, a drink to remind myself that I haven't given in to Layla.

It's well past midnight by the time I go up. In the bathroom, I have a quick shower and walk into the bedroom. I expect Ellen to be asleep but she's sitting on the bed, dressed in one of my old shirts, waiting for me. I come to an abrupt halt. I've never been shy about being naked in front of Ellen but now, I feel awkward.

"I thought you'd be asleep," I say.

"I decided to wait up for you."

"You shouldn't have. You're tired, you need to sleep."

"Maybe, but I want to talk to you."

"It's late. Can we talk tomorrow?"

"No. Tomorrow you'll be in your office, where you seem to spend all of your time now." She looks sadly at me. "What's happened to us, Finn? Why do you never come up to bed until late? If you come up at all."

"Because I can't sleep."

"Because of Layla?"

"Yes, because of Layla. It's not been easy, these last few weeks, not knowing if she's going to suddenly turn up."

"Do you love me more than you loved Layla?" she asks, an echo of what Layla asked me in her email all those weeks ago.

"What kind of question is that?"

"A perfectly normal one, given the circumstances, given the fact that Layla is my sister."

"She always has been, yet you've never asked me before."

"Because I was too afraid of what the answer would be."

I grab a T-shirt and some boxers from the drawer. "The love I had for Layla was different."

"In what way? Better, worse?"

"Just different. Look, can we have this conversation tomorrow? I'm tired, I want to go to sleep."

"When was the last time we had sex, Finn?" I don't say anything, because I can't remember. "Shall I tell you when it was? It was before Layla left that Russian doll on the wall, before she came back into our lives." She gets off the bed, comes over, takes the clothes from my hand and throws them down. "Make love to me, Finn."

I stare at her, because she has never asked me to make love to her before. Also, I know I'm not going to be able to, not while my head is all over the place. Not while my head is full of Layla.

"We haven't had sex for so long." Her hands move to the buttons on her shirt and she begins to undo them one by one, her eyes never leaving my face. She lets it slide off her shoulders and onto the floor. "Make love to me, Finn. Make love to me like you used to make love to Layla."

It's the word Layla that does it, the word Layla that triggers desire in me, that makes me crush her to me, that makes me pick her up in my arms and lie her down on the bed. It's the word Layla that drives me to make love to her in a way that I never have before, not even that first time, when I had imagined she was Layla. It's the name that I murmur, the name I cry out, the name that beats in my brain when it's all over.

And it's the sound of Ellen crying quietly beside me that brings me back from where I disappeared to.

Burning with shame, I get out of bed, grab the boxers from the floor, and go heavily downstairs to the kitchen. I want to tell Layla that she has won, that I've done as she asked, that I've killed Ellen, because that's how it feels. I open the back door and cross the garden to my office. Opening my computer, I see that there's a message waiting for me, from Layla.

Come to the cottage

When?

Now

Relief washes over me—I have somewhere to go. I can't stay here, not after what I've done. If I leave now, I won't have to face Ellen. If I go now, Layla will be waiting for me.

Except that my clothes are upstairs, in the bedroom. I cast my mind around, wondering if there are any downstairs that I can wear. But I need my car keys and they're in the pocket of my jeans.

I go back to the house, hoping that Ellen will be asleep. In the moonlight coming through the window I see her curled up on the bed, in a fetal position. Layla used to sleep like that and I would unfold her and take her in my arms, hold her body against mine. Layla. No need to banish her from my mind anymore. Soon, I will see her. Soon we'll be together.

I dress quickly, trying to make as little sound as possible. I feel in the pocket of my jeans—my keys are there. I take my phone from where I left it on the side.

"Where are you going?"

I freeze. Ellen sits up, turns on her lamp. A soft light bathes the room and red-hot shame floods my body. I want to say something, apologize, tell her how sorry I am. But how can sorry make up for what I did, for making love to her as if I was making love to Layla, for calling out for Layla? I think about turning and leaving without saying anything. But she deserves more than that.

"Out," I say, my voice thick with secrets.

"To Layla?"

My heart thumps. I don't want to lie but I can't tell the truth either.

"Why do you say that?"

She opens the drawer in her bedside table, scoops something out with both hands. There's the sound of wood on wood as she throws a pile of little Russian dolls onto the bed.

"I found these in your office."

Anger surfaces. "You went rooting around in my office?"

"I wanted to know why you spent so much time in there. What else have you been keeping from me?"

"Nothing! I kept finding dolls, I didn't tell you about them because I didn't want you to worry."

Her voice rises an octave "No, you didn't tell me about them because you wanted to keep Layla to yourself!"

"No!" I yell. "It wasn't like that!"

"Have you been in contact with her?" Unable to answer, I start to leave the room. "Finn, come back!" But I'm already running down the stairs. "Finn!" Her voice follows me down to the hall and out of the front door. "Don't go!"

There's a light on in Mick's house, from one of the upstairs windows, and I wonder if he heard us arguing. Voices carry at night.

I use the drive to Devon to push my anger aside. There's hardly anyone on the road, just a lone traveler or two, like me. I drive fast, but not faster than I should. *Come to the cottage*, Layla had said, which means she's already there, waiting. When did she arrive? Did she go there as soon as she'd posted the last little doll to me?

It's just gone three in the morning when I arrive in St. Mary's. I had expected to see a light on in the cottage but it's in darkness. It doesn't mean anything, I tell myself, it doesn't mean she isn't there. But there is a sense of foreboding as I get out of the car, which increases when I see the garden. Even in the darkness I can see that the flowers Thomas so carefully planted are dead, as are the ones in the window boxes. Another omen. Even to my desperate eye, the cottage looks deserted.

No one opens the front door at the sound of the gate scraping on the ground, no one comes running down the stairs in answer to my heavy knock. It's then that I realize I don't have my keys. I'd believed so completely that Layla would be waiting for me that it hadn't mattered.

I take off my jumper, wrap it round my fist and punch a hole in the kitchen window, snap off the remaining glass and use the light from my phone to look around the room. Everything looks just as it did last time I was here. I stick my head inside, listen. There's nothing to tell me anyone is there.

I don't want to believe I've been brought all the way here for nothing. I check my phone for emails—Layla might have been delayed, she might be on her way. But there's nothing from her, so I send a message.

I'm here, at the cottage.
Where are you?
I'm here
Where?
IN SIMONSBRIDGE

FORTY-NINE

LAYLA

I won. Finally, I won. But it's a hollow victory. The fight took too much out of me. It was bitter and bloody and now I'm scared I'm going to disappear again, this time forever. I can feel myself getting weaker by the minute. I wait for the voice to tell me what I should do but it remains silent. I'm on my own.

Ellen is here, though. Finn might have chosen me but Ellen is still here. And there's not enough room for both of us. She needs to disappear.

So I give Finn what he's been waiting for, a time and a place. I tell him to come to the cottage and I watch him leave. I watch him leave Ellen to come to me.

I am not at the cottage, of course. I am close by, waiting to explain to Ellen why she has to go. It's not going to be easy because she won't understand. Of course she won't, the voice says, suddenly appearing again. All those years ago, you made a bargain with her. You told her that if she could get Finn to love her, she could have him. You told her that as long as she looked after him, you would stay away, you would never come back. So she made herself perfect and got him to love her, she looked after him and cherished him. And how did you repay her? You came back.

But that was Finn's fault, I tell the voice. If he hadn't decided to marry Ellen, none of this would have happened. Besides, he never loved her, not really, not as he loved me. Ellen knows that. She'll understand.

And the voice laughs.

FIFTY

FINN

I stare at the message on my phone. Simonsbridge? What is she doing in Simonsbridge? And if she's in Simonsbridge, why did she make me come to St. Mary's? The truth stares me in the face. She needed me out of the way.

For what? To speak to Ellen? It's normal, Ellen is her sister, they have things to talk about. But why banish me to St. Mary's, a three-hour drive away? I feel horribly apprehensive. What if there's some darker purpose in luring me so far away from Simonsbridge?

The image of the doll with the smashed head looms in my mind. I need to get back. I drive faster this time. Layla will have guessed I'm on my way, that I'd drive straight back. My driving borders on the dangerous and I'm conscious that I'm putting my own life at risk. But I'd be a fool to think Layla will be waiting for me in the kitchen, chatting to Ellen over a cup of tea. I shouldn't have left Ellen alone. I need to call her, warn her.

I pull over, call her phone. It goes straight to voicemail. I leave a message, asking her if Layla is there, asking her to call me urgently. I send her a text, asking the same things. I wait a couple of minutes in case she replies; then, conscious that I'm wasting time, I drive on.

My worry increases with each mile I drive. I pull over again, call Ellen's phone, leave the same message, trying not to yell with frustration at not being able to get hold of her. I stop for a third time; there's still no response from her. Then, about twenty minutes from the house, my phone beeps, telling me an email has come in. Please let it be Ellen, I pray silently, as I pull to a stop, even though I know she would call or text, not send an email. If it's from Layla, is it to tell me that she's on her way to St. Mary's, to wait for her there?

YOU SHOULD HAVE GOT RID OF HER

Dread seeps into my pores. My fingers fumble on my phone as I try Ellen's number again. Come on, Ellen, answer your phone, please answer your phone! But she doesn't pick up so I leave a message—if you can, get out of the house. Take your car and drive as far away as you can. Don't stay in Simonsbridge, don't trust Layla.

I ram the car into gear and drive as fast as I can toward the house. The street is quiet. There is no unfamiliar car parked in the road, no cars in our drive. Ellen's car has gone and there's no sign of her coming out of the house.

Leaping out of the car, I run to the front door and let myself in.

"Ellen!" I shout. "Are you here?" I check the kitchen and sitting room. Both are empty, as is her study. I take the stairs two at a time. The bedroom is exactly as I last saw it—the pile of Russian dolls is still on the bed, the shirt she was wearing is still on the floor—except that she's no longer sitting on the bed. I check the spare bedroom next door; it's empty. As I turn to go along the landing, I see a lone Russian doll standing halfway along, in the middle of the floor. I pick it up, noting only that it's exactly like all the others that have appeared over the last few weeks. I check the bedroom at the other end of the house, and the bathroom. Both are empty and there's no sign of a struggle.

I go back down to the hall, my feet pounding on the stairs. I stand a moment. The only place I haven't checked is my office. Please let her be there, please let me find her sitting at my desk, unharmed. Unharmed. Am I mad to think that Layla would harm her? Maybe, possibly. But who knows what Layla could do? I should never have trusted her.

My office is empty and there's no one hiding in the garden. I go back to the house, into the kitchen. I sit down at the table, trying to think what I should do. Where is Ellen? Is she with Layla? Have the two of them been together in this all the time? Have they been stringing me along in some kind of revenge game? Revenge for what? I don't know, I don't know. My mind feels as if it's spiraling out of control.

The other possibility is that Layla has taken Ellen somewhere. But where? Does she even exist? Or is it only someone pretending to be her? My mind goes back to Ruby—where has she been for the last ten days? I reach under the table, searching for Peggy, desperately needing comfort. But she isn't there.

Like Ellen, she has disappeared.

FIFTY-ONE

LAYLA

Ellen wouldn't listen. She was stronger than I expected her to be. I thought the knowledge that she had lost Finn, that he had chosen me over her, would weaken her and she would go quietly. But it seemed to give her new resolve; as I had already seen, she was tenacious when it came to Finn. She wasn't going to let me walk back into his life that easily. If she couldn't have him, she was determined that I wouldn't either. I tried to explain to her that Finn had made his choice, that it was me he wanted, that he had never stopped loving me. But no matter how hard I tried to persuade her, she refused to leave. Go! I screamed. Go! But she wouldn't.

I could feel my mind splintering, fragmenting, sapping the little strength I had left. Ellen wouldn't stop shouting at me, telling me I had to leave, that I should disappear back to my hiding place, back to the place where I had sought refuge all those years before. But the thought of going back to being a nothing person terrified me. If I could just hang on until Finn came back, it would be all right. He would save me and banish Ellen forever.

If only he had done what I'd asked, if only he had got rid of Ellen. I sent him a message telling him as much. But Ellen saw and was angry. Again, she tried to make me leave and when I refused, we began to struggle. All I could think of was Finn, about how he would come back to find he had lost everything. Part of me felt he deserved to. He should have brought me back while he had the chance. But the other part of me knew that my expectations had been too high. He didn't know my story. I should have told him the truth right from the beginning.

Now it's too late. Finn can spend hours, days, months, looking for me but he'll never find me. Not unless I give him some sort of clue, not unless I start him off on the right track. I have a Russian doll in my pocket and as Ellen begins to overpower me, I put it where Finn will find it. Ultimately, it will lead him to the truth about the Russian dolls. And if he discovers the truth about the Russian dolls, he'll know the truth about me.

And maybe, just maybe, he'll know where to find me.

PART THREE

FIFTY-TWO

FINN

It hits me hard, Peggy being gone too. Again, I try Ellen's mobile, and again it goes through to her voicemail. Who else can I call? Tony, I should call him. I'll tell him everything, come clean about the emails from Layla, tell him Ellen has disappeared. The word thuds into my head. *Disappeared.* Ellen has disappeared, just as Layla had. I sit down heavily on a chair. One woman in my life having vanished is suspect enough; for it to have happened to another would be damning. There are still those who believed that I killed Layla and disposed of her body somewhere. I have no proof that she's back. All I have are Russian dolls that could have been left by anybody, emails that could have been written by anybody. Nobody has actually seen Layla, not even me.

Fear numbs me. I can't phone Tony, not until I've thought everything through. In the end, I decide to phone Harry, not Tony. I know Tony believed from the start that I didn't have anything to do with Layla's disappearance but even he might begin to have doubts when I tell him that Ellen has gone missing too. She might not be missing, she might have left with Layla of her own accord. But if that were the case, surely she would answer her phone? I know Ellen; she wouldn't be so cruel as to not answer my messages if she heard them.

Harry will know what to do. He knows as much as Tony does and once he knows the whole story, he'll be able to advise me. I check the time; it's just gone seven. He's usually up at this time. I dial his number. Unbelievably, I get the international ringtone. Harry has gone abroad and hasn't told me? I wait impatiently but he doesn't pick up, so I leave a message asking him to phone me, trying not to sound as panicked as I feel. I pace the kitchen, waiting, waiting, and when he hasn't called within twenty minutes, I call him again. But when he still doesn't get back to me I begin to get a really bad feeling because I've never known Harry to be inaccessible before, even when he's abroad. If ever he can't talk, because he's in a meeting, or in bed with a woman, he always triggers a standard "I'm currently unavailable" text. I try a third time, and a fourth. It's eight in the morning now and it suddenly occurs to me that it probably isn't eight in the morning wherever he is in the world. So I try his office number, to find out where he is, how long he's gone for, but nobody answers, because it's too early.

And where is Peggy? I'm hoping she's with Ellen, because Peggy won't let her come to any harm. But what if she's run off, what if something happened here last night that made her afraid?

I want to go and look for her instead of just sitting here, waiting, but I need to stay here to speak to Tony. But I want to go through everything with Harry first.

At eight thirty I phone Harry's office again. I'd begun to feel as if I was the only person left in the world so I'm relieved when one of his assistants answers.

"I'm afraid he's away," Alice says, confirming what I already know.

"Away where?" I ask.

"I don't know, he said he was going abroad for a few days."

"Well, does anyone know where he is? I wouldn't normally insist but I need to speak to him urgently."

"Hold on a minute, I'll find out."

She comes back to tell me that nobody knows where he is or when he'll be back, just that he walked uncharacteristically out of the office two days ago. I ask her if he checks in from time to time and she says he has once, so far. She promises to tell him that I need to speak to him next time he phones. I hang up, unease spreading through me. First Ruby, then Ellen, now Harry. All three of them have gone somewhere, yet no one knows where. Is there some kind of conspiracy going on? Has all this been about Harry and Ellen, as I'd once thought? But where does Ruby fit in? Or maybe she doesn't, maybe Ruby is simply away on holiday somewhere. The only two things I know for sure is that I'm on my own and that time is marching on.

Tony plays on my mind. If I'm to tell him the whole truth, I need to phone him within the next hour because once he knows about the last email from Layla, the one saying I should have chosen her over Ellen, he'll wonder why I didn't phone him straightaway given the underlying menace in the message. But if I don't tell him the whole truth, I have a few hours. In a few hours I can phone him and tell him that last night, Ellen and I had a row, I went storming off to the cottage and when I came back, Ellen was gone, that she hasn't been answering her phone, and that I'm now getting worried as I would have expected her to be back by now. The truth, the whole truth? Or only part of it?

I give myself until lunchtime. If I haven't made any headway by then, I'll phone Tony and tell him the whole truth. I go through to the sitting room and look out of the window, watching for Ellen's car coming down the road, trying to get my thoughts in order.

I start with Layla. First, is it really her or someone pretending to be her? I go back over everything, from the appearance of the first Russian doll to the last email I received, and by the end, I can't bring myself to believe that it wasn't her. Only she and I knew about the tree stump shaped like a Russian doll on Pharos Hill. Next, I try and work out where she could have been for the last twelve years—but I quickly realize that the most important thing is to work out where she's been for the last six weeks, since the first Russian doll appeared. Ellen had seen her in Cheltenham, yet Layla had said that she was closer than that, so where? How had she been able to leave Russian dolls on the wall without anyone seeing her? I'd heard a car driving away one day but that was before her CLOSER THAN YOU THINK message, when I had presumed she was in Cheltenham, so it had been logical to presume that it was her. But maybe it hadn't been, maybe the car had nothing to do with her, maybe she'd been on foot, because she was already in Simonsbridge. Or maybe she got someone to leave the dolls for her.

I'm back to Ruby again. It would have been easy enough for her to leave the dolls. Did Layla ask her to leave them? Or is Ruby working alone? What about the couple that Mick saw walking past the house? Was Layla one of them? I need to go back and speak to Mick, ask if the woman had red hair, ask if he's seen anything suspicious since. But not now. At this time in the morning, he'll be giving his wife—Fiona, I think he said—her breakfast.

Fiona. That was the name of Layla and Ellen's mother, I remember.

There's a sudden explosion in my brain, the sound of every theory I've just considered being blasted apart, leaving nothing but a roaring in my ears. And then I'm running out of the house and across the road to where Mick lives with his invalid wife, his invalid wife who is called Fiona, his invalid wife that I've never seen and I hammer on the door, shouting to be let in. And of course, it takes Mick a while to open it, and of course, he has a bowl of porridge in his hands, his weapon against intruders. Enraged, I lift my hand, wanting to knock it away, and Mick steps back in alarm.

"Where is she?" I yell. I try to push my way into the hall but Mick slams the door into me, blocking it with his foot.

"For God's sake, man, what's got into you?" he cries, looking frightened. But I see through his act and give the door another almighty shove.

"Let me in!" I yell. "I want to see her!"

"What are you talking about? If it's Ellen, she's not here."

"What do you know about Ellen?" I snarl.

"I heard you arguing last night, then I saw you drive off. She's not here, I promise."

"Let me in!" I push against the door. "I want to see your wife!"

"My wife?" He stares at me, bewildered. "What has she got to do with any of this?"

"Let me see her!"

"No." His whole demeanor suddenly changes. He draws himself up to his full height, which is still eight inches shorter than me. "Go away, Finn. I'm sorry about Ellen but if you don't leave, I'm going to call the police. Ellen isn't here."

"No, but Layla is!"

"Layla?"

"Yes, Layla!" I give the door an almighty shove and Mick stumbles back. "Where is she?" I cry, stepping into the hall. "Where's your wife?"

"Please don't do this." Mick is almost in tears. "You can't, you have no right."

"I have every right!" Pushing past him, I head down the corridor. "Layla! Where are you?" I open the door to the sitting room but there's no one there. I turn to Mick, standing in the doorway, the bowl of porridge still in his hands, and knock it onto the floor. "Where is she?" I roar.

And then I hear it, a kind of whimpering coming from a room further down the corridor. I manhandle Mick out of the way and head for the room.

"No!" he cries. "You can't! Leave us alone!"

But I'm already flinging the door open.

And there she is, struggling to sit up from where she's been lying in her bed, a clawlike hand clutching the front of her nightdress, a look of absolute terror on her face. And as I look at her, I can feel the absolute horror on mine.

FIFTY-THREE

FINN

"Mick, Mick!" She claws at her nightdress.

Mick barges past me, "It's all right, Fiona," he soothes, rushing to her side, pushing her gently back against the pillows. "I'm here."

"Who's that man?" Her voice is shaking with stress.

"It's all right," he says, swallowing his anger. "He's our neighbor, he lives across the road. He just wanted to say hello to you." He looks over at me, his face drained of color. "But he's leaving now."

"Why was he shouting?"

"I'm sorry." My voice comes out a whisper. "I'm sorry." I

begin to back out of the room. "I wanted to say hello, that's all. But I'm going now."

"I'll go and see him out," I hear Mick explaining. "Then I'll come back and finish giving you your breakfast."

He follows me to the door.

"Mick, I'm so sorry," I begin, but he cuts me off.

"Get out. If you ever come near us again, I'll call the police."

I stumble into the front garden and see Mrs. Jeffries on her doorstep, a phone in her hand.

"I'm sorry," I say to her. "I'm sorry." I want to ask her if she's phoned the police but she's looking worriedly at Mick and I can feel them watching me as I cross back over the road.

In the house, I sink onto the stairs and put my head in my hands. Waves of shame flood through me as the whole nightmare scenario plays through my mind over and over again. I can't get the look of terror on his wife's face out of my mind, nor the distress on Mick's as he pleaded with me to leave them alone. How could I have done what I just did, how could I have acted in such a brutish, bullying manner? What if Mrs. Jeffries has phoned the police and they're already on their way? They'll find out that Ellen is missing and Mick will attest to us having an argument last night.

I take out my phone, call Ellen's number. Again it goes through to voicemail, again I leave a message asking her to call me back urgently. I check my emails in the hope that there's something from Layla but there's nothing.

I don't know how long I've been sitting there when my phone rings. Please let it be Ellen, please let it be Ellen, I pray as I fish it from my pocket. It's Harry.

"Is everything all right, Finn? Alice said you were looking for me."

"No, not really. Can you talk?"

"The thing is, I'm a bit tied up at the moment. I'm abroad."

"Yes, I know." I wait for him to tell me where he is and when he doesn't it quickly turns into awkwardness.

"Can I phone you back? In about ten minutes?" Harry asks, breaking the silence.

"Yes, of course."

"I'll call you back."

He hangs up and I sit with my phone in my hand, playing over the conversation again. Something isn't right. He didn't even ask what the problem was when I told him something had happened. Why was that? And why hadn't he called me back until his secretary asked him to? He must have seen that I'd tried to get hold of him earlier, he must have listened to my messages asking him to call me straight back. Did he already know what the problem was, did he already know that Ellen had disappeared?

How many times am I going to wonder if there's something going on between Harry and Ellen before I actually believe it? When I'd asked Harry if he was in love with Ellen, he had denied it, said she wasn't his type. Had he been lying, had I been right all those weeks ago when I thought he was behind the Russian dolls? Was it him who lured me to the cottage so that Ellen could leave while I was away? But why bring me back to the house so quickly? The answer stares me in the face. To frame me for her disappearance, to make it look as if I killed her.

Realizing the precariousness of my position, I feel ill. If Ellen doesn't turn up soon, if the police become involved, not only could Mick attest to our argument last night, he could also attest to me leaving soon after in the car. And then the police might start wondering if Ellen's body was in the trunk and if I dumped it somewhere before coming back home. They might think my visit to Mick this morning was some kind of ruse or distraction, part of a plan to cover my tracks.

My phone rings, making me jump, because it's still in my hand. I take a moment to compose myself, because I have a horrible feeling Harry is going to tell me something I don't want to hear.

"Harry?"

"Look, Finn, there's something I need to tell you."

"Is she with you?" I ask dully.

"Yes." He gives an awkward laugh. "I'm sorry, I should have told you—we should have told you," he corrects. "But we didn't know how you would feel about it."

I close my eyes, hardly able to believe that what I feared was true.

"How do you expect me to feel?" I explode. "I've been betrayed by my best friend."

"That's a bit harsh," he protests.

"Harsh?" White hot anger rises in me. "Why couldn't you just have told me instead of playing all those stupid games?"

"What stupid games?"

"You know damn well! All those stupid Russian dolls, all those emails. Why make me think that Layla was back? Do you realize what it's been like for me? How could you be so cruel?"

"Whoa, buddy, I think you need to calm down. First of all, I don't know anything about emails and secondly, the only Russian dolls I have any knowledge of is the one I found and the ones you told me about." He stops and I hear a woman's voice in the background. "Hold on," he says, "I'm going to pass you to Ruby. Maybe she can work out what you're on about."

I feel as if I've been hit with a brick. Ruby?

Her voice comes down the line. "Hello, Finn." She sounds hesitant, wary. "Is everything all right?"

It takes me a while to answer, to get my thoughts in some sort of order.

"No, not really," I say eventually. "Ellen's gone missing and when I couldn't get hold of Harry, I thought—well, I thought she might be with him."

There's a stunned silence. "Harry and *Ellen*? No, that just wouldn't happen." In the background, I hear Harry groan. "But listen, Finn—when you say that Ellen's missing, what do you mean? Since when?"

"We had a row last night. I left for a bit and when I came back, she was gone."

"But she'll be back, surely, once she's cooled off? I mean, it's only a question of hours. It's not as if she's been missing for days."

"I think she might be with Layla."

"Layla? So she's turned up, then?"

"Yes, I think so. Last night, she told me to go to the cottage in St. Mary's, so I went, but she wasn't there. When I messaged her to see where she was, she told me she was at the house—here, in Simonsbridge. So I turned around and on the way back a message came in saying that I should have got rid of Ellen. And when I got back here, Ellen was gone."

"She didn't leave a note or anything?"

"No. But because of the message I got from Layla, I'm worried she might be in some kind of danger."

She's silent for a moment. "You don't seriously think that Layla would harm Ellen, do you?"

"I don't know. I hope not. But Layla's actions over the last few weeks suggest that she's not exactly rational."

"I take it you haven't told the police that Ellen is missing."

"No, I was going to give it a few more hours. Peggy's missing too," I add.

"Oh, Finn," she says softly, because she understands how much of a blow that is to me.

"It's OK," I say. "I'm hoping she's with Ellen. She won't let

Layla harm her." I hear Harry saying something to her in the background.

"Harry says to tell you that we'll leave in the next few hours and be with you tomorrow. We're in the Bahamas so we can't get there any quicker," she adds apologetically.

"The Bahamas?"

"Yes. We'll check flights and get back to you."

"No, don't come back, it's fine."

"We should have told you," Ruby says, "but it was one of those weird things. When I told Harry—you know, when you brought him to the pub that time and he stayed behind for a drink—that I fancied a break somewhere exotic, he recommended the Bahamas and said that if I went, he'd join me. I didn't think he would," she adds. "Yet here he is."

"So when are you due back?"

"In three days."

"Well, hopefully Ellen will have turned up by then," I say, trying to inject my voice with a little lightheartedness.

"Phone the police. Let us know if you have any news. And if you need to talk, you know where we are."

I hang up. At least I know Ruby and Harry are there if I need them. I take a minute to work out how I feel about the two of them being together and realize that I'm fine with it. Then I remember Ellen and how she's still missing.

I dial her number again, leave another message. As I put my phone back in my pocket my hand comes into contact with the little Russian doll I found on the landing. I take it out and examine it closely, wondering if it comes from the pile that Ellen threw down on the bed upstairs, the ones from my office. Maybe she'd had it in her hand and dropped it on the way out to the car. Not dropped it, put it there, because if she had dropped it, it wouldn't have been standing upright. This doll had been placed as carefully as all the others I'd found. Did that mean that it was Layla who left it, not Ellen?

I go upstairs onto the landing. I had found it about halfway along, bang in the middle of the floor, equidistant from each wall. I crouch down and examine the wooden floorboards, not really knowing what I'm looking for. But there's nothing, and disappointed, I get to my feet. I'm reading too much into it; it's just a Russian doll. It's still in my hand so I stoop and place it in the middle of the floor, more or less where I found it. Straightening up again, I look down at it. Why there? I ask it silently. Why were you standing there? I look up and down the corridor, up and down the walls, up at the ceiling. And see, directly above where the Russian doll is standing, the trapdoor to the attic.

FIFTY-FOUR

FINN

The hairs on the back of my neck, on my arms, stand on end. I haven't been up to the attic since I first moved into the house when Harry asked me whether I'd mind if his friend, the owner, kept some of his things up there. As far as I'm concerned, it's out of bounds and Ellen, to my knowledge, has never been up there. The weirdest thought comes to me—what if Layla has been hiding up there? It would take her CLOSER THAN YOU THINK message to a whole new level. It would also explain how she'd been able to leave the Russian dolls so easily. I dismiss the idea almost at once. I've been wrong about many things today but to think that Layla could have been living in the attic without me and Ellen knowing is ridiculous. There's always one of us around. Before, Ellen and I would take Peggy for a walk every afternoon, and be gone for at least an hour, but we hadn't been doing that lately. One of us usually takes Peggy on our own, so there's always someone here. Even though I spend a lot of time in my office, I could come in at any time. Unless Ellen had helped Layla hide. Maybe Layla turned up one day and begged Ellen to hide her. But why? And would Ellen really have hidden Layla in the attic without telling me?

There's only one way to find out. I stretch up, push the trap door open with one hand, release the ladder that's there and pull it down. I go up the first couple of rungs, testing it for my weight, then carry on up and into the loft. The roof is too low for me to stand upright so I stay hunched over, looking for the light switch. I flick it on and a dull gleam fills the attic.

I look around. Nothing seems out of place and there aren't any signs of someone having lived up here, no mattress, no personal belongings, no remnants of food lying around. I walk over to the carefully labeled boxes stacked against the far wall and, using my phone to throw a little more light over them, I check that none have been displaced. Everything seems in order; they don't look as if they've been disturbed in all the years they've been up here. I turn to the wall on the right where a couple of chairs, an old writing desk and a chest of drawers are propped. I go over and take a closer look. They're covered in a thick layer of dust, reminding me of the cottage in St. Mary's. In the writing desk I find a couple of old pens, and in one of the drawers, some old coins. But the others are empty.

I cross the attic to the left-hand wall. There's a large wooden chest, about five feet by three, with a pile of blankets neatly stacked on top. Nothing out of place there either. I take a last look around, glad that my fears about Layla hiding up here are unfounded. I'm just about to go back to the trapdoor when I find myself taking another look at the wooden chest. Nothing out of place—yet there's something about it that doesn't seem quite right. It's the dust, I realize. Or rather, the lack of it. I reach out and run my finger along the edge of the lid; it comes away clean.

I bring my hand down hard on the top blanket, expecting dust to fly everywhere but there is very little. Which means they were protected by something until very recently. My heart quickens. Had they been in the chest and were taken out to make room for something else?

Something else. Unease prickles my spine and I find myself taking a step back, away from the chest. My heartbeat slows to a dull thud, a response to the horror that is spreading through my body. I try to close off my mind, to not go where it wants to take me, but everything—the countdown, Layla's last message telling me that I should have chosen her, the little Russian doll placed directly under the trapdoor as a kind of clue—all seem to point to one thing. It isn't possible, I mutter to myself, it isn't possible, Layla wouldn't harm Ellen. But hadn't she told me to get rid of Ellen, hadn't she given me ten days? Had she ended up doing what I couldn't?

I can barely breathe. I need to call the police, now, before it's too late. But it is too late. If Layla has done what I think she's done, it's already too late. Unless she hasn't—I can hardly bear to think the word—*killed* Ellen, only hidden her.

I drop to my knees in front of the chest. I don't want to open it but I know that I have to. Please God, please God, don't let Ellen be dead, please don't let her be dead.

My hands are shaking as I move the blankets from the top of the chest and lay them on the floor. My breath judders in my throat, stopping air from reaching my lungs. I grip the edge of the lid, steadying myself. Then, dragging my courage from where it's residing in the pit of my stomach, I throw the lid open and look inside.

My mind spins in disbelief, draining the blood from my face.

FIFTY-FIVE

FINN

I stare down at the dissected corpses of hundreds of Russian dolls, wondering if I'm hallucinating. I reach out and touch one. The feel of the painted wood against my hand tells me they're real. But my mind won't accept it. I was so sure that I'd find Ellen trussed up inside the chest, dead even, that I begin digging underneath the dolls, scooping them to one side of the chest, then to the other, believing that I'm going to find her. And then, when I finally accept that she isn't there, I let out a howl of pure rage at being fooled by Layla yet again. I can't believe that I'm no nearer to finding Ellen, or that I'm still part of Layla's macabre game, that now I'm going to have to figure out why she's left a chest full of Russian dolls for me to discover, and try to work out the message behind it.

A message. On my knees, I begin rifling through the wooden carcasses, hoping to find something, a doll still intact with a piece of paper hidden inside, maybe. But they've all been pulled apart and it suddenly dawns on me that I haven't come across a single one of the tiniest dolls. What I have in front of me are their left-behind, unwanted relatives. Which means that unless Layla brought them all to the house with her earlier this evening, took them up to the attic and hid them in the chest—which is possible but not likely, because there are so many of them—the little Russian dolls that Ellen and I found outside the house, or received through the post, all originated here, in the attic.

Shock rocks me back onto the floor. I sit, my elbows on my knees, staring at the chest, while the truth ricochets through my brain—that Ellen is somehow involved in all this. Layla couldn't have got the dolls into the attic without help from someone. She's never been to the house so she wouldn't have known the attic existed, or that the dolls could be hidden there. Only Ellen could have told her.

During all those weeks when Layla had been in contact with me, it had never occurred to me that she might also have been in contact with Ellen, sending her emails just as she'd been sending me emails. Manipulating Ellen just as she'd been manipulating me. When she'd been urging me to tell Ellen she was back, had she been urging Ellen to tell me the same thing? Had she been playing us off against each other? Had she arranged to meet Ellen somewhere, just as she had arranged to meet me? Is that where Ellen had gone those times she'd left a note on the table for me, the notes saying she had gone shopping? She never normally left notes, she always came and told me if she was going out, yet those two times she hadn't. Was it because she didn't want me to know she was going out in case I asked to go with her? Maybe she had only asked me to join her for lunch to give her notes a more genuine flavor, counting on the fact that I probably wouldn't see the notes until it was too late, or not at all. And if I had, and had phoned her, she would have told me that she was already on her way home. Not only that, when she'd come back that time, I'd thought she was upset with me. But maybe the reason she was upset was because she'd gone to meet Layla and Layla hadn't turned up, like she used to do with me.

I leave the attic, desperate to disprove every theory I've just come up with. But the absence of signs of a struggle in the bedroom or anywhere else in the house again suggests that Ellen left of her own accord, that Layla didn't force her to leave. I check her office and find that not only is her computer switched off, it's also unplugged. It's useless to me anyway; even if I get it up and running again, I don't know her email password. There must have been something incriminating on it—emails between her and Layla, perhaps—for her to have turned it off so completely. Or perhaps it's a statement of intent, as in "I'm never going to use my computer again because I'm never coming back."

What had happened here, just a few hours ago? Had Layla asked Ellen to choose between me and her, just as she had asked me to choose between Ellen and her, and had Ellen chosen Layla? I couldn't blame her, not after what I'd done, not after I'd chosen Layla over her.

My mind plows on relentlessly, finding new theories to torment myself with. Maybe Ellen was part of it all along, maybe she's always known Layla's whereabouts. Maybe my whole relationship with her was a farce; payback for the hurt I caused Layla, even though Layla had hurt me first. Is that really what this is all about? Revenge? It's hard to believe.

A wave of exhaustion hits me. I check my phone and see that it's midday. I try and work out how long I've been awake but my mind is so fuddled it takes me a while. I didn't sleep all night, so nearly thirty hours. Suddenly, more than anything I want to sleep, because when I wake up I might find it's all been some terrible nightmare. But first, Tony.

I psyche myself up so that I'm not disappointed if I can't get through to him, now that I've decided to tell him everything. But he answers almost at once.

"I need your help, Tony."

"Fire away," he says. "But first, take a deep breath." And I realize how agitated I must sound. It's nothing to how I sound when I begin speaking, though. Even to my ears the whole, unabridged story—the Russian dolls, the emails, my trips to St. Mary's and Ellen's subsequent disappearance—sounds mad. I sound mad. When I eventually get to the end of my monologue, because Tony didn't interrupt me once, there's only silence, confirming what I thought, that I sound completely unhinged.

"I'm coming down," he says, putting me out of my misery.

It's as if a huge weight has been lifted from my shoulders. "Thanks, Tony, I really appreciate it."

"But I need you to do something for me."

"Of course."

"I want to check a few things this end first so I'll be a few hours. Make yourself something to eat and get yourself to bed. You sound as if you're at death's door. Leave the key under the mat and I'll let myself in."

"Thanks, Tony," I say again.

"See you later."

I feel as if I could never eat again so I go for a long, hot shower instead. After, I feel so hungry that I get through half a loaf of bread, making slice after slice of toast. Then I go upstairs to the bedroom, push the pile of Russian dolls off the bed and climb in. I'm asleep before my head has even touched the pillow.

When I next open my eyes, I think I've only slept for a few hours because it's still light outside. Just as I'm wondering if Tony has arrived, I hear his voice coming from downstairs. I pull on some clothes and find Ruby and Harry sitting in the kitchen with him.

"When did you get here?" I ask, giving them both a hug, realizing they've cut their holiday short.

"A couple of hours ago. Tony let us in." Harry sees me trying to work it out. "I chartered a plane," he explains.

"Even so," I say. "What time is it?"

"Around seven, I guess." I look at him in bewilderment. "In the morning," he adds.

I can't believe I slept the rest of yesterday afternoon and the night away. I look at the three of them, genuinely touched that they've rushed to be with me. "Thanks for coming, all of you."

"You might not be so grateful when you hear what we've got to say," Ruby says. My heart plummets and catching the look on my face, she hastens to reassure me. "No, nothing like that. All I mean is that the three of us have been discussing everything and seem to have come to the same conclusion."

"Give the man a chance to have a cup of coffee first," Harry protests.

I pull out a chair and sit down. "It's OK, I'd rather know."

Tony clears his throat. "Despite our best efforts, we haven't found a single trace of Layla anywhere in Cheltenham. We've looked at the guest records from every single boardinghouse and hotel, we've shown both her old photo and a digital reconstruction of what she might look like now around in cafés and restaurants and have come up with nothing." He pauses. "And then there's the chest full of wooden dolls you found in the attic—I went up to take a look, by the way."

"Yes, of course," I say, wondering what he's getting at.

"Logically, they can't have got there without Ellen knowing about them," Ruby says. "I mean, how would Layla have got them past both of you?"

"You think Ellen was helping Layla," I say dully. "Don't worry, I've already thought of it." They exchange uneasy glances. "What?" I ask.

"We actually think it might be a bit simpler than that." This time it's Harry.

"What do you mean?" I ask, wondering what they're so reluctant to tell me.

"That maybe Layla was never back. That maybe, there was only Ellen."

FIFTY-SIX

FINN

I look around the table at them, thinking they're having a joke. When I see that they're deadly serious, I realize that Tony didn't understand anything I told him. Irritated that I'm going to have to explain it all again, I cut to the best piece of evidence I have.

"If you remember," I say, "Ellen saw Layla in Cheltenham."

"But *you* never actually saw her," Tony points out.

"No, but Thomas did, outside the cottage at St. Mary's."

"Maybe it was Ellen he saw."

I shake my head stubbornly. "Thomas wouldn't have made that mistake."

"Ellen could just have pretended to see Layla in Cheltenham," Ruby says, almost apologetically.

I open my mouth, ready to protest, then close it again quickly. Ruby is right, it's possible that Ellen only pretended to see Layla.

"So how did the Russian doll get onto the car that day?" I ask. "I dropped Ellen off at the hairdresser and she had only just finished having her hair done when I went back to pick her up."

"She could have nipped back after you left, pretended to the hairdresser that she'd forgotten to pay for the parking."

I search my mind for something else. "Seriously, you expect me to believe that the emails I received, every single one of them, even the ones that told me to get rid of Ellen, came from Ellen herself?"

"It's possible," Harry says.

"Don't forget that she got a Russian doll in the post. She'd hardly have sent it to herself."

"Why not?" Harry counters. "Surely it would be the sensible thing to do, to make it seem as if she was being targeted by Layla too."

"You're mad," I tell them. "You've lost your minds. Of course Ellen isn't behind this. And if what you say is true, how would she have got into the cottage? Only Layla and I had keys."

"Maybe Ellen found yours and had a copy made."

"Not possible—they were in a safe in the bank."

"Then maybe Layla had a copy made and sent them to Ellen before she disappeared."

"She would have asked me first." I look around the table at them. "Look, Ellen isn't that kind of person. She's not devious, or cruel. And she would have to be a bloody brilliant actress to pull it off." They still don't seem convinced and because I trust their judgment, doubt begins to worm its way in. It would, after all, explain so much. It would explain how the dolls were left outside the house with such ease, without anybody seeing. The first doll that appeared, Ellen only needed to pretend that she found it on the wall for me to believe it, the second she could have put on the wall once I'd left to go to the village that morning. Ruby has already worked out how she could have got the third doll onto the car in Cheltenham. I continue onto the fourth, the one left in The Jackdaw. She could easily have slipped it on the plate before leaving for the toilet. The dolls that came in the post—she only had to walk down to the post office in the village while I was in my office, a matter of ten minutes at the most. I wouldn't have noticed that she was gone—hadn't she reproached me for not noticing that she'd gone into Cheltenham those couple of times? And on the two Sundays, when there wasn't any post, she had simply left dolls on the wall again, the first once I'd left to go to the village for bread, the second as we'd left together. She only had to lag behind me slightly and stretch out her arm. I wouldn't have noticed a thing.

I continue rifling through my mind. What about the Russian doll I'd found on Pharos Hill, how had that one got there? Ellen had been at home when I'd left that morning. But I'd gone to the cottage in St. Mary's first, so she would have had time to get to Pharos Hill before I finally worked out that that was where I was meant to be. Had she been laughing when I'd hurried off for my secret meeting with Layla, knowing that I'd automatically assume she was referring to St. Mary's when she said that I had the address?

The odds that Ellen could be behind these nightmarish few weeks are stacking up against her. A wave of fury hits.

"I'm going to check her computer," I say roughly. "See if the emails came from her."

"Do you know her email password?" Ruby asks.

"No, but I'm going to have a damn good try working it out."

I get to my feet. "But if she's as devious as she appears to have been, I doubt we'll find anything."

They follow me into Ellen's study. I plug in her computer, sit down at her desk, start it up and log on using the Rudolph Hill address.

"I can't mess up the password or I'll be locked out," I say, realizing. "Any ideas?"

"I don't think she'd choose something abstract, I think it's more likely to be something connected with everything," Ruby says.

"Pharos Hill, maybe?" Harry suggests. "Where you had the ceremony?"

"Yes, but Pharos Hill what? A date?"

"Try Pharos Hill and the date of the ceremony."

"OK." I type in *PharosHill140413*. It doesn't work.

"How about Pharos Hill and Ellen's date of birth? Or Layla's?"

"We're sticking with Pharos Hill, then."

"It's probably our best bet," Harry says.

I type *PharosHill* in again. "Which date of birth?"

"Layla's," Ruby says. "It was her memorial."

I add *260486*. It doesn't work.

I try to get myself into Ellen's mind-set. What other date could be linked to Pharos Hill? Other than the date of the ceremony, I can't think of a single one.

"Last go," I say. I type *PharosHill*. "Any suggestions for what comes next?"

"Try the year of the ceremony, just the year," Tony suggests. "2013. People tend to use years, not actual dates."

I tag *2013* onto *PharosHill*.

"Oh my God," breathes Ruby. "It's worked!"

"It's almost as if she wanted you to be able to access her

emails," Harry remarks. He lapses into silence and stares at the screen. Because the inbox contains only messages from me.

My heart thumps dully in my chest. I don't want to open the sent messages but I know that I have to. I click on the box, praying it will be empty. But there they are, in all their glory, each and every one of Layla's messages to me.

The silence in the room is absolute.

I run a hand through my hair. "Fuck."

"I'm sorry, Finn," Ruby says quietly.

I look at the screen again. "No. This isn't the Ellen I know. She's one of the sanest people I've ever come across." I twist in the chair, search out Harry. "You know her, Harry. Do you think she could do something like this?"

"Not really, no," he admits. "But how well did we actually know her? She had a troubled past, losing her mother, then Layla, then her father. Who knows how that affected her?"

"We already worked out that whoever was behind the dolls and the emails was unbalanced," Ruby reminds me.

"Yes, but to do something like this? I mean, why?"

"I don't know—revenge for Layla's disappearance?"

"Could be," Tony says. "In a warped kind of way. As in—you were responsible for her losing her sister."

"But I paid the price!" I say, furious. "I already paid the price! Why make me go through it all again?"

"To test you?" Ruby says.

"We'll be in the kitchen." Harry puts a hand on my shoulder.

They leave and I sit there in the office of a woman who, in the space of a few minutes, has become a complete stranger. It's a struggle to put aside my emotions but I don't want them to cloud my judgment. I look at the emails again, thinking about what Harry said, about Ellen choosing a password that was easy to crack, as if she wanted me to find them. Because otherwise, she would have deleted them before she left. It's why she unplugged her computer, to get me to look. So if she wanted me to find them, why? Because she was proud of what she'd done and wanted me to know how clever she'd been? Or out of kindness, so that I wouldn't be left hanging? Was that why she left the doll on the landing upstairs, which led to me discovering the dolls in the chest? It seems she wanted me to know it was her all along.

Hopelessness hits me in the gut like a physical force. It's hard enough to accept not only that the relative happiness I'd found with Ellen has gone, but that it was based on a lie. If Ellen had wanted to hurt me, there's no better way she could have chosen. And that's hard too, because it doesn't equate with the Ellen I knew. We had lived and loved together for a little over a year, just as I had lived with and loved Layla for a little over a year. Is it significant that I was with each sister for approximately the same amount of time? Was that the real timing issue? We—Tony, Harry, Ruby and I—presumed that it was the wedding announcement that had triggered the beginning of the "Layla is alive" campaign. Maybe the two were linked—once Ellen had got me to propose to her, it was time to wind up our relationship. Even though she had in a way manipulated it, had she seen my marriage proposal as a betrayal of her sister? It would mean that our whole relationship had been some kind of test, and one I'd failed miserably. But to be that loyal to a sister, to go to such lengths, seems extraordinary.

A flash of anger ignites in my brain. I need to find Ellen. So where has she gone? Abroad? Not if she has Peggy with her. To the cottage in St. Mary's? Or somewhere else, somewhere she thinks I won't be able to find her? If she left as soon as I went tearing off to St. Mary's, she could be halfway up the country by now. She wouldn't have gone south, it wouldn't be far enough away. She must have had a destination in mind, she wouldn't be driving around aimlessly, not in the middle of the night. Is she in a hotel, sleeping the sleep of an innocent while I'm condemned to hell? On impulse, I pull her keyboard toward me and bring up her search history, hoping to find a link to Booking.com or some other accommodation website. There isn't, but there's a link to a CalMac Ferries website. I open it quickly and find they run services between the mainland and the Scottish Isles. And when I look further, I find the timetable for services between Ullapool and Stornoway, on Lewis.

"Harry!" I yell.

"You OK?" he asks, coming through in a hurry.

"What's the quickest way of getting to Lewis?" I ask urgently. "Is there a flight or something?"

"I have no idea. I don't even know if there's an airport on Lewis. Why do you want to go there?"

"Because that's where Ellen's gone. She was looking up the ferry crossings, so she'll have driven up, or got the train part of the way. But there has to be a quicker way." I go onto Google and type in: *flights to Lewis*. "Yes—there's an airport at Stornoway. I can fly to Glasgow and take another plane from there."

I start looking up flights, aware of Harry hovering uncertainly behind me.

"What time is it now?" I ask. "There's a flight that leaves for Glasgow from Birmingham at eleven forty—can I make it?"

"Maybe," Harry says reluctantly. "It's only eight thirty. But even if Ellen is there, are you sure it's a good idea to go charging up to see her?"

"Definitely! I need to speak to her, I want to know why . . . why she set up this whole charade to make me believe Layla was alive. I want to ask her how she could be so damn cruel!"

"So why not wait a few days? There's no rush, is there? Why don't we see what Tony says?"

"No." I shake my head vehemently. I turn my attention back to the screen. "If I don't make the Glasgow flight there's another at twelve forty, to Edinburgh."

"You might not get a ticket for today," Harry warns, as if he's hoping I won't.

"Then I'll charter a plane," I say fiercely. "I'm going, Harry, and nobody is going to stop me."

"Then I'll come with you."

"No—hold on, there's a ticket for the Glasgow flight, just let me get it." It takes a while to complete the transaction and when I've finished, I raise my head and find him watching me. "Thanks, Harry, but I'm going on my own."

"Then at least let me drive you to the airport."

I hesitate, then realize I'm too wound up to drive. "Thanks. But we can't tell Ruby and Tony where I'm going, OK?"

The look of resignation on his face tells me he was hoping they'd be able to dissuade me but he nods his agreement. We go through to the kitchen where Ruby and Tony are sitting, their hands clasped around mugs of hot coffee, as if bracing themselves for the coming storm.

"Good idea," Ruby says encouragingly, when we tell her we're going for a drive to clear our heads, and Harry and I both know she'll kill him when she finds out the truth.

I don't even take a change of clothes with me. I don't intend staying on Lewis. I'm going for one reason, and one reason only.

FIFTY-SEVEN

FINN

It takes just over an hour to get to the airport and I use the time to work out the whereabouts of Ellen's house on Lewis. I know it's along the Pentland Road and I remember Layla telling me that when they were young, whenever she and Ellen went on walks with their mother, they would stop to run sticks along a metal grating, a cattle guard, just below their house. She also mentioned a loch nearby, so using Google Maps I try and locate roughly where the house might be. It isn't easy because the Pentland Road splits in two at one point, but somewhere along the left-hand turn I eventually find a cattle guard, a loch, and a stone house all within close proximity of each other.

Harry wants to come into the airport with me but I persuade him to go back to the others.

"Be careful," he says, giving me a man hug. He keeps his tone neutral but the warning is there and I know it's not me he's worried about.

I nearly go mad on the journey. Stuck on a plane, then at Glasgow Airport, then on another flight, all I can think is that Layla isn't back, that she never was, that I'll never see her again. The words go round in my head—*Layla isn't back, she never was, I'll never see her again*—building on the anger I feel toward Ellen. When I finally land in Stornoway, and find driving rain sweeping across the airfield and a mean wind whipping itself into a frenzy, my mood, already black, becomes darker still.

It's another frustrating hour before I'm driving through the small village of Marybank toward the Pentland Road. My fault. I should have thought to organize a rental car on the way to the airport instead of expecting to pick one up the moment I arrived. The landscape, which at first is dotted with sheep and low-slung white stone houses, soon becomes bleak and unforgiving, an endless expanse of peat bogs with nothing to provide relief for the eye save the distant hills, brooding and menacing, mottled with bare rock. The fact that I don't pass a single vehicle only lends to the feeling that I'm driving into the back of beyond, to the end of the earth.

My mind keeps going back to the keys. There's something that isn't adding up. If Layla had wanted Ellen to have a set, in case she wanted to come to St. Mary's at a time when we weren't there, she would have told me. There was no reason for her not to; she would have known I wouldn't mind. So it's more plausible that Ellen has only had Layla's set of keys since Layla disappeared. Did Layla send them to her after she disappeared from the parking lot? Or—and now my heart starts racing—did Layla give them to her in person?

The car skews to the left as I momentarily lose control, distracted at the implications behind my last thought—that sometime after Layla disappeared, she and Ellen met up. Is that why Ellen never questioned me about what happened that night, because she already knew? Why she never speculated about where Layla might be, if she had been kidnapped, if she was dead or alive, because she knew? I had put it down to a sensitivity for my feelings—but could her reserve have been for a darker, secret reason? Had Layla somehow made her way back to Lewis after she disappeared from the picnic area? Is that why Ellen has brought me here, why she left the link to CalMac ferries on her computer, because this is where Layla is?

It's a struggle to exercise caution, to not get carried away. I remind myself of all Ellen has done, her subterfuge, her secrets, her lies. Isn't this what she's wanted me to believe all along, that Layla is alive? But whatever the truth is, I'm certain Ellen knows more about Layla's disappearance than I could ever have imagined.

The road becomes a single-track lane and each jolt, each bump, fuels the fury that has been steadily building inside me since I saw my emails to Layla on Ellen's computer. Through the rain, my eyes pick out the inky waters of a loch to my left, black reeds jutting through its surface like a three-day growth and I reduce my speed, searching for a cattle guard. Seconds later, my wheels find it, jarring my concentration. I pull in on the other side of the guard. As I get out of the car, adrenaline courses through me.

I look around, shielding my eyes from the rain. Fifty yards or so ahead, on a hill to my right, there's an old stone house with a corrugated roof, reddish in places with years-old rust. Even at this distance, I can see it's deserted. I make my way along the road and up the rough footpath to the house anyway, my shoulders hunched against the foul weather. I'd given no thought to rain when I'd thrown a thin jumper on over my T-shirt as I left for the airport, and I'm already soaked through. As I approach the cottage, the feeling that I've come to the wrong place deepens; there's no sign of life, no light at a window. I realize that there's no trace of Ellen's car—the logical place to park it would have been where I parked mine, by the cattle guard—and it occurs to me that the link to CalMac Ferries might be another of her ruses, a trick to deter me from finding her true destination. Overcome with frustration, I give a cry of pure rage.

Something—a sound—stops me in my tracks. It comes again—a small bark.

"Peggy!" I call. The door to the house, slightly ajar—I can see that now—is nudged open and Peggy comes lumbering toward me.

"Peggy!" I crouch down so that she can lick my face, telling her she's beautiful, that I've missed her because, somewhere deep in my heart, Peggy has always represented Layla.

Layla. "Where's Ellen, Peggy?" I ask. She nuzzles my face a last time then squirms from my grasp.

I follow her into the house. The first thing I notice is how cold it is. There's a room to the right and through the open doorway I see Ellen huddled on a sofa, a blanket drawn up around her. She must have heard me arriving, she must have heard Peggy bark, she must know I'm here, yet she doesn't move. After a moment, she raises her head, as if only just aware of my presence, and the look of delight on her face—that she has succeeded in dragging me all the way to Lewis—infuriates me.

I take a step toward her.

"You came," she says, her voice shaking with cold. Or maybe nerves.

"How could you, Ellen?" I ask harshly, aware that Peggy has curled up at Ellen's feet. Another betrayal. "How could you be so cruel?"

Her face, so full of expectancy, sags, and I feel a savage pleasure that she has underestimated me.

"I thought . . ." she falters.

"What?" I snarl.

"That you'd come to bring me back."

"Bring you back?" I look at her uncomprehendingly. "To where?" She stares back at me, a blank expression on her face. "Simonsbridge?" She drops her head—was that a nod? "I haven't come to bring you back, I don't want you back. Not after what you've done." She flinches at my anger. "Why did you do it, Ellen? We were happy, weren't we? We were going to get married, for God's sake! Why wasn't that enough for you?"

"Because you didn't love me, not like you loved Layla."

I ignore the hopelessness in her voice and take another step toward her. "I could never love you like I loved Layla," I say, looming over her. "Why did you have to make me think Layla was alive? I might have been able to forgive you anything, but not that. Not making me believe Layla was alive."

"Layla is alive," she whispers.

My heart thuds. So where is she?

Ellen takes her hand from under the blanket and raises it to her head. "Here," she says, tapping the side of it.

I give a harsh laugh. "You're mad." I reach down and grab her shoulders, bring my face closer to hers. "Tell me, Ellen—how did you get Layla's keys?" She doesn't answer, so I give her a shake. "How did you get Layla's keys?" I repeat, louder this time.

"She gave them to me."

"When?" I bark. "Before she disappeared or after?"

"After."

"Did she come to Lewis, Ellen? Did Layla come to Lewis?"

Her eyes brim with tears. "Yes," she whispers.

My breath comes juddering out of me. Be careful, a voice warns. Remember, she lies.

"So how did she get here? How did she get from France to here?"

That blank look again. I'm still gripping her shoulders so I lift her to her feet. She stumbles against me and I have to stop myself from pushing her away.

"Answer me, Ellen! How did Layla get to Lewis from France?"

"A lady took her." Her voice trembles. "Then she hid in a caravan, then she got a lift, then she got the ferry, then she walked."

"You're lying! There was no lady!"

"Yes." Ellen nods her head. "The driver of the car."

"It was a man!"

"No, no." Another vigorous shake of her head. "It was a lady."

I stare down at her. Could she be right, is that why the police never found him?

"So if Layla came to Lewis," I say, moving on, "why didn't the police find her?"

A crafty look comes over her face. "She hid."

"Where?"

"Here."

"Why? Why did she hide?"

"So he wouldn't find her."

"Who?" I cry, suddenly afraid.

"Him." I wait. "Our father."

Not me then. I look hard at her, barely recognizing her, wondering if she's mad, or just very clever?

"How long did she stay hiding?"

Ellen smiles at this. "Forever."

There's something about the smile that chills me. "Is Layla dead, Ellen?"

She makes a noise, half-laugh, half-sob. "Almost."

A terrible dread takes hold of me. "Where's Layla, Ellen?"

Her eyes dart toward the door and before I can stop her, she wrenches herself from my grasp and runs from the room.

"Ellen!" The roar in my voice matches the roaring in my ears. I tear after her. "Ellen!"

Dusk has arrived, dragging a dark sky behind it. The wind whips my face as I follow her, the ground soft beneath my feet. I catch up with her by a stone wall, grabbing her arm, pulling her back toward me, spinning her round to face me.

"Where's Layla?" I yell, aware of Peggy behind me, growling, something she never does. "Tell me where she is!" I'm shaking her so hard she can't answer but I can't stop, I can't stop the rage, because somewhere inside me, I want to kill her. "Where is Layla!"

"Don't, Finn!" she screams. Something in her voice stops me in mid-shake. I push her blindly away from me. She cries out, I hear a thud—no, not a thud, a crack, the sound of a skull on stone. I can't see, there's too much mist, not in the air, in my eyes. I lift my face to the sky, letting the rain wash it away, my breath juddering in and out of me, fighting for control. I claw my way back, lower my head, open my eyes. They come into focus and fall on Ellen, lying motionless on the ground. My heart leaps in fear.

"Ellen!" I crouch on the ground beside her, bend my body over her, protecting her from the elements. "Ellen!"

Her eyes flicker open. Her skin is waxen, nothing to do with the rain.

"Layla," she whispers. "Layla."

I put my hand under her head, lift it slightly so that she can see me. "You'll be all right," I promise desperately.

"Layla."

"Layla isn't here," I say gently.

She shakes her head. A trickle of blood seeps from her nose.

"Layla," she says again. "Not Ellen, Layla."

Her eyes fix on mine, then close. I stare down at her, my fear doubling in size. Still cradling her head, I check her neck for a pulse with my other hand, my fingers trembling on her wet skin. It's there, but faint, so faint. Next to me, Peggy whimpers.

"It's all right, Peggy," I tell her. "It's all right."

I reach into my pocket, take out my phone, switch it on. As I feared, there's no network. I twist my head this way and that, looking for a house, for someone to help. There is nothing and no one, so I gather Ellen into my arms and carry her down to the car, trying to hurry, trying not to slip, or trip over Peggy, who is walking too close to my heels. I open the door, lay Ellen on the back seat, pull my jumper over my head. And as I fold it into a rough pillow, I see that my hand, the one that had cradled her head, is stained with blood.

Peggy climbs in and lies down on the floor. I close the door behind her, try my phone again. There's still nothing.

I drive as fast as I can, as fast as I dare, talking to Ellen over the sound of the wipers, telling her that it's going to be all right, that she's going to be all right, my mind chewing feverishly over what she had said. Not Ellen, Layla. Not Ellen, Layla.

"No." Someone moans—me, not Ellen. "Please God, no, don't let it be that, don't let it be that."

I reach the end of the single-track road, driving faster now because the road is better. As I get nearer to Stornoway, I hear the sound of what seems like a hundred messages arriving on my phone, and realizing that the phone signal has kicked in, I pull quickly to a stop so that I can call for help. There are missed calls from Harry, Ruby and Tony, text messages asking me to call them but I ignore them and turn to check on Ellen. And my heart lurches, because her face is death-white and she is still, too still. Throwing my phone onto the passenger seat, I lean into the back of the car and take hold of her hand, feeling clumsily with my fingers for a pulse. I can't find one and I force myself to calm down, to stop my fingers from shaking, and try again. Still nothing. Letting go of her wrist, I wrench my door open and as I get out, the wind slams me back against the car. Opening the back door, I bend over Ellen, shielding her from the rain, and this time, search her neck for a pulse, praying that I'll find something, just a flicker, to tell me that she's still alive. But the towel under her head tells me otherwise; it is no longer stained with her blood, but soaked with it. Another moan escapes me. My phone starts ringing and I reach into the passenger seat and answer it in a daze, my eyes never leaving Ellen's face.

"Finn, thank God! Listen, Finn," Harry says, his voice urgent. "You need to look at your emails. I've sent you something, something I found on Ellen's computer. You need to read it, do you hear me? You need to read it before you see Ellen. Finn! Finn, are you there?"

I hang up. He's too late. I need to phone for an ambulance. But it's too late, far too late. I sink back onto the road. Ellen is dead. The words beat in my brain. Ellen is dead, Ellen is dead. Ellen, not Layla. Not Layla. Please God, not Layla. I need it to be Ellen. If I've killed Ellen, I can take it.

I know, though. Even before I look at the email Harry sent

me, before I even look at the attached file, I know. I read it anyway.

> I'm still here. Ellen didn't overpower me, not completely. I was stronger than she thought, stronger than I thought. She hasn't gone away though. She's still around, lurking in the shadows, I can feel her. But for now she is quiet and while she is quiet, my mind is clearer. So I'm going to use the time I have left to write to Finn, in case things don't work out as I hope.
>
> So, Finn, this is for you. When I disappeared that night, I didn't think about what I was doing or where I was going, all I wanted was to get as far away from you as possible. I thought you were going to kill me, you see. I know now that you weren't, I know that you walked away so that you wouldn't hurt me. But I didn't know that at the time. I only understood once I'd read your letter.
>
> The man that you saw coming out of the toilet block wasn't the driver of the car parked outside; he must have been one of the truck drivers. The driver of the car was a woman and as I ran down the access road onto the motorway, she nearly ran me down. When she screeched to a stop beside me, I opened the passenger door and climbed in. She looked terrified, but then a truck came down the access road behind us and she had no choice but to drive off.
>
> She wanted to drop me at the next service station but I was too afraid that you would come looking for me so I made her drive on until we reached another one a couple of minutes later. As I stood on the forecourt, my one fear was that you'd arrive at any moment. I didn't know how I was going to get to England. I didn't have my passport on me, all I had were the keys to the cottage in St. Mary's, because I was wearing

the jeans I'd been wearing the day we left. Even my little Russian doll was missing and I realized I must have dropped it when you were shaking me. It distressed me more than the lack of a passport, because it was the only thing I had to remind me of Ellen.

I decided to worry about the lack of a passport later and try and get to a port. All I could think of was getting to Lewis and this surprised me, considering how desperate I'd been to leave. But I suppose home is home and there wasn't anywhere else I could really go. Around the back of the petrol station, at the far end, I saw a couple of camper vans and a caravan parked there. The camper vans were impenetrable but when I tried the door of the caravan, it swung open, so I got in and groped my way to the back.

I must have drifted into sleep because I was woken by voices, a man and a woman talking together as they approached the van. The next thing I knew, we were moving off.

Nobody came to check inside the caravan at the port, but I suppose twelve years ago, there'd been no reason to. And it was the middle of the night. The motion of the boat soon rocked me to sleep. I only woke when we were docking, and the knowledge that I'd managed to get to England relatively easily made me confident I could get the rest of the way to Lewis.

When we eventually came to a stop a couple of hours later, the couple went straight into their house, leaving the caravan on their driveway. I looked around for some money. I knew I could probably hitchhike all the way to Ullapool but once there, I would need to take the ferry across to Stornoway. I found a few crumpled bills in the pocket of a pair of trousers and in a black handbag, a purse containing sixty pounds and a few coins. In the end, I took the whole bag, and because I was cold, a man's anorak which I wore over mine, and a woolen hat to cover my hair.

It was early morning and I remember wondering where you were, if you were back in St. Mary's, glad to be rid of me, or if you were still in France. I could hear some light traffic in the distance so I headed toward it, hoping I'd be able to hitch a lift. I immediately thought of Ellen and how horrified she'd be if she knew that I was about to do something so potentially dangerous, and a sob caught in my throat. I could hardly believe that I was about to return to the man who had so brutally murdered her and dumped her body in a peat bog. Because that's where Ellen is, Finn, in a peat bog. You have never known her, only my version of her.

My father was a violent bully of a man who tolerated Ellen and hated me. The only one who could control him was our mother and when she died, our world, already fraught with difficulty, became a nightmare. Because of my father's nature, we lived pretty much in isolation on Lewis. Although Ellen and I went to school, we had no friends. We were oddballs, part of a family who lived on the margins of society. At my mother's funeral, there were four of us, my father, me, Ellen, and a teacher from school.

Ellen was sixteen at the time of our mother's death and I was nearly fifteen. Ellen never went back to school and nobody came looking for her. Instead, she filled our mother's shoes, caring for me and our father. My mother's death had a profound effect on me. Something pinged in my brain, like an elastic snapping. I refused to accept that she was gone and would speak to her, then answer back in her voice.

"Can we have macaroni for dinner?" I would ask.

"Yes, of course," I'd say in my mother's voice, before Ellen could answer.

It drove my father into a fury and Ellen would implore me to only talk to Mum when he wasn't around. But it was my coping mechanism and I was as incapable of stopping as my father was of not drinking. I began to adopt her mannerisms and she ended up sharing my head with me. As for school, I gave up going and nobody came looking for me either. They were too afraid of my father.

Before she'd died, our mother had given Ellen a box containing money she would take from my father's wallet when he was too drunk to notice. It was her present to us, our ticket for getting away from our father, and as soon as there was enough money, we were leaving, Ellen and I together. Ellen began to calculate how much we would need to get to London. I wanted us to leave as soon as I was sixteen but Ellen wanted to wait until I was eighteen. I thought of London as a big adventure but Ellen was more cautious. We might not be happy where we were, but at least we were relatively safe. As long as we didn't do anything to annoy our father. When he was around, Ellen kept within sight and I kept out of sight. If he couldn't see Ellen he would yell for her, demanding to know where she was. If he saw me, he would roar at me to go away. I never knew why he hated me so much but I didn't care; I would have hated for him to even tolerate me.

Ellen's target was a thousand pounds. There'd been over seven hundred in the box when Mum had given it to Ellen and it took us almost three years to get the rest. By that time, our father's eyesight had begun to deteriorate but he refused to do anything about it. Often, when dusk approached, I took great pleasure in leaving things lying around so that he would stumble over them, hoping he might fall hard enough to smash his head open on the stone floor. But it didn't happen and I became desperate to leave. I wanted to spend Christmas in London but Ellen felt that it wouldn't be right to leave our father before Hogmanay. I thought we could leave without telling him—but again, Ellen felt that it wouldn't be right. Whatever he was, she said, he was still our father. Besides, she explained, if we just disappeared he might call the police and they might make us come back. I doubted he would, or that the police would make us come back if he did, but if there was the slightest risk of either of those things happening, I didn't want to take it. So I deferred, and it cost Ellen her life.

It was my fault. A week before Christmas, our father flew into a furious rage when Ellen told him there was no milk for his tea. He began to attack her verbally, in a way he had never done before, calling her the worst names he could think of. And unaware of what I was doing, I began shouting at him in Mum's voice, swearing at him in a way that she wouldn't have dared, telling him that he was a bully and a lazy good-for-nothing and that she was glad we were leaving him.

"You should go now!" I said in Mum's voice, turning to Ellen. "Go on, take Layla, before it's too late!"

I don't know if he actually believed we were going to leave but he was already thundering toward me, his arm raised. I tried to move out of the way, but he felled me with a single blow and as I lay winded on the floor, he bent over me and began hitting me with his fists. As I tried to protect myself with my hands, I heard an almighty thwack, followed by a grunt of pain from my father. Looking up, I saw Ellen holding a shovel, which she must have grabbed from outside the door. Even from the floor I could see murder in our father's milky eyes and I shouted at Ellen to run. But she was no match for him. It didn't take much to wrestle the shovel from her, nor to hit her with it. She keeled over like a bowling pin, splitting her skull open on the stone floor, and as blood seeped from her head, my father hit her over and over again with the shovel until she was nothing but a pulpy mess. Then he threw the shovel down, gathered up her lifeless body and carried her out of the house, trailing blood behind him.

I didn't move. Paralyzed with shock, I didn't even cry. I stayed exactly as I was, curled up on the floor, my hands still raised above my head. I don't know how long it was before my father came back.

"Let that be a lesson to you," he said, coming to stand over me. "Try and leave and you'll end up in the bog, like your sister. Now get to bed." When I didn't obey, because I couldn't, he yanked me up by my arm, dragged me to my bedroom and threw me inside.

The next few days were a blur. I took over Ellen's chores like an automaton, cooking and cleaning as she had done, barely noticing what I was doing. I knew that at some point I was going to have to wade through the sludge in my brain, but I took comfort in the sludge because it stopped me from accepting what had happened to Ellen. It allowed me to pretend she had merely gone away for a while, as I had pretended with Mum.

The sludge eventually moved to one side, allowing me enough clarity to work out that I needed to get away. It wasn't difficult; I left in the dead of night while my father was drunk, walking all the way to Stornoway, and when I got there I used the money from the tin to buy a ferry ticket across to Ullapool, and then a train ticket down to London.

I was so naïve when I arrived. Still in shock, I hadn't thought anything through. If you hadn't come to my rescue, I'm not really sure what would have become of me. I couldn't accept that Ellen was dead. It was why I wrote postcards to myself from her, postcards of Lewis she had bought from the store in Stornoway, to take with us when we left, to remind us of where we had walked with Mum. I also bought myself a birthday card, and one at Christmas, and when I read them out to you, I honestly believed they were from her.

You made me feel so safe, so loved, that I quickly fell in love with you. So if I truly loved you, how could I have slept with someone else? Having had too much to drink was only part of it. The speed at which our relationship was moving was the other part. I had come to London to experience life and there I was, already settled down. My friends that night joked about it, and when they dragged out of me that I'd been a virgin when I met you, they were appalled that I would never know what sex was like with anyone else. I'm not going to blame them, but I was aware they were trying to get me a little bit drunk, aware that they were pushing a man—I don't even remember his name—at me. And suddenly, I wanted this other guy, I wanted to have sex with him. It sounds terrible now but I was young and stupid and in the end, my stupidity cost me everything. It cost me you.

If someone had told me back then that fifteen months after I first left, I would be back on Lewis, caring for the father I was so terrified of, I would have thought them mad. It took me two days to hitchhike to Ullapool. Nobody on the ferry over to Stornoway recognized me—why would they? It wasn't as if Ellen or I had been well-known members of the community. Anyway, with my distinctive hair hidden under a hat, wearing clothes that I would never have chosen to wear, I looked nothing like my former self.

As I made my way down the Pentland Road toward our

house, I prayed that my father had drunk himself to death, or that he had died from complications arising from the cancer or from the diabetes. He hadn't, but I was about to witness firsthand how a relatively short amount of time can ravage a person's mind and body to such an extent as to render them unrecognizable. My first inkling of this was when I pushed open the door and stepped into the hallway.

"Ellen, is that you?" a voice called, and it took me a moment to realize that it was my father speaking, not some stranger as I'd first thought. Taking a breath, I walked into the room on the right and found myself staring at a man I barely recognized. He was so diminished he was only half the man he'd been before.

"Ellen?" he said again, leaning forward in his armchair, and I realized, from the way he was squinting at me, that he couldn't actually make me out. And my heart leaped, because if I could make him believe I was Ellen, I would have a much easier time. But surely he knew that Ellen was dead, surely he remembered he had killed her?

"Yes, it's me," I said, inflecting my voice with Ellen's softer, more gentle tone, glad he couldn't see that I was shaking, because being so close to him again brought all the old feelings of terror back.

He relaxed back into his chair. "Make me a cup of tea, then."

I escaped to the kitchen, wondering if it was all some trick, if he knew very well I was Layla and was playing with me. But when I opened the cupboard, I saw that my father was barely capable of looking after himself, let alone playing tricks. The cupboards were bare apart from the tea and a huge sack of porridge, and the sink was piled high with crockery. While I was waiting for the kettle to boil, I went to his bedroom and pushed open the door. The sour smell told me not only that my father hadn't changed his sheets for months but that he was incontinent.

I took his tea to him. It was black and, remembering how the lack of milk in his tea had led to Ellen's death, my hand shook as I handed it to him.

"So where you been, then?" he asked.

"Edinburgh," I said, marveling that Ellen's voice came so naturally to me.

He grunted. "That sister of yours, she upped and left too."

"She went to London," I said, realizing that not only had diabetes robbed him of his sight but that his abuse of alcohol, or maybe the cancer, had begun to erode his brain. I felt no pity, only relief.

The next day I cut my hair to my shoulders, because that's how Ellen had worn hers. I still needed to make it darker like hers so when I went into town to buy hair dye and food, using Ellen's old bicycle, I wore her clothes and a scarf around my head.

I only realized that I was the subject of a missing person's search from a discarded newspaper I found on a bench outside the supermarket, a week or so after I returned to Lewis. It sent me into a complete panic. There was no mention then that I was from Lewis, the article only mentioned London. A few days later, however, the police turned up, swiftly followed by a reporter. I quaked with fear that someone would know I was Layla but with my father yelling "Ellen" at me, demanding to know what was going on, the only thing they asked was when I'd last had contact with my sister and to let them know if she contacted me again. The strange thing was, I already felt like Ellen, so it wasn't hard to speak of Layla as my sister. I didn't want to be Layla anyway. I was ashamed,

ashamed that I'd blown my chance to make a better life for myself. I didn't deserve to exist.

The reporter didn't stay around long; the only thing he gleaned before my father told him to piss off was that Layla was a bad 'un. After, when I read in the newspaper that you had supposedly asked me to marry you, I was angry and upset. I understood why you hadn't told them the truth—if you had, the police would have thought you'd killed me in a fit of anger. But I hated that you'd lied and in the photos that appeared in the newspapers, I thought you were faking your grief. Nevertheless, I was glad when I learned from Tony that no charges were being brought against you. The theory put forward was that I'd been abducted and that suited me fine. So I wrote to you, as Ellen, telling you I knew you wouldn't have done anything to hurt Layla, because I wanted to see what you would say, if you would tell the truth about our argument and express remorse. But you only spoke of how happy you had been with me and I knew I couldn't let you go, not completely, so I was grateful to get snippets of information from Tony, whenever he contacted me to update me.

By the time Tony suggested the memorial ceremony, I'd almost forgotten that I was once Layla. My father had been dead for nearly a year and I was renting a comfortable flat in Edinburgh, thanks to a couple of fields he had owned further down the Pentland Road, which I sold after his death. I trembled inwardly at the thought of seeing you again, worried it would bring Layla back from where I'd buried her, even though I now inhabited Ellen's skin completely. Her mannerisms and gestures had come as easily to me as my mother's had. When I ate, spoke, walked, stood, I was Ellen. When I slept, I slept on my back, with one arm stretched above my head, not curled into a ball as Layla had. I thought like Ellen, laughed like Ellen, smiled like Ellen, a smile less wide than Layla's because Ellen was more serious. But something deep within me—a remnant of Layla perhaps—wanted to go to the ceremony.

Do you remember how you barely glanced at me? If you had, you might have seen Layla in me. But you didn't—yet she saw you. She yearned to reach out and touch you, to kiss the creases at the corners of your eyes, smooth her hands over your hair as she used to do. And after, when I returned to Edinburgh, she wouldn't leave me alone. I could feel her clawing her way back, wanting to be part of your life again. So I reminded her of what she'd done, how she'd betrayed you. He wouldn't want you back, I scorned. But you could have him, she said craftily, making me jump, because I hadn't heard her voice for a very long time. You could have Finn. I quaked at the thought, because wasn't he violent, just as our father had been? If you make yourself perfect, if you never do anything to anger him, he could be yours, she insisted. And you won't mind? I asked. You'll go away and never come back, you'll leave me alone, leave me to be Ellen? Yes, she said. As long as you promise to love and cherish him.

I was excited by the prospect of having you back. I didn't want to spend the rest of my life on my own. But I knew it would be a long process, and that I might not succeed. I started by keeping in touch with Harry and while I waited for my friendship with him to flourish, I doubled my efforts to get my fledgling career as an illustrator off the ground. After eighteen months of pounding the pavements of Edinburgh, Glasgow, and London with my portfolio under my arm, I was eventually taken on by an agent in Finsbury and whenever I knew that I was going to be in London, I'd let Harry know. By then, you'd gone back to work for him and were living at the flat during the week, so Harry and I would meet in the bar of my hotel. I think he felt sorry for the life I'd led and because I had no family.

One day, when I had my shirtsleeves rolled up, he happened to remark that I had the same skin as Layla. I saw at once he was referring to my freckles; the ones on my face weren't visible under the makeup I wore but it alerted me to the fact that physical traces of Layla still remained. What would happen the day you saw me without makeup? Over the next six months, I had laser treatment to even out my skin tone. I wasn't worried about my body shape; my years of living frugally with my father meant that I weighed a stone and a half less than I'd been before. There wasn't much I could do about my eyes, but instead of simply wearing mascara and shading my eyebrows, I started having them tinted so that they would look different.

Eventually, Harry began inviting me to stay at the flat whenever I was down from Edinburgh. You kept your distance at first but after my fifth or sixth visit, you began to relax and when I began to discuss jazz artists with you, I could see I had your interest. Then you invited me to Simonsbridge for the weekend, to meet Peggy, because I'd told you how much I loved dogs. And Peggy was so easy to love that I lost Layla's fear of them.

I knew from Harry that you were in a relationship with Ruby and I could tell that she was more enamored than you were. But it made me determined to move things along. So one evening, I kissed you and we ended up in bed.

We were happy together and I was elated when you asked me to marry you, because I remembered that you hadn't asked Layla. I was curious as to whether you would have one day but you denied this and I was glad, because it meant that you loved me more than you'd loved her. But Layla wasn't happy about our forthcoming marriage and to my alarm, she began to make her presence felt. Worried that you might decide to sell the cottage, she wanted to see it one last time. I tried to resist but she wouldn't let it go and I thought that if I gave in to her, if I let her have this one thing, I would be able to bury her once and for all. But seeing the cottage again had the opposite effect. Not only did she refuse to go away, she also wanted you to know she was back. Then she found the letter, where you asked her to marry you, and the ring. And the fight for you began.

It's time for me to go now. I don't know how all this is going to end, if you'll find me, if you'll bring me back. But in case you don't, there's one thing I want you to know.

I always loved you, Finn. We both did.

EPILOGUE

FINN

I did bring Layla back. I brought her back to St. Mary's, to be buried in the little churchyard there. I was handcuffed to a police officer at the time but at least I was present, thanks to Harry, who once again pulled strings for me. He wanted to try and get me off the manslaughter charge, but I wouldn't let him. Anyway, the bruises were there on Layla's shoulders, proof that I had gripped her, shaken her, pushed her.

I'm kept alone in a cell, on suicide watch, with plenty of time to dwell on what might have been, if only I'd understood. I deserve my life of solitude. I shun all visits, from Harry, from Ruby, from Tony. My only comfort is knowing that Peggy is loved and cared for at The Jackdaw.

I used to think it was the not knowing which was the worst; not knowing what had happened to Layla, not knowing where she was, if she was alive or dead. But the knowing is so much worse; knowing how much she must have suffered, knowing that I failed her, knowing that in the end, I killed her. Yet there's one thing that plagues me above all else, and it's this: if I had truly loved Layla, surely I would have known her anywhere.

ACKNOWLEDGMENTS

It seems that the more books I write, the more people there are to thank. As always, at the top of my list are the hugely talented Camilla Wray and Sally Williamson, my agent and editor respectively. Without their enthusiasm, encouragement, and endless patience, I wouldn't be living my dream of becoming an author. I'll never be able to thank them enough. They really are the best. Grateful thanks also to the amazing Lisa Milton and Kate Mills.

I'm indebted to the rest of the teams at Darley Anderson and HQ, who work tirelessly to ensure that my books reach the widest possible audience, both in the UK and abroad. I'm only sorry that I can't name each of you in person, because the list would be too long. But you know who you are!

It has been a pleasure this year to meet some of my editors in other countries, and to have participated in book festivals around the globe. Thank you not only for inviting me, but also for making my time with you so enjoyable. Special thanks to my publishers in the United States, St. Martin's Press, notably

Sally Richardson, Jennifer Weis, and Liza Senz, and to Bertrand Pirel and Marie Dêcreme from Hugo et Cie, my publishers in France.

Huge thanks to the unsung heroes of the book industry—the bloggers and readers, retailers and librarians, whose support is so vital. Thank you for buying my books, for reading them, for recommending them, for your reviews. I couldn't do it without you.

Thank you to my fellow authors, many of whom I've been able to meet this year, and who have become such wonderful friends. It's a real pleasure to be able to talk all things book-related over lunch or tea! And to my friends outside the book world, both in the UK and in France, for always being interested and supportive.

I owe special thanks to Nina Phipps, from the isle of Lewis in the Outer Hebrides, who kindly suggested the Pentland Road as a possible location for the house where Layla grew up. Also to Dominique Oddon, who shared her expertise in psychology to give me insight into personality disorders.

Last but not least, I'm indebted to my family. First of all, to my truly lovely daughters Sophie, Chloe, Celine, Eloise, and Margaux for being my first readers and for letting me talk ad nauseam about my books. To Calum, for his unfailing support and for still making me laugh every day, no mean feat after thirty-five years of marriage! To my parents, for still being here, at ninety-four and eighty-seven years old, to read another of my books—keep eating that porridge, Dad! To Christine, my sister, and my brothers Kevin, Francis, Philip, and Dominic, for always asking about my writing, with a special mention to Francis for giving me that best and most satisfying thing in the world—the last laugh!

Philippe Matsas

B. A. Paris is the internationally bestselling author of *Behind Closed Doors* and *The Breakdown*. She grew up in England but has spent most of her adult life in France. She has worked both in finance and as a teacher and has five daughters. *Bring Me Back* is her third novel.